T0078021

LINKAGES

ELAINE CHANDLER-HARRIS

Order this book online at www.trafford.com
or email orders@trafford.com

Most Trafford titles are also available at major online book retailers.

Print information available on the last page.

ISBN: 978-1-6987-0972-7 (sc)
ISBN: 978-1-6987-0971-0 (hc)
ISBN: 978-1-6987-0970-3 (e)

Library of Congress Control Number: 2021920578

Trafford rev. 10/06/2021

Trafford
PUBLISHING   www.trafford.com
North America & international
toll-free: 844-688-6899 (USA & Canada)
fax: 812 355 4082

CONTENTS

BOOK II
Lottie's Children

CHAPTER 1

The sun shone brightly that morning, blinding Lottie as she sat staring out of her bedroom window. It had rained the night before, and water prisms hung from the trees; daffodils sprouted upward, worshipping the Maker of such a glorious day; and birds of all kinds sang, forming a chorus of pure joy. Smoke from the cigarette Lottie held at her lips hung in the air like a heavy mist, irritating her eyes. Turning away from the view, she looked at the black dress that lay across her bed. It contrasted starkly against the busy patterns of the quilted comforter that framed her bed. The straight, simple black dress was her favorite and had been Spanky's too. It seemed to her improper for a funeral, but it was what she wanted to wear. Spanky's death had become, to her, another horrible scene played against a backdrop called life. Despondent, she walked to the bed and sat down. She crushed her cigarette out in the tobacco-filled ashtray on her nightstand. Since she had awakened at six that morning, she had smoked a dozen cigarettes, and it was just a little past eight.

It was very real to Lottie that Spanky was gone. She had held his lifeless body in her arms. She and her brother Julian had made the arrangements for his funeral. She herself had chosen the suit for his burial. It was she who kissed his cold lips; it was she who cried warm, salty tears as she left the funeral home, dreading the ride back home to the place that she had shared with Spanky and their children. *What will I do without Spanky? Will I know who I am without him?* she silently asked herself.

"I . . . I hate to see Mamie there," she said to the light-blue carpet beneath her bare feet. "I hate sharing this pain with her, I hate knowing how she feels, and I hate caring how she feels."

Just as Lottie stood up to get dressed, Teddy, her seven-year-old son and the youngest child, burst into her room unceremoniously. "Can I go, Mama?" he asked.

"No, Teddy," she answered. "Remember, we talked about this. You, Raphael, and Vicky will stay with Millie today. You're too young. Mama just doesn't want you children there. A funeral is a very sad thing. Try to understand, sweetheart," she said as she embraced her dejected son. Teddy's disappointment almost broke her already too fragile heart. Lottie sought to appease her son. "Look, why don't I take you kids to the park later."

Somewhat distrustful, Teddy gave his mother a brief smile and ran out of the room to tell his ten-year-old sister, Vicky, and his twelve-year-old brother, Raphael, the good news. Lottie gently closed the door behind him. She could never get Teddy to close her bedroom door or ask her permission before entering. He burst through her door just like he burst through life.

Lottie disrobed. She knew Teddy didn't really believe her about the park. *Now that Spanky is dead,* she thought to herself, *maybe the children and I will spend more time together.* Until Spanky introduced her to cocaine and the night life, she and the kids had had lots of fun together. She played with them. She loved playing catch with Raphael. He was so cute as he tried to hold the ball in his little hands, but he was determined to be the best at whatever he did. She and Vicky played dress-up with Vicky's dolls—sack dresses with ribbons for sashes. When Raphael started school, she helped him with his homework. She cooked for them, washed their clothes; she literally made her housekeeper unnecessary. Her kids were the envy of the neighborhood. All that changed as Spanky became more demanding

2

of her time. When she wasn't with him, all Lottie did was stay in her smoke-filled room getting high, watching television, and waiting for Spanky to come home.

"Spanky," she breathed his name rather than spoke it, seeing his smirking, charming smile, seeing his dreamy brown eyes, which hypnotized and spellbound her, eyes that locked her into him, into silence and submission, joy and guilt, guilt and ecstasy.

"Enough!" she admonished herself. Shaking Spanky off, Lottie dressed. "I'll be fine," she told herself.

She looked at the bed and imagined herself lying there with Spanky as he caressed her and held her tightly in his arms. Tears streamed down from her eyes. She glanced at the side table and moved toward it. She hesitated for a moment and then opened the drawer. She stood looking at the vial of cocaine nesting there, inviting her to use it, to stop the pain. She slammed the drawer shut and pulled herself away. Lottie went to her dresser and stared at her image in the mirror. Her hands trembled slightly as she struggled to hook her pearls around her neck. She finally had to fasten them from the front. Preoccupied with her reflection, Lottie reached for a cigarette and lit it. She was more than mildly captivated by the reflection of herself. She was pretty, although too thin. She no longer knew who the medium-brown woman in her mirror was. The mirror shook as she leaned against the dresser, causing her image to momentarily collide with her person. She was affected by the moment. Lottie saw and witnessed her own fragmentation and was frightened by it. Void of makeup, her shiny long black hair framed her magnificent face. Lottie looked at the time. She didn't want to be late. She dressed hurriedly, grabbed her purse, and rushed out of the room.

In the living room, which belonged to her kids now—for she never entertained and rarely occupied it herself—sat Teddy, Vicky, and Raphael eating a breakfast of peanut butter and jelly sandwiches while

3

watching Saturday-morning cartoons. Lottie hated to disturb them. They were such good children. Even Teddy, with his volcanic energy, was sweet and accepting. Vicky was a bit withdrawn, preferring the company of her brothers to other children. She was a beautiful child with her father's dreamy eyes and her mother's long black hair. Her skin was the color of caramel like her grandmother's. She had been the delight in her father's heart (the least desired child by Spanky, yet she was the conqueror of his heart). Raphael was a brilliant boy with a propensity for reading and a passion for baseball. He always carried his mitt and ball with him, anticipating the opportunity to play catch with a friend or anyone who would indulge him. He had recently joined a Little League Baseball team. If not for his uncle Julian, he would not have gone to the tryouts. Nonetheless, his uncle signed him up to play. Lottie had not the interest in taking him or his siblings anywhere. Those jobs went to her brother, Julian, and best friend, Millie. Spanky never considered spending time with his kids and didn't care that he had stolen their mother's time from them. Lottie felt extremely sad as she watched her children. She knew for sure that Raphael and Vicky understood death. They knew their father was gone for good. Teddy, on the other hand, didn't seem to understand or care. He acted as if his father were on one of his "business trips." For the first time, she considered the seriousness of her relationship with Spanky.

How will her children react when they become wise to Spanky's true identity? To them, he was their father, a frequent visitor who sometimes lived with them and sometimes not. He didn't play with them and wouldn't let them near their mother when he was around. His only interest seemed to be in their mother and Vicky, of course. He would come into the house calling for Princess Vicky. He wasn't like their friends' fathers who took them places and asked about school and homework and ate breakfast and dinner with them.

Raphael learned early about Spanky's peculiar ways. On one obscure day, lodged in his memory, Raphael, excited about his new baseball glove that was given to him by his uncle Buddy, hurled himself onto Spanky's lap, eager to share with him his gift, only to be shoved onto the floor and told, "Don't dirty up my suit, boy! Shit. What's the matter with you?" Raphael was only five at the time and intensely hurt by his father's abruptness and insensitivity. He ran to his mother in tears, accusing Spanky of pushing him down and hurting him. Lottie did nothing. She told Raphael that was the "way" his father was and that his father did not mean to hurt him and not to feel bad. She said Spanky didn't have much patience with kids. Raphael didn't know what "patience" meant, but he understood preferential treatment as he would observe his father with his baby sister. He could not help noticing the kisses and love Vicky received from Spanky. In his innocence, Raphael discerned that it must be he and he alone that his father disliked and disapproved of. In the years that followed, Raphael made no attempts to win his father's affection. He resorted to calling his father "Spanky" instead of "Daddy." He learned to find solace in the make-believe world of books. His uncle Julian had bought him several books when he was but a baby, explaining to Lottie that it was of the utmost importance that Raphael learn to read early so that he would have an edge on life and could do well in school and in this world, which was against black boys. Therefore, Raphael, by age six, had learned to read incredibly well. By ten, he had read such classics as the *Adventures of Huckleberry Finn, Learning Tree, Black Boy*, and more. He was a young boy who seemed at peace with his life and expected only what he received from his true environment.

"Hey, guys, you haven't finished eating yet?" asked Lottie, a rhetorical question and one treated as such. Raphael shrugged, and no one else bothered to answer her. "You'll have to take your sandwiches with you to Millie's," said Lottie, not affected by the lack of response.

Dutifully, they took their breakfast in hand and got up to go. Lottie turned off the television and joined her children, who waited patiently for her at the door.

Lottie knocked on Millie's door and rubbed Teddy's head, smiling down nervously at him as she waited for Millie to answer.

"Well, troopers, here you are finally," said Millie affectionately. She had always been very fond of Lottie's kids and let them visit her at will. Millie and Lottie were close in age and had bonded immediately upon meeting. "Don't you look nice," she said to Lottie as she appraised her best friend. "And if I didn't know better, I'd say you are straight."

Choosing to ignore Millie's tug at her conscience, Lottie said, "I will see you guys later. Thanks, Millie." And she left.

Lottie had gotten in her black Mercedes and was prepared to pull off when she suddenly had an attack of foreboding. She ran back inside her house, closed the door with her body, and sighed. Her whole frame trembled. She went straight to her bedroom. She opened a nightstand drawer and extracted a glass vial containing, what was for Lottie, fortification. She sat on the side of the bed and poured the powdery substance onto a mirror. Carefully she separated the cocaine into rows, and then she took a small brass tube and snorted the drug up her nose. She inhaled deeply, gratefully basking in the numbness that caressed her body and soothed her. "I can handle it now," she told herself. Replacing everything neatly back in its place, she left, this time without a backward glance.

Mamie Wallace was beyond herself. The funeral was only two hours away, and she hadn't even dressed. She couldn't move. She was still in shock. Only a few days before, Spanky had lain with her in her bed. Sure, their relationship was tumultuous, to say the least, but she loved him with all her heart, always had, always would. If she had truly believed in God, she would have been very concerned for his mortal soul and hers, but she had never let her parents' devoutness become a part of her. Somewhere deep in the cavern of her soul, she knew without a doubt that God existed. It was just that she could not afford to allow Him or anyone to be a part of her life, to determine for her the right or wrong of her love for Spanky. She and Spanky had always felt that the love they shared for each other was perfectly natural. All Mamie was sure of at that moment was that she had lost what was most dear to her. Only Spanky made her feel complete, not her kids, not anyone else could ever do that for her. She and her brother had attacked each other viciously when she last saw him. Her demands that he leave Lottie had fallen on deaf ears. She knew her crusade to end Spanky's relationship with her daughter was a futile cause. She had been trying for fourteen years to find a way to lure Spanky from Lottie's arms. "I'll never forgive her," Mamie promised herself. "Never."

Mamie allowed herself to remember the beginning, to pinpoint the exact moment when her brother became more than just a brother to her. They had always been close. Roger "Spanky" Fielder was three years older than Mamie and her idol. She literally worshipped him and would do anything for him.

2

Mamie and Spanky were raised by a mother who spent most of her time in silent prayer. She leaned so heavily on the Lord that she had become totally oblivious to those around her, especially her children. She hadn't always been that way. When Mamie was only a baby, two years old to be exact, and Spanky five, their ten-year-old brother Raymond Jr. was killed in a hunting accident. He had gone hunting with their father, which he did often, and somehow got separated from his father and the others. Unaware that Raymond Jr. was about and on his own, cohunters Mr. Morrow and Mr. Willis came upon what they thought was a deer in the shadows of the woods. They opened fire. When the deer fell, they leaped for joy and ran to fetch their game. They were stopped in their tracks by the figure of a young boy lying on the ground where their deer should have been—a young boy with half his face torn off and blood soaked from the two shots assailed at him from the hunters' rifles. Denial was their first instinctive reaction. It just couldn't be Raymond Jr.'s lifeless and mutilated body at their feet. Raymond Sr. came running when he heard the shots. Fear stirred in his heart and fought with his mind, which told him that Raymond could not have ventured that far from him, that it was indeed the sought-after deer that formed the massive heap lying visible to him from the place where he stood. Momentarily frozen, Raymond Sr. crept closer, shaking his head as nearness dispelled all hopes of it being a deer lying there. It was indeed his son. Painfully and mutely, he bent down and extracted the lifeless body of his son from the bloodstained earth, which formed his bed.

He took him in his arms, leaving a trail of his son's blood as he took him home.

Never, ever recovering from her loss, Ester Fielder turned to the Lord for comfort and away from her family. Overwrought with guilt, Raymond Sr. catered to his wife's every need, which left him little to no time for Mamie and Spanky other than to bark commands to work and do their chores. Consequently, the two turned to each other for security and love.

Rural Mississippi in 1939 was a bleak place for the Fielder family. Their income came from their father's sharecropping and their mother's job cleaning houses for white people. By the time Mamie was fifteen and her brother eighteen, they had experienced a life of daily chores, infrequent schooling, and little, if any, guidance at all. As long as they worked hard, the rest of their time was used in activities that they enjoyed and plenty of mischief.

Ester, who never missed a Sunday of church or a Wednesday-night prayer meeting, did not force her dedicated rituals on her children. She felt that they were needed more at home to do the chores neglected by her work schedule and their schooling. However, every Saturday night, they gathered as a family to pray and read the Bible together, an exercise that Mamie and Spanky found to be unnecessary. Their attention was, as usual, on each other. They snuck pinches on and made weird faces at each other until their father made them stop, for their mother was the one reading from the Bible and did not notice their behavior. With this performance, Ester believed that her obligation to expose her children to the Lord had been accomplished. After all, they each had been baptized at age twelve and did go to church once a month for three months of Sundays, when the crops did not need constant tending. Raymond was Ester's constant companion, not so much for his religious commitment but rather to keep an eye on his wife.

Mamie and Spanky never went hungry. Ester brought home plenty of food, given to her by the women she worked for. They had clothing donated by those same families for whom their mother worked. Their only needs were supervision and love. Ester had decided that after the death of Raymond Jr., love was too costly. What if she lost Mamie or Spank or Raymond Sr.? She was never going to take that risk again.

Spanky was, for the most part, very kind to Mamie, although there were times when she fell victim to his pranks. He enjoyed tying her up with hemp rope and watching her squirm and tussle. One time, he tied her too tightly, and she bled from her too constrained legs. Satisfied that she had suffered enough, Spanky finally released the rope and helped Mamie attend to her wound. Mamie carried a constant reminder of that incident, a scar. It had been easy for Spanky to explain away Mamie's injury to Ester. He told his mother that Mamie had gotten tangled in the rope, and through his effort to free her, he had tugged too hard on the rope. Ester believed him, and that was the end of that. In spite of the occasional cruelties, Mamie endeavored to please her brother. Part of her need to please Spanky came from the fear that he would abandon her and she would be left alone. (Spanky often talked of running away from home.) Equally important to her was the joy Spanky brought to her heart. He would sing, read, and play fantastic games with her that took them away from their squalid and mundane existence into worlds filled with richness and beauty. She was always a princess and he a king. They would sometimes play husband and wife, facing their enemies together, overcoming all obstacles to their joy and pleasures.

Mamie felt secure that nothing would ever interfere with her relationship with Spanky, but someone inevitably did. Spanky acquired for himself a best friend, Tony. Tony and Spanky's relationship had started to develop when they were twelve years old. The two would rush through their chores so they would have time for fishing and any other pastime activity in which they chose to participate. More often than not, Tony would come to their house because of Spanky's obligation to care for Mamie. Tony's visits were sparse because he lived far away. As Mamie matured, she became more independent, but in the beginning of Spanky and Tony's friendship, she wanted to be a part of the things they did. Spanky, of course, had let her know for certain that he was not going to share Tony with her. She would just sit and watch them wrestle and play ball. When watching them became too much to bear, Mamie would run to her room and cry. She refused to let them know how rejected she felt. She did not know what to do with herself. She had never felt so totally alone. Soon bored of moping around, Mamie busied herself with drawing and books. As she grew older, she also acquired more household responsibilities. She learned how to cook and wash.

It was a while before Spanky and Tony realized that they had lost their one and only fan. They spied on Mamie, eager to learn the source of her contentment. Once discovered, they took pleasure in ridding Mamie of her preoccupations. If Mamie was in her room reading, the two teenagers would come in and snatch the book from her hands. If she was mopping, they would walk on her clean floors with dirty feet, and she would have to start over again. After several of these antics, Mamie decided to never speak to her brother again. Unfortunately for Mamie, her silence only made Spanky more determined to terrorize his sister. While Mamie endeavored to stay away from them, Spanky and Tony vandalized her possessions. They ripped off the heads of her childhood dolls and spewed their guts, they hid her mirror outside in the barn, and they stole her books. Each incident brought the culprits to hysterics. They laughed so hard at Mamie when they took the books that she stopped crying to wonder at the creatures that stood before her. For the very first time, Mamie hated her brother.

Spanky and Tony grew past this stage, to Mamie's relief. They decided, instead, to indulge themselves in the fascinating world of sex. They then saw girls in a new light. Tony had acquired some sexually illustrated magazines from his uncle, which he promptly shared with Spanky. Tony's uncle was aware of his nephew's growing interest in sex and encouraged him to seek answers by perusing his personal stash of sexually illustrated magazines. Spanky and Tony would often spend their time talking about sex and how they couldn't wait to try their newly acquired sexual techniques on some wanton females. Isolated from most girls, except at school and church, they contented themselves by mutually masturbating. When not together, each would seek the seclusion of his bedroom or whatever secluded spot known to relieve themselves of the tension mounting in their developing bodies.

Mamie was not looking for anything in particular when she ventured into her brother's bedroom. She walked around looking at everything, touching everything. Spanky, as with herself, kept his room clean and neat. Their mother, Ester, would have it no other way. Mamie especially liked his Native American blanket, procured from one of the many Native Americans who came into town to sell their wares. Tepee and buffalo images enhanced the rich gold and brown sand, and a yellow-and-orange sun hung in the midst of a blue sky. Mamie got on her knees and looked beneath the bed. She expected to find a pair of old shoes or, at the most, a pair of long-forgotten dirty socks. Instead, she found a box of mystery and intrigue. Mamie was flabbergasted by what she saw. She flipped through the magazines, amazed by the sexually explicit contents. Mamie had never seen a grown person's naked body, nor had she ever seen men and women touching each other in a private moment. Unconsciously, she felt her own body while transfixed by those she saw. Her hand moved slowly, exploring, touching herself for the very first time. She noticed that when she touched her hidden and secret places, it felt good to her. She was captivated by the intimacy suggested in the magazine pictures. The couples' bodies seemed to be drawn to each other by a magnetic force. The liberties the couples took with each other's body were unimaginable for her. Mamie grew faint. Her pulse raced. Something stirred inside of her. Her stomach felt like tiny fingers were inside of it, stroking and tickling it. She closed the magazine abruptly, composed herself, and went to find Spanky.

Almost inaudibly, Mamie shrieked. Spanky turned, saw her, and scurried to adjust his clothing. "What are you doing?" she asked with a look of utter disbelief on her face. Too embarrassed to answer her, Spanky busied himself with the task of milking the cow. Mamie turned and left. She walked slowly back to the house. The image of her brother and those in the magazines were superimposed in her mind, clouding her thoughts. She was bewildered.

When Spanky came inside the house, he had already prepared himself for the onslaught of questions he would surely be asked. Giving Mamie no time to bombard him, he took her by the hand and led her to his room. Mamie told him what she had discovered while prowling his private space. She bent down, reached under his bed, and pulled out Spanky's personal treasure. She pulled out a magazine and let it flop open as she dropped it on the bed.

"What were you doing in my room?" he demanded of her. Not waiting for an answer, he snatched the book from the bed. "Sit down," he commanded. "I'll tell you everything."

Still irritated with Mamie's intrusion into his private world, Spanky exposed his and Tony's new interest in sex to Mamie from his limited perspective. She had understood, at least, what he had been doing in the barn, because she herself had experienced the same pleasure when she touched herself. She could not understand the physical need that was agonizing her brother and herself beyond self-control, and Spanky could not fully explain it to her, only to say that he did not know any girls other than her. Spanky told Mamie he wanted to be with a girl. Almost simultaneously, the fact that she was a girl registered with them both. With her interest in sex piqued, Mamie was eager to let her brother experiment with her body. Neither knew exactly what to do, so they thumbed through Spanky's magazines for more detailed and visual instructions, following the graphic illustrations as exactly as possible. They began to experiment with each other's body. Eager to complete the process, Spanky forced his manhood into Mamie.

Mamie screamed as Spanky began to have intercourse with her. "It hurts!" she cried. "Stop! Stop! You are hurting me!"

Spanky wanted to stop. He paused for a moment and tried to force himself to withdraw from her, but he couldn't. So consumed was he by the one experience that he had longed for, for so long. After the pain subsided, Mamie began to feel pleasure. They held on to each other while they both moaned and sighed. It was brief. The same lack of control that would not let Spanky release Mamie from his embrace would also not let him prolong his assault on her body. Utter panic and fear seized them both when they saw the blood that lay sticky and messy on Mamie's thighs and on the bedspread beneath her. Spanky was sure that he had mortally injured his sister. Sweat poured from every pore of his body. He sat on the side of the bed shaking, wondering what he would tell his parents when they discovered that he had—although unintentionally—killed his sister.

"Oh, Mamie, I am so sorry," said Spanky. Do you think I've killed you?"

Mamie eased herself off the bed. She felt pain when she stood up and reacted to it by bending over and holding her stomach.

"No, no," said Spanky.

"Relax, Spanky. I am not dying," said Mamie. "If sex could kill, there wouldn't be very many women or men alive at all. I have heard girls and women talk. It's natural for a virgin to bleed during her first time."

"A virgin?" asked Spanky. "Like the virgin we hear about in church?" said a very shaken-up Spanky.

"Yes, I am a virgin too because I never had sex before."

Mamie left her brother's room to wash herself and change her clothes. She came back into her brother's room with a bucket of soapy water and a towel and began cleaning the blood off the bedspread. Spanky stood watching her as if he didn't know what to do next.

"Spanky," said Mamie, "you have to give me your clothes to wash, and you have to go wash yourself clean. There's blood on your penis also. I will wash our clothes when I'm finished with the blanket. Our parents cannot know about this."

Spanky willed himself back to reality and followed his sister's advice. He did not fully trust his calm and practical sister. She didn't know anything about sex. He decided to talk to Tony's uncle for more expert advice.

Tony was as frightened and uninformed as Spanky, so he agreed that they should talk to his uncle, who would undoubtedly know if Spanky had injured his sister. Spanky was totally against exposing the fact that he had slept with his sister to Tony's uncle. Therefore, they decided to approach the situation in a hypothetical manner. Relieved to the point of giddiness by the extended education on how to perform sex for the first time and what to expect after deflowering a virgin, Spanky was about to hurry home and let Mamie know she was right when he was stopped in his tracks.

"Did you use a rubber, son?" the uncle asked.

"What's a rubber?" asked Spanky.

The uncle went into his bedroom and came back with a pack of rubbers. "These, son, are essential. Tell your friend that if he don't want no babies, he better wear this on his dick to catch the sperm so it won't enter into the girl's womb and make a baby." The uncle placed a few packs in Spanky's hand and told him to give them to his friend. He told him if his friend needed more to come and see him.

Spanky wanted to shit. His tongue became petrified. He needed to faint but couldn't. He asked for a glass of water. The idea that he could have impregnated his sister was more than he could bear. He and Tony left after he drank his water.

"Man," said Tony.

"Boy," said Spanky, "we just have to wait and see. I wonder if Ms. Know-It-All knows about the pregnancy thing."

"Are you going to discuss it with her?" asked Tony.

"Nah, dude. This shit is too complicated as it is. I just hope she doesn't end up pregnant."

The unsophisticated lives that Spanky and Mamie lived, coupled with their lack of moral scrutiny, allowed them to feel guiltless about what had happened between them. Mamie blamed Spanky's roughness for the pain she suffered. It was over a week before the aching stopped. She accepted the brutality of her brother just like she had in the past when he caused her pain emotionally and physically, so she did not hold a grudge against him for very long. What curtailed and delayed future sexual explorations between them was the fact that each of them needed time to digest what had already occurred and come to terms with his and her own sexuality. At eighteen, Spanky was invariably in need, but he hesitated to approach his sister. Mamie, on the other hand, had been distilled by it all and subconsciously desired to return to her innocent state, so over a year passed before they knew each other again. Although they remained close, they each kept a physical distance from the other.

It was cold and dreary that night. Rain pounded on the roof of the house. The wind pressed against the windows and doors and howled like a banshee. Mamie was sprawled in front of the fireplace, gazing into the flames. Her mind wandered from the life of Jane Ayers and dwelled instead on her own fantasies and dreams. She was sixteen and often found herself thinking of Spanky in a carnal way. A strong stirring grew inside of her, an insidious gnawing that she could not identify. It seemed to intensify whenever she thought about her brief and savage experience with Spanky, which seemed so long ago. Sex had been pleasant for Mamie, but she had been left with a yearning, which she suppressed over time. Her body often betrayed her, and she struggled against her desire to distance herself from her brother and to be with him willingly. Such were the thoughts that consumed Mamie as she stared into the fire.

In his room, Spanky lay on his bed. The ceiling above him appeared to undulate as the rain assaulted the roof. His head pounded, and his heart raced as he thought of being with Mamie. Masturbation had become ungratifying. Lately, every time he looked at his sister, desire overtook him, causing him to perspire and tremble. Sometimes he felt like forcing himself on her. Their parents had left early that evening for prayer meeting. He and Mamie had not expected them to go out in such severe weather, but Ester had insisted, so Raymond Sr. acquiesced. The knowledge that he and Mamie were alone only made matters worse for Spanky.

As he struggled to reason with himself—*What if our parents come home too soon? What if Mamie wants to be left alone?*—Spanky was not able to stop his desires from overtaking him. At the moment when he could not stand it any longer, he heard a soft knock at his door. He sat upright, startled. "Come in," he managed to say in spite of the dryness of his throat. Mamie opened the door and shyly peeped inside of Spanky's room.

Mamie and Spanky's memories of all that followed was blurred. The sensation of their bodies merging and rising to levels of passion never imagined and the alarm of their parents' discovery of them together became meshed, leaving each with a sense of what it must feel like to die briefly and awaken in hell. Mamie's strongest memory was the look of absolute disbelief and disgust reflected in her mother's eyes—those eyes that shot out and met her soul, reducing her to ashes.

3 CHAPTER

Ashes, ashes, and cinders best described what Mamie's soul was filled with that day—the day of her beloved brother's funeral. A part of her had died too, leaving in its place a residue where her heart once dwelled. She looked about for something, anything to verify that she was alive or at least awake. There was a knock at the door. She was almost sure, but her body wouldn't rise to answer it. Shortly after she failed to get out of the bed, Calvin "Buddy" Wallace Jr. entered her room.

"Mama," he said as if questioning why she was sitting there. Impatient, he said, "We don't have much time. You should get dressed."

Mamie's eyes followed the direction of his voice, but she couldn't see him. The trancelike state, which had seized her, blinded her and dulled her hearing.

"Mama, are you all right?" Buddy asked as mounting concern for her caused him to feel inept and useless. Angry with himself for not coming sooner or even realizing how deep the effects of Spanky's death had on his mother, he advanced upon Mamie and shook her, trying to rattle her mind back from wherever she had hidden herself.

Buddy never really left home. After he returned from the service and when the former tenants moved out of the third-floor apartment in their three-flat building, he moved back home. He wanted his own privacy, but he did not want to be far from his mother. His father had deserted them years earlier after a stormy confrontation with Mamie, an incident that Buddy preferred to forget.

Buddy pulled Mamie from the bed and literally finished dressing her. He did not feel good about his mother attending Spanky's funeral.

He thought it would be too much for her, especially since Lottie, his sister, was going to be there. After he got Mamie situated, he called his brother Julian.

"Jules, man, the old girl is zonked. She's not functioning at all. She couldn't even dress herself. I had to dress her, man. You know I am not cut out for this shit!"

"I know, Buddy. I spent the night with her last evening. She didn't get out of the bed. I had to wait on her hands and feet. I thank you for taking over this morning. I had to leave early to get dressed for the funeral," said Julian.

"She's just sitting here staring at nothing. Have you talked to Lottie? Is she all right?"

"I haven't spoken to her this morning, but when I saw her last evening, she was prepared to come," responded Julian.

"I hope we all get through this today. As far as I am concerned, we should have put the bastard in a pine box and sent his ass floating down Lake Michigan," said Buddy with conviction.

"I get you, man. We just have to get our family through this," responded Julian as he sighed from exasperation.

"We have really never talked about our family, Jules, but this is some fucked-up shit. To be honest with you, I'm glad that son of a bitch is dead," confessed Buddy. "I should have killed his ass a long time ago. I wanted to real bad, but I knew Mama couldn't take it. I knew she loved him more than anything in the world. Look what that love did to all of us. She is as dead right now as Spanky is."

"Man, do you want me to come by there?"

"Yeah, Jules, if you can," said Buddy. "Are you bringing Christine?"

"Buddy," said Julian, with a hint of sadness in his voice, "she doesn't know anything about all this. She knows that my uncle passed. She'll have to eventually be told about my family, but things are new right now, so I feel it is too soon to give her certain revelations."

"I understand, man. That's why I never let a woman get too close to me. The skeletons in my closet chime a little bit too loud," empathized Buddy.

"Lottie isn't straight. She's on that stuff real tough. I know one thing, Buddy. The worst hasn't happened yet. The police may be wondering, but I'm sure I know who killed Spanky," said Julian cryptically.

"Oh, Jules, who?" asked Buddy.

"This is not the time to discuss that subject, man. We will talk after the funeral," said Julian. "I'm on my way."

"Jules, wait. Was it Lottie?" pressed Buddy. "It couldn't have been Lottie. She loved that bastard."

"Later, Buddy," said Julian, evading the question.

Buddy did not know how to take this last bit of revelation. Julian was a brilliant young man. Only twenty-five years old, he had already made a moderate success of himself at the bank where he worked. He had recently been promoted to assistant to the vice president of Finance. Although he kept his distance from Spanky, Julian was extremely close to Lottie and her children. He could very well be privileged to information not available to Buddy. He was anxious and eager to hear what his little brother had to say.

<hr>

There were many people attending Spanky's funeral to Julian's surprise: employees from his various business interests, his guys (friends), several female acquaintances, and others not known to the family. Julian sat at his mother's right, gently holding her hand, as the many attendees came by to greet them. The chapel minister stood before them and eulogized his uncle, his mother's brother, with words befitting any stranger. Buddy, to her left, pressed his shoulders against his mother as if to offer her his strength. Out of the corner of his eyes, he stole glimpses of her, photographic imprints that projected a full picture in his mind. His mother's sardonic profile seemed to embellish her fine looks. Over fifty, she was slim and petite next to his 6-foot, 3-inch, 215-pound frame. Looking no older or younger than her age, Mamie Fielder-Wallace's medium-brown complexion was augmented by the long coal-black hair reflected throughout her family line. A few strands of silver lay in perfect contrast to her ebony tresses. Her eyes turned downward at the corners, creating a hooded effect to her medium-brown eyes—eyes that always seemed to be dreaming. Her small pug nose added emphasis to her full lips. She was a fine-looking woman who, by all standards, could have had anyone or anything she wanted.

Buddy suddenly felt angry. At first, he had been horrified by his family's life, but as time went by, he found himself adjusting and accepting the oddity of their way of life. As his eyes fell on Spanky's corpse, he shuddered at the impact that the man had had on his family and always would, in spite of his demise—his uncle, his mother's brother and lover, his brother's father, his sister's lover, his niece and nephews' father.

"You were a motherfucker," he whispered beneath his breath while glaring at Spanky's lifeless body.

Mamie had not seen Lottie sitting at the end of the pew; nonetheless, she knew for sure that her daughter was there because she felt Lottie's presence. Mamie felt as if her entire soul had left her body and collided with that of her daughter's, bruising upon contact.

Mamie thought she would hate Lottie forever, but she truly didn't. In her opinion, they both were losers in the game they had played. Directing her attention to her brother, Mamie remembered the day when Spanky came to Chicago and knocked on her door. She knew it was him even before she opened the door. She wished that she had sent him away . . . the way her mama and daddy had sent them away.

Going back through the painful depths of times already lived, Mamie found herself face-to-face with her mother. She met Ester's eyes—eyes that bore eternal coldness and condemnation, eyes that promised Mamie a tormented soul and spiritual death.

"Well, Mama," said Mamie to the ghost of the woman she had not spoken to in over thirty years, "your prophecy came true. My life is a living hell. No matter what I did or did not do, hell was going to be my home anyway. You knew you were sending me there when you and Daddy gave me to Calvin Wallace, ported me off like the shameful piece of trash you proclaimed me to be. First, you sent Spanky away from me, 'to the devil' as you put it, then you pondered my fate and plotted my demise, me, your 'trashy, sinful daughter.' Fortunately for you, heaven does smile on its righteous children. Heaven sent you Calvin Wallace, a thirty-year-old handyman who needed a wife, who heard that you had an eighteen-year-old daughter, a virgin daughter. Calvin took one look at me, and you knew you had him. And if he found out after the wedding that I was not exactly pure, it wouldn't matter. 'He would be too in love to care,' according to Daddy."

Calvin was too much in love to care. In fact, he just took Mamie on that first night, grunting and sweating. He never even took notice of her less-than-chastened state. All he said afterward was that it hadn't been too bad for the first time. He thought Mamie's soft crying was perfectly natural.

Nine months after her wedding night, Mamie gave birth to a son. They named him Calvin Wallace Jr. after his father. Calvin Sr. had great hopes for a close relationship with his son, so he nicknamed him Buddy.

"That's what we'll always be, buddies," said Calvin, slightly short of bragging.

Calvin wanted a better life for his son than the one he had been living himself. He had heard about all the great opportunities for black men up north, so he sold his small house and 10 acres of land and took his family to Chicago, where he made arrangements for them to stay temporarily with his first cousin and his family.

Calvin soon found that Chicago really offered a black man very little. Without the benefit of having one's own, a black man such as himself could only aspire to being a janitor, porter, elevator boy, dock hand, in general, common labor, if one found employment at all. Calvin longed for his previous existence, which he had bartered off for a chance at the rainbow. His ambition was his salvation. Calvin's cousin had managed to help him get a job at the steel mill. He worked in steel by day and as a janitor at night. He saved every extra dollar, determined, if nothing else, to at least purchase a house or an apartment building that would generate additional income as well as provide his family with lodging. Within five years of moving to the "big city," Calvin achieved his goal. He purchased a three-flat building on the south side of Chicago.

Life just *was* for Mamie. She existed daily in an absentminded state. She lived for Calvin and Buddy, attending to their needs. She cleaned, cooked, read a great deal, sewed some, and daydreamed most of the time. When Mamie left the house, it was with purpose, such as grocery shopping, shopping for clothing, and buying furniture and adornments for her new home. She loved going to the beauty shop. People always complimented her on her beautiful hair, and she could listen to the stylists and customers' gossip for hours. The pedicures and manicures she got made her feel spoiled. She could have talked herself out of the necessity of getting those extras, but everyone she knew insisted that she be completely beautiful from head to toe. She was able to buy many of her clothes at the shop because the owner also had a boutique. Beverly, the owner, chose gorgeous outfits for Mamie and encouraged her to get out of the house and show herself off. Mamie settled for a few dates with Calvin when she felt like it. She was not accustomed to drinking alcohol or dancing. She went with Calvin to nightclubs for the entertainment. She would have much rather been at home.

Mamie thought about Spanky constantly, wondering where he was, how he was doing, and whether or not he had married and had children, but mostly, if he ever thought of her. She had not seen or spoken to him or heard from him since their parents threw him out of their home.

On June 30, 1961, three days after her twenty-second birthday, Mamie gave birth to Lottie Marie Wallace. Lottie was hailed the most beautiful baby ever born. Her father could not take his eyes off his daughter. Her mother felt true love for only the third time in her life. The first being her deep affections for Spanky, and the second time was with her son Buddy. He was so energetic and happy and fun-loving that Mamie found her heart leaning toward her firstborn child and finally bonding with him. The third time was at the moment she beheld Lottie. She was a mirrored image of Mamie with Spanky's eyes. Mamie could never utter what was on her mind as she held Lottie for the first time. She had to convince herself that Lottie was Calvin's daughter, not Spanky's.

Mamie had come to terms with her life and marriage to Calvin. She was pleasant to those around her and attentive to her husband and children. She had even begun to will herself to not think about Spanky so much. After Lottie's birth, Mamie felt that she had been given a part of Spanky that she would never lose. Such was Mamie Wallace's world on the day that Spanky strolled back into her life.

Mamie had been feeling disconcerted. Everything around her seemed like a dream as she lay in bed that morning, drifting in and out of sleep. Between the portholes of sleep and consciousness, Mamie reached for something that was not there. Calvin gently caught her wrist and guided her hand to the treasure she evidently sought. Mamie felt his manhood and snatched her hand away. Calvin was confused at first, then he assumed that his wife was still sleepy and didn't want to be bothered. He arose from bed and took a cold shower and started his day early.

As Calvin's shadow crept from the bed, Spanky's took its place, enrapturing Mamie, caressing her, warming her body to his presence. Her body moved rhythmically. When Calvin emerged from the bathroom and saw Mamie's writhing body, he did not hesitate to join his wife in bed; eager was he to take advantage of her sudden passion. He made love to her, carrying Mamie's pleasures to heights they as a couple had not felt before. She held him tightly and smothered him with kisses. At her peak, she screamed Spanky's name. Mamie's cry for Spanky echoed in Calvin's brain, resounding and pulsating like the quaking of the earth. He pulled himself from her, wondering if she were mad or he. Had she called for Spanky? Why would a woman scream out her brother's name while making love to her husband?

Dread seized Mamie as she came to herself. Without a doubt, she had made love to Calvin's body, yet his image was Spanky's. She had called out Spanky's name for sure. She allowed the light of the world to slowly enter her pupils. It took a moment for her to focus on Calvin. She was not the least bit surprised by the expression on his face. She told him that she had been worried about Spanky lately and had been dreaming about him before she started to make love to Calvin. Although a part of him knew this to be untrue, Calvin accepted his wife's explanation. He let the warmth and pleasure he felt earlier to invade his body and mind, urging him to take his wife's body again and again.

By the time Mamie had gotten out of bed, Buddy (then seven) had dressed himself for school. Four-year-old Lottie sat in her bed, chewing her nightgown and giggling at her brother, who made funny faces at her. Mamie scooped Lottie in her arms and ran her hand over Buddy's fuzzy turf and gently guided him into the kitchen, where she made breakfast for them before rushing Buddy out to school and Calvin to work.

Mamie had just sat down with Lottie to comb her daughter's hair, which already hung beneath her shoulders, when the doorbell rang. Seized by an uncanny sense of foreboding, Mamie put Lottie down and went to the outer door to see who was calling on her. Spanky's face flashed in her mind. Her heart started racing uncontrollably when she saw Spanky standing outside with a suitcase in his hand. Her emotions webbed inside of her. Instantly she wanted to close the door, but her desire to see her brother was the strongest of her feelings. Spanky grinned broadly at Mamie. He had not realized before how beautiful his sister was. It had been twelve years since he last saw Mamie. She had developed into a gorgeous woman. Gone forever was the exotic teenager whom he had known and loved. Observing with a keen sense his sister's reticence and discomfort, Spanky launched into the reason for his visit.

Over the years, Spanky had managed to keep in touch with his father through infrequent letters and calls. It was through an impromptu call that he learned of their mother's death. She had died of kidney failure. Offering to return home to console his father, Spanky was surprised when his father told him not to come. Instead, their father told him to contact Mamie and let her know. Spanky knew that a simple letter would have done, but he wanted to use the occasion to see Mamie. He longed to see her for a long time, but he wasn't sure how he would be received. After his tenure in the army, Spanky took a job in Detroit. One of his army buddies asked him to come there when his service was over. He had practically ensured Spanky a job at an automobile factory. For five years, Spanky had worked there. For twelve years, Spanky had ached to be near Mamie. When he left Detroit, he left for good. He had managed to save some money and was intent on opening a liquor store. He had hoped that Mamie would let him stay with her and her family until he could get settled.

Mamie was not moved by her mother's death, and unlike her brother, she had no desire to return to Mississippi for the sake of her father—a father she had not heard from or talked to once since they shipped her away. She found it inconceivable that Spanky could even wish to see their father again. She didn't know what to say to her brother when he asked to live with her. She told him that she would have to talk it over with her husband. (She secretly wished that Calvin would object, for even at that moment, Spanky cast a powerful spell over her.) When he reached for her at the door, she drew back, not yet willing to trust herself in her brother's arms. The yearning that had seized her earlier that morning had not subsided but rather intensified when she first saw him. Yes, she still loved Spanky more than anything in the world.

Calvin did not hesitate at all to offer Spanky a temporary home. He thought that having him there would please his wife, and he would do anything to make Mamie happy. He spent a great deal of his free time, which wasn't much, helping Spanky look for a place to open up his liquor store. As relaxed as he was about having Spanky around, Calvin could not help notice how quiet Mamie was, how thoughtful and nervous she appeared. Calvin attributed this to the news about her mother's death and the pain of being away from her father during what must be a difficult time for him. Until then, Calvin had not thought much about the fact that Mamie never mentioned or communicated with her parents. In fact, he had taken for granted that she had been in contact with them. How could it be that such distressing news had come to her via an estranged brother? He realized that he would never totally know his wife.

Days alone with Spanky were excruciating for Mamie. Without openly doing so, she observed his every move and hung on to his every word. The heartiness of his voice caused her body to tremble. His excitement about everything dared her to want to live within that hurricane with him to feel exhilarated and free. He could always entice Mamie into his mania. His charm was irresistible. Fighting to subdue her emotions was exhausting Mamie. She refused to get carried away by Spanky again.

Spanky doted on Lottie. He gave Buddy minute attention. When he could get Mamie to look at him, he would smile broadly and let his lazy eyes linger on her body. She became alarmed every time Spanky looked at her, because it was obvious that he desired her. It was the same desire that she herself fought constantly, an unmerciful and powerful feign that crept upon her like a thief in the night. The day that Spanky came home and announced that he had found a place for his liquor store on Forty-Seventh Street was a day of relief for Mamie. It would only be a matter of time before Spanky would move out. Mistaking Mamie's illuminated smile as a show of openness and love, Spanky grabbed her in his arms and whirled her around. He lowered her gently. Their eyes locked, trapping them once again. They kissed. So sweet and natural was their love for each other that the years that had divided them perished in an instant. Enraptured, they made love on her living room floor.

After it was over, Mamie told Spanky that they could not allow themselves to become lovers again. She told him how much she respected Calvin and could not let her feelings for him interfere in their marriage. Deep down inside of him, Spanky knew what she said was only right, yet he could not make himself promise her that it would not happen again. Already beside himself with longing, he brushed her words aside with kisses and tenderly made love to her again.

As Mamie and Spanky lay together, time passed. Time had become as obscure to them as their surroundings. They were nowhere yet everywhere. They seemed to float boundlessly into infinite ecstasy. Neither heard the door unlock nor Calvin's heavy steps as he entered the house and into the living room, where they lay, still joined together. The thunderous sounds resounding in the air had no reference point. It was the sharp pain of Calvin's foot as it struck Spanky's head and Mamie's ribs and the yanking of Spanky's embedded body from her that made them aware of his presence. Scurrying to clothe themselves while fending off Calvin's wrath, Mamie and Spanky's minds filled with mortification at being caught together once again.

Spanky seemed too peaceful for Buddy. He felt badly about the fact that he hated the man, but there was no forgiveness for his uncle, dead or alive. He would never forget that awful morning.

The day that Buddy lost his father was as clear to him as if it had been yesterday. Buddy's intense dislike for his uncle began at the tender age of ten. No one had seen or heard him when he came home from school that day. He was petrified with fright as he saw his father slap his mother and turned Spanky's half-clothed body into a punching bag. Buddy could not catch all the melee because he had to check on Lottie, who was in her room alone and crying. She had been awakened by the noise in the living room. She was calling for her mother. Buddy had heard enough to know that the chaos had started because of his father's discovery of Spanky with his mother. Buddy was bewildered. He could not imagine what was so awful about their being together. He assumed from his father's ranting that something wrong had happened. His father was a kind and loving man. Buddy had never even heard him raise his voice, much less strike someone. Calvin Sr. was not likely to go into such a rage without provocation. Buddy had been upset by the fighting, but he was wrecked when he heard his father tell his mother that he was leaving, that he would never stay in the house with a "sinful witch like you." He told Mamie to keep the house and the money. He told her that he would only take what he needed to "get the hell out of Chicago and away from her." He said he would be tempted to kill her if he stayed too near.

"You low-down whore! You and your brother can do anything your hearts desire. You can lay here naked on the floor and satisfy your lust until the devil meets you in hell. I could have been one of the children. What if Buddy or Lottie had walked in on you instead of me? Let me go before I kill one of you," hollered Calvin.

Buddy panicked. He ran to his father, who was in his parents' bedroom, pulling his clothes out of the drawers and off racks and stuffing them into his bag. "Oh, Daddy!" cried Buddy. "Please don't leave. Don't leave me, Daddy," pleaded young Buddy. "Mama will be good. She didn't mean to be bad. Please don't leave us, Daddy." Buddy weakened from his efforts to persuade his father to stay. He sank to his knees and cried inconsolably.

With a heart as heavy as lead for his life had just been shattered, Calvin Sr. struggled for words. Buddy was his son, his firstborn; nonetheless, he had to leave him. He couldn't stay with Mamie another second. The thought of her made him physically ill. He fought nausea. He told Buddy, "I have to go, son, and you have to be a big boy about this. I know you don't understand why I am leaving, and I hope you never have to know. I love my family, Buddy. I can't live here anymore. There's too much pain here for me. I can barely breathe as it is. I'll send for you, Buddy, as soon as I get settled. You'll stay with me then."

"Where will you go, Daddy? How will I know where you are?"

"I don't know, son. I'll travel until I find a home. Maybe I'll find a job as a truck driver. Until I decide where I want to live, I will have to call and write you. I don't want to live in Chicago anymore. That will be okay, right?" With a hug and kiss, Calvin left the room. Buddy heard him in Lottie's room as he said goodbye to her too.

Of course, it was okay. What else could he do, except hold on to his father's words? Crumbling to the floor with pain and disappointment, Buddy cried pools of tears. He heard the door slam as his father left, and he almost died inside. When his mother came into the room, she tried to comfort her son. Buddy scooted away from her and buried himself beneath the bed, finding comfort in the dark, in the coolness of the floor. He stayed there whimpering like a wounded puppy until he became exhausted and fell asleep. His mother did not enter what used to be hers and Calvin's bedroom again that evening.

The next morning, Buddy emerged from his place of solitude and went into the living room. He saw his haggard-looking mother stretched out on the couch asleep with Lottie at her feet. Her face was swollen and red. Spanky, with a bottle of liquor next to him, slept soundly on the floor. Buddy searched him over. He knew without a doubt then that he would hate his uncle forever.

Although it had been nine months since his father left, Buddy still anticipated the day when Calvin would walk through the door. He knew for sure that the arrival of a new baby would bring his father home. The birth of his brother Julian was not exciting for Buddy at all. He had been overcome with joy when Lottie was born, but the birth of this little quiet, bright-eyed baby was nothing special. His father had not been there to stand over the bed and light up the room with his fascination and joy. Lottie simply loved her little baby brother. His mother acted as if he were a dream come true. It seemed to Buddy that the only person around who was less enthusiastic about the birth was his uncle Spanky. Both left the doting to the women in the house.

Buddy discussed the possibility of his father's return home with his mother, only to be told the same thing over and over again. "He won't be back, baby," repeated his mother nonchalantly. Gently lifting Buddy's chin to face him eye to eye, Mamie said, "He has been gone for a long time now, honey. He's not coming home anymore. He still sends us money and pays the bills and always asks me to give his children a kiss for him. He loves you guys very much."

"But what about the baby?" pressed Buddy. "Does he know about him? Doesn't he want to see Julian?"

"No, Buddy. Your father doesn't know about Julian. He wouldn't want to know," said Mamie.

"Wouldn't want to know?" That didn't sound like his father to him. As a young boy, Mamie's cryptic statement had not made much sense at all to Buddy, but as time went on, he figured out the mystery—Julian was Spanky's baby. After overhearing many conversations and arguments between Spanky and Mamie over the years, Buddy contented himself with the fact that someday Spanky would leave. He had seen Spanky coming out of his mother's bedroom many times. He came to the conclusion that his father's place beside his mother in bed had been absconded by Spanky. Buddy eventually accepted Spanky's presence but confided to his mother that he did not think it was proper for his uncle to be sleeping in his father's bed. In the ensuing time, Buddy's innocence shed away like a butterfly shedding its cocoon, and he realized that his mother and Spanky were lovers.

One day when he and Spanky were alone, Buddy asked his uncle why he did not date or have a girlfriend or a wife like other men. Brushing aside the seriousness of Buddy's question, Spanky told him that he did have a few women in his life. Sixteen years old by then and more familiar with the codes of love, Buddy wittingly told his mother that Spanky was seeing other women. He had hoped that this bit of information would forge a breach between the two of them that would ultimately lead to Spanky being evicted from the house. He, instead, caused more turmoil, constant arguments, and plenty of bitter tears for his mother, who was already suffering emotional distress because of her suspicion that Spanky was being unfaithful. His mother was dedicated to her brother. The affirmation that he had indeed been cheating on her was so devastating to Mamie that she lost all reasoning. Her attention, which had once been lavished on her children as well, was now given to the task of keeping Spanky away from other women. Mamie's desperate struggle to hold on to Spanky consumed her.

Buddy did not want to go to college when he graduated from high school, so he joined the army. He wanted to get away from it all. The constant bickering and emotional distress was not the environment in which he wanted to live anymore. He packed his things and moved into a transit hotel until he could finish his enlistment procedures. He enlisted in the army and was out of Chicago on his way to Lubbock, Texas, in no time.

Buddy stayed away for four years. He rarely wrote his mother and never came home during that time. Once he left the army, the first thing he did was to go see his father. Calvin's whereabouts had been known by him for years. When he went away to the service, Buddy took one of Calvin's letters to Mamie with him.

He had intended to stay with his father. Calvin was living with a woman in St. Louis, for he never divorced Mamie or aspired to marry again. The relationship that he and his father had begun to establish was bonded by their hatred of Spanky. It was a connection that they both had wanted but did not know how to have, so when Buddy decided to return to Chicago, the two ultimately drifted apart.

After Buddy returned to Chicago, he had no intentions of staying in the house with his mother and Spanky. He was twenty-three years old and had saved a little money and was ready for his independence. He took a room at the local YMCA and found himself a job at a local trucking company, repairing trucks and sometimes driving to deliver merchandise. His experience in the army had served him well in civilian life. His employer paid him well because he was a true asset. Later, Buddy would become part owner and then owner.

Buddy eventually found himself lured back to the place he grew up in and had once called home. The third-floor tenant had passed away, and the apartment was vacant for the first time. When Buddy arrived at the apartment building, he could not help but swell up inside. The building was well-kept. One of only three apartment buildings on the long block, it loomed three stories high. It was a brick building trimmed in blue and adorned by blue-and-white-striped awnings. It was a working-class man's achievement, positioned in a working-class man's neighborhood. Its quaint veneer masked its tainted inhabitants. His father might not have kept his promise to send for him, but he continued to take care of Mamie and her children. The building had long been paid for, so his financial generosities were more than the family needed. When Buddy had matured enough to put himself in his father's shoes, he knew that he had done the natural thing and had taken the only road to freedom, sanity, and happiness. His father had appeared to be happy when Buddy saw him in St. Louis. He could attest to how unhappy one was who was forced to be a part of Mamie and Spanky's lives.

Buddy was shocked, to say the least, when he saw his mother. She made no pretense of joy at his arrival home. During the time that Buddy had been away, Mamie had turned into a joyless and troubled woman. If not for her natural beauty, she would have seemed much older. Lottie greeted her big brother with enthusiasm. Buddy could not look at Lottie for long. His last encounter with her was fresh in his mind. In fact, the incident was often on his mind. He felt embarrassed in her presence. She was a young woman now, a gorgeous young woman. Julian, the proverbial bookworm, barely raised his head from his book long enough to welcome his brother home.

Buddy remembered the night he left home. He was nineteen years old and had graduated from high school. He had planned to take his time deciding what to do with his life. He had settled into a lifestyle that kept him away from home. He hung out with his old friends from school and made new ones easily. He was not a heavy drinker; however, he liked to party. He was not looking to marry anytime soon and have children, so he kept his feet moving when dealing with the women. One particular evening, he decided to sit in his car for a while, listening to music and enjoying still the feelings from a wonderful evening spent with his favorite girl and their friends. He checked his watch; it was six minutes past one o'clock. When he went inside the building, he noticed that the lights were still on in the house. The whole family was usually asleep by that time.

Buddy heard a crashing noise and raising voices. In an instant, he found himself grabbing his mother's arm while unclamping her fingers from around the base of a lamp, which was positioned to be thrown at Spanky. Mamie wept hysterically in Buddy's embrace. In between spells of crying, she muttered, "He was with Lottie! I caught him in bed with *my* daughter," said Mamie. Buddy eased Mamie to the couch, and then he turned to address Spanky only to discover him gone. Buddy told himself that he would deal with him later. In the meantime, he would check on his sister.

Buddy did not bother to knock on Lottie's door. He found her sitting up in bed, crying silently and heaving. "Are you okay?" he asked. Lottie nodded to indicate that she was fine. "Did he hurt you?" Lottie shook her head. "What happened here, Lottie? What happened between you and Spanky?" Lottie did not answer her brother. She slid down in her bed and turned her back to him. Buddy plopped his 230 pounds of solid weight on Lottie's bed, causing her to accidently roll against him. She scooted herself away from him. "Look, Lottie," pressed her brother, "I want to know what happened between you and Spanky. This shit is serious, Lottie. You and Spanky? This crap never ends, does it? First, Mama, and now you? That bastard is going to die when I see his ass again." Lottie never spoke. Buddy sat there for long moments, seething. He could not absorb all that had occurred. He placed his hand on Lottie's shoulder. She did not respond, so Buddy left her with her secret.

When Buddy returned to the living room, Mamie was calm. His anger was not reserved for his uncle alone; his mother had an equal share, and Buddy vented on her. "You are such a slut!" he pronounced to his mother. "It's because of you and your sick ways that this is happening to Lottie. How long has he been using and abusing her? When did it start, Mama? Your daughter does not even know what this is all about. Hell, her mother sleeps with her uncle. Because he is not your husband or her father, she thinks that it must be okay for her to sleep with him too. I'm sure he seduced her, just like he seduced you. You turned your back on your husband to sleep with that poor excuse of a man. You're sick. This whole household is sick. It is not over, Mama. He'll be back. He will keep charming Lottie. That son of a bitch will have Lottie eating out of his hands the same way he has you doing. She has always worshipped him. The transition from niece to lover was very easy for Spanky, I'm sure. I asked her what had happened between them, but she would not answer me." Mamie's eyes never rose to meet her son's; words never parted from her lips.

Buddy sat on the couch next to a silent, tearful Mamie for the rest of the evening, thinking. He thought about how wonderful his life would have been had he left with his father, for his life was sorely stressful. He worried about his family. He felt hopeless against the will of his mother and now his sister. He worried about Julian's quietness and detachment. To Buddy, this house was unwholesome and vile. He thought about all the years he had sat and endured things as they were. Basically, Buddy was a gentle person, yet he wanted to kill Spanky on a serious level, more than anything in fact. He couldn't stay any longer; he couldn't save his mother or his sister. He just wanted to move away from them so that his stomach could settle down and his nagging headache would go away. He fell asleep with these thoughts on his mind.

The next morning, Buddy wanted to change his mind and stay, but he couldn't. He didn't want to leave Mamie and Lottie alone, but if he stayed, he had no power to change things. Nonetheless, if he did stay, he could at least keep an eye on his he family. Perhaps, he could keep Spanky at a respectable distance from Lottie. The nays won, and Buddy packed his bags and left.

CHAPTER 6

Mamie wanted to die as Spanky had. She had grown used to the other women, because she knew that Spanky loved her and would always come home to her, but when he decided that he had to have Lottie too, that was too much for her to bear. Her heart ached from the betrayal. The fact that he had turned his attention to her daughter was something that she had never fathomed. Mamie had noticed the way that he used to watch Lottie and stare at her with lust glaring from his eyes. She said nothing and did nothing. She just knew he would never act on any desires that he might have had for her one and only daughter. She was sure that he would never touch her baby girl, her Lottie.

That night, when Mamie had awakened and discovered Spanky absent from their bed, she initially thought Spanky had crept out in the middle of the night, as he often did. She assumed, rightfully so, that he had gone to see another woman. She was not wrong about that prediction. However, it next occurred to her that he might be in the kitchen getting something to drink. When she passed Lottie's room and heard voices, the fact that he was with Lottie leaped out at her. She closed her eyes as she opened Lottie's door, fearing the worst. Within her heart, she knew the truth, yet when she opened her eyes and saw him there, she was disabled by the stroke-like symptoms that attacked her body, the mind-blowing evidence of him caressing and kissing her daughter, and their nakedness. She felt deceived by both of them.

Lottie could not control the tears that drained from her eyes, which sprang from her soul. She had never known loss, had never felt such pain and longing before. Seeing Spanky lying there lifeless was unbearable. She wanted to run away screaming. She tried to tell herself that it was a bad dream, that she would awaken with Spanky's arms around her. The effects of the drugs had diminished. Through tear-filled stares, she looked over at her mother, who sat surrounded by her bothers, hoarding them. Lottie felt bitter and alone. She had rarely felt threatened by Mamie when Spanky was alive. She knew that her mother had long ago lost her control over him, yet it annoyed Lottie that Mamie would be the one treated like the widow in mourning.

Lottie seldom felt badly about taking Spanky away from Mamie. Spanky told her in the beginning that he only stayed with Mamie because she needed him. He told her that he had grown tired of Mamie clinging to him, but he knew that she would be hurt if he completely pulled away. Therefore, Mamie would always be in his life, and he would always take care of her and, frankly, love her. Lottie asked him if he was still intimate with Mamie. Spanky told her that he would always be with Mamie.

$$\sim\!\!\mathit{m}\!\!\sim$$

When Lottie was but thirteen, Spanky started to touch her body. He told her he would never hurt her because he loved and adored her and she was very special to him. He told her that it made him feel good to have his "best girl" close to him. He told her that he just needed to hold her and touch her. Lottie was happy to have him care so much for her, for she loved him very much. She catered to Spanky. She worshipped her handsome uncle. She enjoyed sitting on his lap with her arms around his neck. Her body grew warm as he would press his lips against hers, gently massaging her budding breast. His sweet breath made her dizzy. The smell of musk and spice made her swoon. When he abruptly stopped, she would beg him to continue, asking for more, but not really knowing what more was. He would laugh at her eagerness and soothed her injured pride with the promise to fulfill her wishes when she was older. He made her promise to never tell Mamie about their "special time" together because if she did, he would be forced to go away forever. The thought of his leaving her brought fear to Lottie's being. The terror evoked by just imagining her life without Spanky brought dread to her soul.

At sixteen, Lottie's beauty was beyond compare. She commanded the attention of everyone who encountered her. The boys at her school were spellbound. However, they did not exist to her. Lottie simply didn't see them. She was impervious to those around her. She would engage in light conversation with some of the girls in her classes but declined all social invitations. She was soon labeled a snob and ignored. Lottie didn't care. Outside of academics, her preoccupation was Spanky. The hours between when she had last saw him and would see him again were spent trying to imagine what wonders he would bring to her next.

Spanky had been spending long periods of time away from home. Lottie was aware of the growing tension between her mother and him. She had also noticed the constant vigilance that Mamie kept over Spanky and her. Lottie understood what affected her mother: it was jealousy, not unlike the jealousy she herself felt toward Mamie. Mamie was a woman possessed. Lottie had often overheard the confrontations between her mother and Spanky about his "womanizing." Somewhere within Lottie lay the same monster, the fiendish ogre who could not bear the thought of sharing Spanky with anyone. Lottie, however, was pleased to just have him there with her whenever he was available. She had not yet tasted the fleshy fruit of love, the intoxicating juices that ran lucidly through her mother's veins.

Lottie could remember when she was younger that she was the apple of her mother's eyes. Mamie approved very much of the love and attention she received from Spanky, but now her mother did everything she could to keep them apart. Lottie remembered her sixteenth birthday. Her mother had thrown her a birthday party. All her family was there. She had received such lovely gifts: an ornate brass comb and brush set from Julian; a beautiful nightgown and robe set with matching house shoes from Buddy; a pearl necklace, earrings, and bracelet set from her mother; and best of all, a diamond and ruby ring from Spanky.

That night, Lottie was extremely excited. She had anticipated Spanky coming to her bedroom to see her. He had promised her something more precious than a "mere gift." He had promised to make her a woman. Lottie wanted more than anything to be Spanky's woman. She was distraught when he did not come to her. He had been waylaid by Mamie that evening, who insisted that he stay home with her. Lottie could hear her mother's soft plea for Spanky to come to bed. To Lottie's dismay, he acquiesced.

As Lottie lay in her bed, she tried to envision Spanky and her mother together. Her heart pounded at the thought. Never before had she entertained the idea of their being together intimately, but it was her birthday, and Spanky was to be with her, not Mamie. At that time, Lottie had not considered taking Spanky from her mother or replacing her, because she knew that she already held a special place in Spanky's heart. She was secure with his love for her and her love for him. A virgin in body and mind, Lottie could not fathom what took place between Spanky and her mother in sensual images. She could only guess what was going on from her own limited contact with Spanky. The thought of him kissing and caressing her mother instead of her was enough to bring a veil of misery over Lottie's entire being. Sex was not a topic discussed in the Wallace household. Lottie was as ignorant about intercourse as she was about her quasi family's lifestyle.

Days and weeks passed; still no Spanky. When she went to bed, he was still at the liquor store or elsewhere, and when she arose, he was already gone. She grew morose by his absence. Mamie, on the other hand, radiated with happiness. For the first time in her life, Lottie hated her mother.

Lottie had been crying silently for some time when Spanky entered her room. He didn't knock; he just walked in like he was expected. Lottie smiled broadly at him. Frightened by the fire in his eyes, she wondered what he might do to her. Unceremoniously he took her in his arms and kissed her so hard that she could hardly breathe. It was a passionate and long kiss. His tongue explored her mouth and her ears and her breast. Lottie groaned. Abruptly he stopped and looked down at her. He stroked her hair, her face, and her body until she lay limp and trembling beneath him. It was all so wonderful—the joy, the ecstasy. Spanky's hand traveled the length of her body, seeking a particular spot. He found it, and Lottie lay tortured. He slipped his finger inside of her, and she wanted to scream, but he stopped her, not wanting to wake up Mamie and Julian. He pushed her legs apart and warned her that it was going to hurt at first, but eventually, it would feel very good. He was right. Lottie had never felt anything that painful before and then that good. Her body rose, and she writhed beneath him. After they finished, Spanky held her in his arms, tenderly kissing her face, her eyes, and her lips. She wanted more of him; however, he pulled away from her and told her it was too soon, that she needed to rest and heal first. He told her that he loved her, that she was now his, and that he would always come to her. While they lay there in silence, naked and contented, chaos claimed the moment.

Lottie covered her mouth. The silence almost compelled her to scream as Mamie stood at her door, looking at Spanky and her. Spanky got up and slowly dressed. His eyes never left Mamie, who was still fixated by what she had seen. Spanky took her by the arms and gently led her away. He closed Lottie's bedroom door behind him. How awful she felt. Someone was going to die; she was sure of it. She pleaded with a god she did not know to not let it be Spanky. She heard the outrage in her mother's voice. She heard glass break and slaps and screams.

The days that followed were endless. Mamie was so overwrought that she was rendered helpless. Julian, unwilling to participate in the upheaval, buried himself in his room and books. Buddy came home in the middle of the melee and ended up physically attacking Spanky. When he came to Lottie's room to question her, she refused to talk to him. Buddy left home at the break of sunlight, and Spanky had disappeared. Lottie tried to avoid her mother at all cost. When it became apparent that Spanky was not going to return, Lottie grew resentful toward Mamie. Two years passed before Lottie and Mamie saw Spanky again. Two years of silent reproach had fashioned Lottie's relationship with her mother. Each spoke only when necessary.

Lottie had done very well academically. She graduated valedictorian of her class. She could have gone to any school she chose. The idea of going away to school was not appealing. What if Spanky came back home? She entered the University of Chicago. She knew that she wanted to teach children, so she focused her studies on education.

Lottie loved school. She excelled in her pursuit to be the best. She was sure-footed and determined to go all the way. She was sitting in the living room that spring, studying and watching television at the same time. She heard the jingling of keys in the door lock. She assumed it was her mother coming in from the beauty shop. It was too early for Julian, who would either be at the library, a friend's house, or at the movies with his friends. He usually arrived home by dinnertime. She half rose when she saw him. The heaviness of shock pressed her back down in her seat. She wanted to run and hug him, but she remembered that she was also angry with him. Spanky did not require encouragement or forgiveness. With two great strides, he was upon her, gazing in her eyes, which grew enormous with wonder and amazement. He drew her close to him. Lottie's knees buckled under his embrace. He lifted her up gently, kissing away her ambivalence. Never speaking, he carried her to her bedroom.

Questions floated through Lottie's mind aimlessly. "Why haven't you called? Where have you been?" Her effort to concentrate was useless. She was being held captive by her own willingness to submit to the one person who had broken her heart.

Spanky talked briefly about his absence. He had moved in with a female friend, from whom he had recently parted company. He had opened a nightclub and bought a four-bedroom house in Pill Hill, a community of well-to-do inhabitants. He had purchased the house with Lottie in mind. "I had some decisions to make, Lottie," he said. "Things couldn't go on the way they were. I knew I had to make a choice between you and Mamie. Sweetheart, I want to make a home with you."

"I want to be with you too," said Lottie. She flung herself into Spanky's arms, knocking him backward onto the bed. She bathed his face with kisses and tears. So happy was she to escape with Spanky into a wonderful and new world.

When Mamie arrived home, she was amazed to see Spanky there reading the newspaper while Lottie worked on her assignments. His eyes rose to meet hers, and his handsome smile and dreamy eyes called, and she no longer felt angry toward her brother. She met him in the middle of the living room where they embraced each other. "Are you staying for dinner?" Mamie asked Spanky and went into the kitchen before he could reply.

Spanky grabbed Lottie by the hand and led her to the kitchen. He hadn't come to eat; he had come to get Lottie and was determined to let Mamie know where he stood. Mamie was standing at the kitchen sink with her back to the doorway. As if sensing that they were there, she turned around and faced them. Lottie could tell that she knew something was afoot. Mamie's eyes focused on not just the two of them but rather the whole of them. Almost imperceptibly, Mamie shivered. Lottie saw it. She grew weak in her stomach. Her emotions were strong; fear, compassion, and love converged on Lottie and made her ill. She rushed into the news that she and Spanky were leaving together. "Mama, Spanky has come for me. He wants me to live with him, and I have decided to go."

Spanky stepped in. "Mamie, you know I love you, but it can't be like it was before, and you know that as well as I do. I want to be with Lottie. I had to make a choice, a hard choice, because I love both of you."

Together, Lottie and Spanky waited for the storm to come. It never came. Mamie, who was clearly surprised and hurt, only said, "Spanky, how is this going to look to your son, Julian, and Lottie's brother, Buddy? You are breaking up my family, your family. Even though you have never acknowledged it, you do know that Julian is your son."

"I suspected as much. He looks just like me. The boy rarely speaks to me. What else could I have done? You live well, Mamie, thanks to me."

"And Calvin," said Mamie.

"And Calvin," admitted Spanky. "No disrespect intended. Mamie, I have caused you all pain. I can't be here anymore. My love, what you and I share, we will always share. Nothing will ever change that."

"So you still plan to be both my daughter's and my lover, even though you will be living with her."

Mamie fixed her eyes on the doorway of the kitchen and left. Lottie felt a chilly breeze when her mother passed by her and Spanky. Neither could speak. Spanky led Lottie to the doorway, gathered her suitcases, and walked out of the house with her.

L ottie quickly fell in love with her new home. There was a spacious living room. To her left was a family room with a floor-to-ceiling fireplace. On the right was a magnificent dining room. Upstairs was the master bedroom and three more bedrooms. The master bedroom was sunny and bright. She adored the bay windows, which framed a large tree that had been fitted with a swing. Flowers adorned the lawn and followed the pathway to the house. The remaining bedrooms had potential. Lottie wanted to start decorating and furnishing her new home immediately. Spanky had put Lottie's name on the deed. It was his gift to her. It was significant to Lottie because it represented her freedom and her first possession.

Lottie sat in her swing one day and imagined herself visiting with Mamie, two friends just sitting around feasting on life. It was this same tendency to fantasize that prevented her from really understanding what Mamie was going through. She thought and hoped that Mamie would be as happy for her as she was for herself. After having Julian's paternity revealed to her, Lottie was able to see a side of Mamie she had not observed before: Mamie's strength had become apparent, as well as her mystique. Lottie and Spanky had never discussed Julian. Lottie had made a few lame attempts, but Spanky was not willing to talk about him.

After three months of silence, Lottie decided to talk to her mother. Mamie seemed pleased to hear from her when she called. She invited Lottie over for a visit. When she arrived, Mamie gave her a hug and kissed her cheeks. The two adversaries smiled at each other. It was awkward, but pleasing. Lottie was reminded of times past when she and her mother were close. For the first time, Lottie noticed how dark her old home was. Although partially opened, the curtains allowed only so much natural light to enter the house. Her old home was tastefully furnished. Mamie had always preferred the dark pallet. The couch, love seat, and lounge chair were of a maroon paisley pattern. The walls were eggshell white. All the wood—the coffee table, side tables, and desk—were made from oak. Maroon shears lay shyly beneath beige curtains with a strip of maroon in the center. To the left was an oak dining table with claw-feet. On top of the table was a maroon-and-gold paisley cloth encircling a gold bowl of fresh apples and oranges. The kitchen was straight back. The hallway led to a small bathroom. All the bedrooms were off to the left side of the living room. Lottie's room was first, then her mother's room was next on the same side of the hallway. A spacious bathroom separated Buddy's and Julian's room, which was on the opposite side of the hallway.

The house was a pleasant-looking home for Mamie and her family, although much too quiet for Lottie. For some odd reason, Lottie wanted to see her old room. She couldn't resist the urge. While Mamie busied herself with refreshments, Lottie went and inspected her former bedroom. Lace and ribbons, pinks and blues assaulted her visual senses. The surroundings were soft and delicate and very infantile. It occurred to her that very little had been updated from her childhood. She had been given a nice queen-size bed when her long legs started to hang over the bed frame. She had not taken much with her when she left, mostly clothes, a few pictures, and her jewelry. On the dresser sat a solitary picture of Mamie and her family, which she had overlooked in her haste to pack. Lottie focused on the mirth expressed in their eyes. They were sitting for a family photo, but Spanky had been making faces while they tried to appear dignified and classy. They were all so young. Julian was a baby. He sat in Mamie's lap, giggling at Spanky. Lottie took the overlooked relic with her when she left the room.

Lottie stopped outside of the room and considered her next impulse, which was to pay Julian a visit. It was afternoon, and she hoped he was at home. She knocked gently on the door. (Julian could become quite incensed when an interloper entered his fortress.)

"Come in," he said dryly. Lottie peeped inside timidly and smiled. "Lottie!" said Julian with pure joy and surprise. Lottie beheld her little brother with pride, for he was far from a little boy. At seventeen, Julian was practically a grown man. Why hadn't she noticed how much he had grown? She had missed him. They embraced. Feeling uncomfortable, they separated. Each started talking simultaneously; each inquired about the other's well-being.

"You know, Lottie," Julian ventured, "I wish I had spent more time with you and Buddy. You have both moved out, and it seems that I hardly know either of you. I can see Buddy often because he lives upstairs, but it's not the same with you. I hate that that man took you away, I hate that he hurt our mother, and I hate that he is going to hurt and destroy you."

"Oh, Julian, Spanky would never hurt me. I'm sorry about Mama too. That is why I'm here today. I want to keep our family together. You must know, Julian, that we all love you. I know things have been strained over the past few years, and none of us has communicated very well, but that doesn't mean that we don't love one another. I'm sure you've been a great help to Mama."

"No, Lottie, you are wrong," confessed Julian. "I haven't been a help to anyone. I've stayed in my little cocoon most of my life. I just couldn't take it out there with you and Mama and Spanky. I just can't be a part of something in which I don't believe. I don't want to be a part of a family that I am ashamed of having. I try to spend time with Mama, but she's so quiet most of the time. She almost never talks, so I never know what she is thinking or feeling. It is tiresome. I ask questions. She doesn't answer. I rephrase the questions.

She doesn't answer. I need my mother to explain herself to me, Lottie. I understand that she doesn't have to tell me anything. Nonetheless, I need her to tell me everything. She told me about Spanky being my real father. He has been around me all of my life, yet she didn't bother to tell me that fact. I thought Calvin was the father of all of us. I see why he never came back. I carry the Wallace name. I thought Spanky was my uncle too. I am a product of incest, Lottie. My uncle is my father. I know that must be wrong, evil in fact. It feels wrong. I feel like I am the main act in a freak show. Buddy tried to explain Mama and Spanky's relationship to me long ago, but I was just too young to understand. Now I do. I hate Spanky, Lottie. I know you and Mama love him, but all I feel for him is hate."

Julian waited for a response from Lottie; none was forthcoming. They sat close together on his bed. Lottie put her arms around Julian and held him. His warm tears fell on her shoulders. She had no words of comfort for him.

"Have you ever noticed, Lottie, that we have no real friends? I mean, the kind that you bring home with you after school, the kind you can invite to spend the night with you? I was afraid to bring anyone to this house. I never knew what the temperament would be. Hell, we are not even friends with each other. We really cannot afford to be. Buddy and I have been friendlier with each other than we ever were since you moved out. The thread of our new alliance is our mutual hatred for Spanky. We even talked about killing him once. Boy, did that feel good! Unfortunately, he and I are both cowards, or should I say, fortunately, for Spanky's sake. I wish we all could have been closer. Spanky alienated us from each other, and he's going to do the same with you. He has made it virtually impossible for you and Mama to be close. When he was away those few years, I began to feel good about us as a family. In a way, we had exorcised ourselves of the one true demon among us. He no longer controlled my mother and my sister," said Julian with a sideward glance at Lottie.

"Why you, Lottie?" asked Julian. "Why do you want to be with him so badly that you would move in with him? If you were free, you could finish school and meet new friends, date guys your own age . . . We could be a 'normal family.' You don't need him, sis. Please come home and let him go. I even think Mama would eventually adjust to his absence if you both agreed not to see him anymore. Even though she is very hurt now, eventually she would heal."

Tears welled in Lottie's eyes and crawled slowly down her face. How could she explain to her brother what was in her heart? Her defense for being with Spanky would have been decimated by her brother's see-it-like-it-is wisdom; this she knew. Her need for Spanky was not easily explained. She never rationalized being with Spanky. As bright as she was academically, she never put her love for him under evaluation. She fed off instinct. There was no place for her in which Spanky did not exist. "I can't live without Spanky," said Lottie. "For two years, I was miserable. I did well in school because I studied to consume myself, to not have to think about him every hour of the day. When he came back, he brought me back to life. My life is with him, Julian. I have never wanted to hurt Mama. I'm just not strong enough to give up Spanky for her sake. He wouldn't stay with her anyway. He had been living with another woman during his time away. He left her to be with me. Spanky does what Spanky wants to do. I plan to talk to Mama. I need to make her understand.

"Yes, Julian, Spanky is your father and our uncle, but I don't feel guilty, bad, or ashamed of that fact. That is just who he is, as far as labels go, but no mere uncle could be who Spanky is. He's so very special, Julian. You just can't see it yet. I have never wanted or needed anyone or anything the way I need Spanky. I don't want anybody else, and neither does Mama. What can be so wrong about two women loving a man so dearly? I wish the same for you, Julian, that you will one day be loved so much."

"No!" said Julian resolutely. "I never want anyone to love me beyond reason or obsessively. I never want to be loved by anyone with so few reasons to live. I've never asked anyone in this house to consider me or how I feel, and I surely won't start now. I have always hoped that you and Mama would one day consider and care for yourselves enough to see how destructive Spanky is. However, I know deep down that it will never happen. As for me, I'll always love you and Mama, Lottie, but I am out of here when I graduate. I will always be available to you and Mama, but I refuse to continue to be a part of Spanky Fielder's life." To punctuate his declaration, Julian opened a book, settled in his chair, and began to read.

"Won't you come and have lunch with Mama and me? Taking his silence as her answer, Lottie left the room. She was saddened by her encounter with Julian. More than anything, she was sad about the loneliness her brother felt, must have felt all his life.

When Lottie went into the kitchen, she heard Mamie fussing about how she needed to warm the coffee and what had taken Lottie so long. "Not now, Mama," said Lottie. "Let's talk." Lottie was nervous, and she could see that Mamie was uncomfortable. Looking at her mother was like looking at a mirror, at an older version of herself. The pain and anxiety that registered on Mamie's face caused Lottie's chest to constrict. "I am sorry if I have hurt you, Mama," said a remorseful Lottie to her mother. "I am in love with him, Mama, and I love you too. I need you in my life. Spanky and I both need you. You are our family."

"I believe you mean what you have said, Lottie," responded Mamie placidly. "But what possible place could I have in your lives? Where do I fit? I knew as a child that I would never love anyone else like I love Spanky. I tried with your father. The truth is, had Spanky never come to me, Calvin would have only had a small portion of me. The more of me would have always belonged to Spanky. Without him, I'm like a plucked rose that's surely destined to die. Loving Spanky has cost me a lot. My love for him has isolated me from everything that was not him. What do I do now, Lottie? Where do I go from here? You see, my dear, Spanky never isolated himself or let the world go by. He is out there, exposed to it all. He likes living that way. He'll never be yours or mine alone. He knows other people, other places. I never had a need of that. However, for you, Lottie, and Buddy and Julian, I want you to be a part of life. If you stay with Spanky, Lottie, you'll never know any world but Spanky's world."

"Mama, I'm already there. I desire no one and nothing, just Spanky's love."

"It's easy to be with Spanky, Lottie. Remember how you felt when he was away from us? That is what being with Spanky feels like. I accepted his being out there, because I knew all paths he took would eventually lead him back home, here with me, where he belonged. Yes, we fought about other women and his unaccountable weekends. Nonetheless, I felt secure that he would always be with me. He always has, and he will be again, Lottie. Indeed, you do have him now, but it's just a matter of time before he starts to miss me, to need me. Spanky and I are of the same soul. Lottie, out of all the things Spanky has done that hurt me, his being with you hurts the most. This is his biggest betrayal.

"Lottie, I'll never stop loving you. You are still my little princess, and I don't blame you for what has happened. Spanky is invariably drawn to the forbidden. He couldn't have resisted you if he wanted to. You are so much like me. In you, he saw the Mamie of long ago. With you, he could go back to the beginning, when there were no bitterness, no betrayals. I won't pretend to be happy for you, Lottie, because with Spanky, there is no long-lasting happiness. You'll suffer greatly. I just hope you are strong enough to bear it."

Anguish settled over Lottie. "Did you think throwing Julian in Spanky's face would make him stay, Mama? Is that why you chose that particular time to tell all of us that Spanky was Julian's father?"

"No, Lottie. Spanky has always known that Julian was his son. I brought it up to remind him that he has a responsibility to be there for me and my family."

"Why did you wait so long to tell us, Mama? Julian is seventeen years old. He's not taking this bit of news well. You need to sit down and talk to your son. His world has come crashing down before his very eyes. He hates Spanky, and you are going to make him hate you too."

Mamie had nothing to say. She didn't want to talk about all that. The topic only added to her misery. What was there to talk about? She loved all her children. Their paternity should not be an issue. Julian came from love. That was all that mattered. Lottie could not just sit there and watch her mother suffer, so she rose to leave.

"There is a price on Spanky's love, Lottie," Mamie admonished her daughter.

Cloaking herself in dignity, Lottie walked gracefully out of her mother's house.

⌒Ɱ⌒

When the morning sickness started, Lottie had been so depressed that she attributed her illness to her emotions. She had formed a friendship with the young couple next door. Millie and James Robinson had filled many lonely hours for Lottie. Millie and Lottie had breakfast together most mornings. Neither of them worked. Lottie had all but dropped out of school. She was only three semesters short of receiving her bachelor's degree in education from the University of

Chicago. Spanky had told her that he needed her close to home and available to him day or night. After hustling James out of the door, Millie would either go to Lottie's or make breakfast for the two of them in her own house. Spanky never rose before eleven, so Lottie was free to do as she pleased. On occasions, the women would go out to eat, but they had to be home before Spanky woke up.

It was at breakfast that Millie first witness Lottie's nausea. Lottie barely made it to Millie's bathroom before she tossed up the omelet she had just eaten. "You are pregnant!" exclaimed Millie.

"What?" asked Lottie, wiping her face with a damp towel.

Millie stood at the bathroom door staring at Lottie in amazement. "How far along are you?" she asked.

Lottie, still baffled, said with forced levity, "Millie, what are you talking about? I'm not pregnant. I've just been worried about Mama and Julian, that's all. Maybe a little homesick too. I'm depressed, girlfriend, that's all."

"You are pregnant," said Millie in a definite manner. "Lottie, James and I don't have children, but I have been pregnant three times, although I miscarried each time. Our three babies are in heaven now. When was the last time you had your period?"

Lottie pondered the question. "I don't remember, Millie. I haven't been keeping up with my cycle. Let me think. Oh! I remember. My period was on the last time I saw Mama. That was over three months ago. Millie," said Lottie, astonished, "I think you may be right. Wow, Millie, I'm going to have Spanky's baby!"

Spanky was not the happiest of pending fathers. He hated the idea of a child coming between him and Lottie. In addition, a baby was going to spoil Lottie's perfect body. "You are more beautiful than any woman has a right to be," he told her. "And you belong to me. How lucky can a man be? You have your child, and then you come back to me. We'll get somebody to help you with the baby."

Lottie's pregnancy did not stop Spanky from taking her body whenever he chose. Every time Spanky touched Lottie, she trembled. His lovemaking was passionate and strong. It grieved her dearly when in her fifth month, she had to refuse him. "The doctor said I am showing signs of early dilation. He doesn't want me to risk a miscarriage," she explained to her irate lover. "I'm mostly to stay in bed for the next few months."

Lottie thought for a moment that he was going to strike her. He rose from the bed, dressed, and left. Spanky stayed away for three endless days. Her greatest fear was that he had gone back to Mamie. During the rest of her pregnancy, Spanky only visited his home. He was away constantly. Whenever he was around the house, he barely spoke to Lottie and often looked at her with disgust. Lottie felt that getting pregnant was the worst mistake she had ever made.

Lottie got out of bed one morning to use the bathroom. As her feet touched the floor, water poured down between her legs, and pain was instant. She climbed back into bed and lay in a fetal position. The pain was so excruciating that she started crying. Lottie called out for her mother and Spanky. Never had pain been so piercing. It was too soon. The baby was not due for six more weeks. The ache in her heart almost matched the pains in her abdomen. She just knew that she was losing her baby. The past few weeks had been very trying for her. Spanky had been unavailable to Lottie. Over a period of time, Spanky new lounge was his main focus. He used the venture to justify to Lottie why he had not been home very much. He also owned a liquor store that housed residents on the second and third floors. Spanky had other investments, but they were not to be discussed with his woman. Lottie grabbed the phone and called Spanky's lounge. Knowing beforehand that he would resent her calling him at work and that he would tell his staff to take a message, Lottie left the news that she was in labor with his partner, Dewy, who had answered the phone.

Lottie had not met Dewy, but she knew of him, and he knew who she was. Moments later, she was surprised when Spanky called back and told her that he was on his way home.

Lottie lay in the hospital bed for hours with Spanky at her side. She was delirious with pain. Spanky sat helplessly in a chair next to her bed, trying to soothe her with light strokes of her hair and aching belly. A doctor had been tending to her, but he had left the room for what seemed to Spanky a very long time. The nurse who stayed with them did her best to ease Lottie's discomfort. She brought ice and rubbed it across Lottie's forehead and constantly monitored her vital signs.

The doctor was a tall, thin, middle-aged man who wore his glasses on the bridge of his nose. When he returned to the room, he asked Spanky, "Is she your daughter?"

"No, she is my niece," managed an ashamed Spanky. He had never been confronted before about his relationship with Lottie.

"Anyway, at the moment, we're trying to determine if she can deliver naturally or if we need to do a C-section. All we can do right now is try to keep her as comfortable as possible."

"Thank you, sir" was all that Spanky could manage. He was a nervous wreck.

Amid her agony was her perpetual concern for how Spanky was holding up.

"Little lady," said Spanky. "We are going to take good care of you and your baby."

"I'm surprised you care," said Lottie. "You have done nothing but abandon me during this pregnancy. You weren't home, you wouldn't return my calls, and you act as if I had done something to insult you. I did not make this baby by myself. Where have you been? Were you with Mama?"

"Listen, Lottie," said a conciliatory Spanky, "it's just that I am used to having you when I want you. I got angry, that's all, and for the record, don't question me about where I go and what I do. I won't have that from you, Lottie, or anyone else."

CHAPTER 8

Lottie never really knew Calvin Wallace. She was very young when he left. Buddy, who loved him so much, told her the most about their father. He told her that he was good and kind. Buddy said unlike Spanky, he was a family man, one who was always there for them. Lottie thought about the early years when Spanky would disappear from home and how frantic her mother would be, how unhappy he made her. She remembered her mother's despair during those episodes of unaccountable absences. Mamie's words were, "He took himself into the world because he wants to dwell there. In that world, family does not exist and is definitely not a priority. When he gives us money, he feels that he has met his obligation to his family."

Lottie decided to call Mamie because she needed her. She needed the warmth of a mother, not the coldness of this man who stood looking out of the window, disengaging himself from her most important experience. "Mama, I am in Holy Angels Hospital. The baby is coming early. Can you come to me, Mama?"

"I'll be there as soon as possible, baby," said Mamie. "Where is Spanky? Does he know you're in labor?"

"He's here with me, Mama," said Lottie. Then she whispered into the phone, "But I want him to go."

"I understand," said Mamie's quavering voice.

When Mamie arrived, relief flooded the room: brooding Spanky started smiling, and Lottie's hands reached out for her. As mother and daughter embraced each other, Spanky gravitated toward the door.

"I'm going to take care of a few things, Lottie, now that Mamie is here. I'll return soon." He leaned down and kissed Lottie's forehead. "Call me, Mamie, when the baby comes," he said and left the room.

"How are you, Lottie?" asked Mamie. She was being kind and gentle with her daughter. Lottie became suspicious. She was about to ask Mamie if she had been with Spanky when her mother said, "When you were born, it was as if Spanky had been given to me again. We were estranged at the time. You looked so much like him to me. I just adored you. When Julian was born, I felt him to be a love child. Now you will have your own love child, Lottie. I never got the chance to enjoy Julian. After he was born, Spanky demanded more and more of me. My baby and my baby's father both competed for my attention, but Spanky was not to be outdone. He required sex from me before I had totally healed, so good luck, Lottie. You're going to need it."

"I just need to know one thing, Mama. Has Spanky been with you during my pregnancy?"

"Of course, he has, Lottie. Just like he was with other women when I was pregnant with Julian," responded Mamie. "I told you. Spanky will always come home to me."

"Well, at least that explains why you are in such a good mood," said Lottie solemnly. "I'm so tired. I just want this to be over."

The universe heard Lottie's cry. In the middle of her searing contractions, the doctor returned with the news that they were going to induce labor. Two hours later, Lottie was presented with a new baby boy. She looked at his face and kissed him. She loved him in her belly, but she was overjoyed when she held him over her heart. Their hearts beat as one, and her existence now had a purpose. She knew love in new ways, pure and unconditional. She named him Raphael. He was not named after anyone in particular. Lottie had always liked that name. To her, it was poetic and mysterious.

Mamie loved her grandson immediately. She had shared in the agony and glory of his birth. Lottie's son reminded her mostly of Julian. He had the Fielder's downcast eyes and long eyelashes. His ebony hair was wispy, with stubborn curls that resisted any attempt to smooth them. His complexion was like caramel candy, and he smelled new. Mamie returned the baby to Lottie and sat and watched her beautiful daughter become a mother. She heaved as she held back the tears that were forming in her soul, for she knew this baby would be neglected and unloved by its father. She was happy that he would have Lottie.

As happy as she was, Lottie felt sorry for her son. Lottie was not clairvoyant, but she felt that her son and his father would never be close. She was all he would ever have. Raphael was premature and showed signs of jaundice. The nurse gently took him out of Lottie's arms and told her that the baby would be examined by the doctor and incubated. Lottie was immediately concerned. The nurse reassured her and advised her that the doctor would speak to her when he had finished evaluating Raphael.

Mamie called Spanky to give him the good news. Since all had gone well, he chose not to return to the hospital. He called Lottie during her brief stay but did not visit. His excuse was, he could not afford to be away from his businesses. He assured Lottie that he would be there to take her and the baby home.

The doctor came to speak to Lottie. He told her that her baby was underweight and did indeed have jaundice. He would have to remain in the hospital for at least two weeks. His diagnosis mortified Lottie.

Mamie did not return the next day for a visit. In the ensuing time, Buddy, Julian, Millie, and James had all come to see her. Julian brought the baby a teddy bear, and Millie gave Lottie balloons and a card. More gifts were waiting for them at home.

Lottie was released on the third day. She was very reluctant to leave her baby behind. Spanky had arranged to pick her up. She took him to the natal unit to see his son. When invited to suit up and go with Lottie inside to say goodbye to Raphael, he declined.

The new housekeeper and ultimate nanny met them at the door. She introduced herself as Florida Whitfield. Mrs. Whitfield, who was dressed in a white uniform, helped Lottie to her bedroom and offered to bring her something to eat, which Lottie declined. Mrs. Whitfield was an affable woman and destined to be a close and loving friend to the growing family.

Lottie went to the hospital daily and spent most of the day with her son. She had not been able to persuade Spanky to go with her. Instead, Millie went with her. Every day Millie had to induce Lottie to leave the hospital long enough for the two of them to have lunch. The day Raphael was released from the hospital was a time of uncontainable joy for Lottie. Once again, Millie substituted for Spanky and took the mother and child home.

As they entered the house, Mrs. Whitfield reached for the baby, but Lottie stepped back. She smiled at the middle-aged woman and said, "The baby is asleep. I'll take him upstairs and lay him in his crib." Mrs. Whitfield followed.

As they ascended the stairs, Spanky, who was still at home, spoke. "I'll be late as usual, sweetheart. Will you be all right?" he asked before leaving out of the door.

Lottie, who was still perturbed with him, said, "I'm fine, Spanky. Go about your business."

⌁

When Julian arrived, Lottie was breastfeeding her baby. Julian touched his little fingers. Lottie fought her emotions. She did not want to distress her baby. Julian sat quietly while Raphael nursed. After which, the baby was taken away by Mrs. Whitfield. He went and sat next to Lottie on the side of the bed. "I tried to get Mama to come with me, but she refused. Has she ever visited you here at your home, Lottie?"

"No, Julian, not once. She hasn't even called since Raphael and I came home," said Lottie.

"I came because I wanted to see you and my new brother. For his sake, I'll be Uncle Julian…less confusing." Julian composed himself and continued, "He's been there with her, Lottie. Several times in fact. Now she's all confused again. He told her he couldn't bear to be around you right now. She lets him stay whenever he wants. I hate him so much. I hate him and I hate her and I hate you. You've brought an innocent child into this nightmare. I'll not neglect the baby or you. I just want you to understand that I am here today just for the baby's sake. He is going to need me in his life. Otherwise, I would stay as far away as I could."

"Is he sleeping with her?" asked Lottie.

"What do you think?" Julian almost hollered at her. He answered with no regard for his sister's feelings. "I got to go now, Lottie. I will see you soon." He left her to ponder the situation on her own.

When Lottie walked into the house that day with Raphael in her arms and Spanky at her side, she thought she would suffocate. She couldn't catch her breath. She was having a panic attack. Her heart was so swollen and tender that it cut off her breath for a moment. She sat down on the sofa to keep from fainting. Mrs. Whitfield, who had witnessed Lottie's near collapse, grabbed the baby and took him to his nursery. Spanky sat beside Lottie and held her in his arms. He kissed her lightly on the lips and told her she had to quit obsessing over Mamie. He told her he loved her above all else.

Lottie couldn't contain herself. Ever since she had been home with the baby, her only contact with Spanky had been via the telephone. Even then, Lottie barraged Spanky with a litany of questions about him and Mamie. She had been shocked when he called and said he was taking her and Raphael out for lunch.

"You don't love me, Spanky," said Lottie matter-of-factly. "You took me from my home, brought me here, got me pregnant, and left me. You turned your back on me when I needed you most. As if that were not enough, you've resumed your relationship with Mamie. I was too fat and ugly for you. The doctor said I should not have sex those last couple of months of my pregnancy. Instead of standing by my side, you went to my mother. Spanky was not going to be denied sex. Oh no! Not for anybody or anything in the world. Is that all I am to you, Spanky, a sex object?" screamed Lottie.

Spanky left his fingerprints on Lottie's smooth face and his course words on her soul. "Don't you scream at me!" he assailed. "How dare you question me and accuse me of anything. Before there was a Lottie, Mamie existed. Never, ever question me about her. I have not and never will leave my first love. She was my first love and lover. She is the queen, Lottie. I didn't ask you for a baby. He's here now, and I accept that, so you take care of him. Thanks your job to take care of me and Raphael."

"In that order, Master?" said Lottie sarcastically. "I didn't make Raphael by myself."

"You could have used protection, Lottie. You wanted to get pregnant. You thought that would tie an apron string around me, to keep me in place. No woman rules me. No woman tells me what to do," reiterated Spanky.

"Perhaps so, Spanky. From now on, I'll have babies strictly for myself."

"There won't be any more babies in this house, Lottie," stated Spanky adamantly.

"You have everything you want, Spanky," retorted Lottie. "I'm going to have what I want also, and I want babies," said Lottie before scaling the staircase to the nursery.

Lottie was a mother who felt that her baby must come first. Spanky grew weary of competing with Raphael and chose to spend most of his time away from home. Lottie became accustomed to him not being there. Because of the club and liquor store, when Spanky did come home, it was usually not until about five o'clock in the morning. Lottie was routinely up feeding the baby. She never knew what mood he would be in. If he was extremely tired, he would go to bed immediately and sleep until about eleven. If he felt amorous, he would insist upon her coming to bed, leaving Raphael's care to the nanny/housekeeper.

One morning, Spanky came home with gifts for Lottie—a beautiful, simple, but elegant black dress and a diamond earrings and necklace set. He told her to wear them to the club that evening. It was time, he said, for his "gorgeous girl" to get out of the house. The occasion turned out to be the first of many. At first, Lottie was flattered and felt good about hanging out with Spanky and his friends at the club. She would sometimes invite Millie and James along for a night of fun. After a while, she started to feel guilty about being away from Raphael.

Spanky would mostly insist on her presence. The lovely clothes and the nightlife were not really what Lottie wanted. She put up a good front for Spanky's sake. Most tedious to her was the continuous battle to keep lecherous men from compromising her position as Spanky's woman. Male customers soon learned that the magnificent woman with the long black hair was not to be approached. The message had been delivered via Spanky's near lethal assault on a guy who sought the favors of Lottie Wallace.

On many occasions, Lottie would go into Spanky's office to take a break from the crowd and check on Raphael. Her congenial nature would succumb to irritability. It was at those times that she sought solitude. One evening, not knowing that the office was occupied, Lottie walked in on Spanky as he was giving a man, whom she didn't know, money in exchange for an aluminum package with white powder inside. The man excused himself and departed without introducing himself to her. Lottie had had no exposure whatsoever to drugs and could not fathom in her mind what the purchased substance was.

"Hey, babe, just in time," said Spanky. "Come here and try this." He scooped some of the powder onto the smallest gold spoon that Lottie had ever seen. He sniffed the substance up one nostril and repeated the action on the other. "Want some?" he asked her.

"What is that stuff?" asked Lottie.

"Coke," said Spanky without hesitation. "Baby, with the hours I put in, I need something to pick me up, and this stuff does the trick. It also makes your man feel real good. Here, try some."

"No, thank you," replied Lottie dryly. "I feel good enough."

"Suit yourself," said Spanky nonchalantly and left the room.

⌁

Lottie was very much aware of her current pregnancy. She had been careful to not get pregnant. Raphael was over two years old, and she was confident that there would be no slipups. When Spanky came home that particular afternoon and carried her off to bed, she pleaded with him to give her a moment to prepare herself. Patience was not one of Spanky's virtues; he selfishly took her in spite of her initial objection.

Lottie gave birth to a beautiful baby girl whom she named Victoria, Vicky for short. Spanky was beside himself. He adored his wonderful little girl. Lottie was totally taken aback by his response to Vicky. She had braced herself for a repeat of her experience with Spanky after Raphael was born. He couldn't get far enough away from fatherhood. The man who had literally ignored his son found his daughter to be irresistible. When he came home, he would go straight to the nursery, eager to see his precious Vicky. He often remarked about how much she looked like her mother. Lottie thought she looked like all of them—Mamie, Spanky, and her.

When Lottie told Spanky a short time later that she was pregnant again, he struck her so fiercely that she reeled. Unable to regain her balance, she tumbled over a chair. She was bewildered and hurt, both physically and emotionally. Her mouth bled, and she clutched her stomach, afraid that the pain she was feeling might indicate a miscarriage. She had erroneously thought Spanky's paternal nature had finally evolved and he wouldn't mind them having more children. Spanky left her sitting on the floor. Still in shock, Lottie dressed, gathered her children, then called Millie and asked her to take her to the doctor.

"I don't understand you, Lottie," said Millie. "Why do you put up with that man? He's too old for you. He's abusive, never at home. I just don't understand."

"You couldn't understand, Millie. All I can tell you is that I am nothing without Spanky."

Lottie was fortunate. Her baby was all right. She herself, though bruised, was fine as well. Lottie didn't want to go back home right away. She asked Millie to drive by her mother's house. She saw the tan Cadillac parked on the side of the building and asked Millie to wait in the car for her. Millie saw Spanky's car too.

"Oh! Lottie, no. I don't think you want to confront Spanky right now."

Lottie ignored her. She gathered Raphael and Vicky from the car and walked up to her mother's house.

Julian opened the door and was astonished to see his sister standing there. He closed the door behind them and blocked his sister's entrance into the house. "I thought that I was taking the kids to the zoo tomorrow, not today," he said, pretending to have mistaken Lottie's reason for being there. "Hi, Raphael," said Julian, picking up his nephew. He gave Vicky a quick peck on the cheek.

"I'm not here about the zoo, Julian," said Lottie. "I just needed to get out of the house for a while."

Julian observed his sister closely. He had only seen her a few times since he had returned home from Howard University, where he had been attending school. He had spent the majority of his time getting settled. He had started a new job, enrolled in grad school, and moved simultaneously. He was at his mother's house to pick up his remaining belongings. He noticed that Lottie's face was swollen and bruised. "Lottie, did he do this to you?" he asked, turning her puffy face toward him to get a better look. "He's a maniac," said Julian. "The man is a fucking animal."

"I don't want to talk about it, Julian. Look, is Mama home? I want to talk to her. Why are we standing out here? Let's go inside, Julian. I'm tired. Are you worried that I will upset Mama? Or are you worried I may see Spanky? I saw his car, Julian. What are you doing here anyway?" she asked, not attempting to hide her irritability.

"My mother does live here," he retorted, angry with Lottie and himself for being in such a precarious situation. "I just stopped by to pick up the rest of my things and to say hello to the ole girl. Why are you here?"

"How is your new place?" she asked, ignoring his question. "Do you like where you live?"

"I love it! Lottie, you look like you could use a little fresh air. Is that Millie with you?" Julian walked over to Millie's car to say hello. "Hi, Millie, are you ladies out enjoying yourselves today?"

"Hello, Julian," said Millie, leaning over to give him a kiss. "No, we're not having fun. Your sister has an agenda," said Millie with a sideways glance at Lottie.

"I'll come with you girls. Maybe we can brighten up the day. We can go eat or maybe to the movies."

"Julian, you're as sweet and considerate as always, but I don't want to go anywhere," said Lottie. "Vicky is heavy, and I'm tired. Let's just go inside. Okay?"

Julian searched his mind for a delicate approach to the dilemma but couldn't come up with one. Unsuccessful in his attempts to dissuade Lottie from going into the house, he decided to tell her the truth. "Lottie, I really don't think it would be a good idea for you to visit Mama at this time," he said.

"Why not?" asked Lottie rhetorically, for she knew the reason. She did not wait for an answer. She brushed past her brother and went inside. Sensing her mother's strong emotions, Vicky started squirming and crying. Lottie did not take the time to console her. She shoved Vicky into Julian's already full arms. Julian struggled to not drop Raphael as he took possession of Vicky. Conveniently occupied, he had no chance to stop his sister before she converged on Spanky and Mamie, who sat at the kitchen table, anticipating Lottie's entrance. They had been alerted by Vicky's crying. He knew what was about to happen in that house was not suitable for children, so he took the kids outside to play while he and Millie watched them and kept each other company.

"What is this, Mama? Spanky?" She all but screamed. "You assault me, Spanky, then run off to be with your other lover?"

Spanky sprang to his feet but stopped short of striking her.

"Go ahead. Hit me," dared Lottie. "It won't be the first time. What's wrong, Spanky?" she shouted, crazed with jealousy and indignation. "Are you afraid that sweet Mamie will see you for what you are, see the real you?" she spat. "Does he beat you too, Mama, or does he reserve that behavior for me?"

"Go home, Lottie" was all Spanky could manage to say. So incensed was he. In an effort to compose himself, Spanky turned away from Lottie's enraged countenance. With his back to her, he said, "Are you following me, Lottie?" Facing her, he said, "What type of mother are you? Did you drag my kids over here to watch their mother act like a fool? Take the kids and go home, Lottie. A word of caution for you, Lottie. Don't ever follow me again."

"I did not follow you," hissed Lottie. "I just came from the doctor, who said my baby will live, even though you tried to kill it and me, so I decided to stop and see Mama to tell her about the baby. I had no idea you'd be here, but how lucky for me that I came. I don't worry about your whereabouts, Spanky," said Lottie, hurling her words like daggers.

"I know for sure if you are not with another woman, you're with Mamie, because you are rarely at home with me and your children. Finally, I understand your game. Why did you buy that big house that I'm in? Why didn't you just leave me here with Mamie? You could have saved yourself a lot of energy and time. You could have just gone from bedroom to bedroom instead of house to house. Isn't that so, Mama?" asked Lottie, addressing her mother directly. "You see, Mama, he never really made a choice between you and me. He didn't have to. He just wanted to broaden his operational base: you over here, me over there—different sceneries, same game. Get it, Mama?"

"Lottie, you are still so naive," responded Mamie. "Did you really think I would give Spanky up to you? I told you when you moved in with him that he would come back to me. He always has, and he always will. You'll have to accept that if you want to keep him. He is the only man I have ever loved. I didn't give him up for you. He is a part of me. He is the only part of me that I care about. There is nothing I won't do for Spanky, including letting him have you if that's what he wants."

Lottie looked at the two of them in utter disbelief. Spanky, in his arrogance, never changed his stance. Fiery darts shot from his eyes and reduced her to cinder. Betrayed and crushed, Lottie turned to leave with shoulders bent.

"I am coming home, Lottie," Spanky said, halting Lottie's exit. "And I expect you to be there." He moved upon her and turned her to face him. Looking down into her tortured soul, he said, "I love you, Lottie, but you must grow up now. I will take care of you and my kids, but you have to stop this insanity. I asked you to live with me because I want you there. You have my kids. We are a family. There is a baby inside of you now, and it's mine too. I will never desert you, dear heart, and I don't want to hurt you. The only way for you not to be hurt is to accept me as I am."

Lottie took a long look at her mother and smiled. Mamie smiled back. They were the type of smiles that said what neither would dare utter. They were smiles that declared war, that promised the annihilation of a relationship, the dispensation of each other.

Julian was happy to see Lottie come out of the house. He and Millie were quiet. They took the children and placed them in the car. "I'll be over tomorrow about ten o'clock to pick up Raphael and Vicky," he said. Lottie nodded in response.

cy

77

Lottie sat at her bay window and watched Julian languidly walk back to his car after dropping her children off. She hurt for him. She knew just how deeply he was wounded. As with herself, Julian would just have to learn to accept things as they were. She could not change things, even if she wanted to. What saddened her most of all was the fact that she did not want to. For the first time, Lottie was truly disappointed with herself. Like Mamie, Spanky was the essence, the power over her being.

When Lottie arrived home that day, Millie was outside waiting for her. Millie had anticipated her friend's early return, because consistently, Lottie was never away from home for very long. Millie met Lottie at her car. She didn't really want to be inside on such a lovely spring day, so she had set refreshments out on her patio for the two of them. She did not notice Lottie's demeanor because she was too busy talking.

Lottie had never had a confidant. In fact, she had never had a true close friend before Millie. Millie was not an intrusive person. She rarely questioned Lottie about the personal aspects of her life. James, too, was older than Millie, but not as much as Spanky was compared to Lottie. Millie was also older than her by about five years. The fact that Lottie and Spanky were not married was not an issue for Millie. After all, many couples chose to just live together. It was a sign of modern times. Sometimes, when Lottie noticed Millie's quiet observation of her, she would imagine the many questions that must be running through her friend's mind. Lottie was grateful to Millie for not asking them.

When Millie turned to accommodate Lottie by giving her ice tea, she saw the bruise on her cheek and stepped without hesitation across the line of pleasant reserve. "Lottie, Spanky jumped on you again?" (Millie remembered the time he assaulted Lottie when he found out about the baby.)

Lottie did not look at Millie or answer her question because it was rhetorical.

"Look, honey," said Millie, "this may not be my business, but what would possess Spanky to do this to you?"

"He is fed up with my babies," said Lottie sarcastically. "He can't stand to look at me with my big belly. He doesn't find me sexy and attractive anymore. He took a disdained look at me this morning and hauled off and slapped me."

"He seems to adore Vicky," said Millie. "I never knew he resented your having children."

"There is a lot you don't know, Millie," said Lottie cryptically.

Millie knew instinctively that she had been given all the information that she would receive from Lottie.

Theodore, affectionately called Teddy, was impatient to arrive. He was born three weeks early with an upper respiratory infection. The doctors assured Lottie that he would recover without serious consequences, but nothing allayed her fears. Lottie rarely left his side. She gave little consideration to Spanky, putting aside her concerns for his whereabouts and concentrating instead on Teddy's needs. When she and Teddy arrived home, they were welcomed with a surprise party staged by Millie. All were present, except Spanky and Mamie.

The next morning, when Spanky came home, Lottie was nursing Teddy. Spanky saw for the first time the newest addition to his family. Spanky lifted Teddy's little fingers, which lay on Lottie's breast, and displayed, for a few moments, a tender and gentle smile. He kissed Lottie and retired to bed. Later, Lottie followed Spanky to the bedroom. She snuggled next to him in bed. He put his arms around her. They lay together for a long time, not speaking. With her heart full and tiny drops of tears trailing her cheeks, Lottie told Spanky that she would never again bear his child. She had elected to have her tubes tied after Teddy's birth. Spanky knew what a sacrifice Lottie had made. He knew that her greatest joy in life derived from having children and being a mother. He continued to caress her, offering her sweet kisses as compensation for her decision.

Spanky started spending more time at home. As Teddy became less demanding of his mother's attention, Spanky became more so. Mornings that Lottie would have spent with her children were given most often to Spanky, satisfying his voracious appetite for sex. Furthermore, he would insist upon her coming to the club a few nights a week. Lottie felt torn between her obligations to her children and Spanky's constant demands.

One evening, as she sat in Spanky's office, exhausted and guilt-ridden, he entered and locked the door behind him. He took from his pocket a vial of cocaine. After separating it into lines of equal proportion, he took a $100 bill from his wallet and fashioned it into a straw and sniffed the cocaine through it. He turned to Lottie and gave her the straw. Lottie did not refuse this time. Imitating Spanky, she inhaled the drug. Subtle was its effect. Lottie didn't feel like she did when she drank liquor. It was rather mellow and smooth and light and gay. She turned to Spanky and smiled her approval.

Spanky took her in his arms and kissed her passionately. He leaned her back onto the couch and raised her dress, stroking her legs and warming his hands between them. He bit her nipples through the sheer fabric of her dress, sending waves of electricity throughout her body. Lottie moaned. He nibbled at her ears and kissed her neck. He slid the ribbon straps of her dress down her arms, exposing her breast. Taking a nipple in his mouth, he bit it gently. Lottie felt that she would lose her mind. Partially clothed, they made love. The loud music and noise from the club muted their screams of ecstasy.

It became customary for Spanky to leave with Lottie enough of the white substance to have on hand at all times. At first, she would only indulge with him. After a while, she started stealing moments out of her day to fortify herself. So much of her old lifestyle began to change. Gone were the morning breakfast with her kids and Millie. Raphael, who was now being taken to school by Mrs. Whitfield, had to wait until after school to see his mother. Vicky and Teddy would be dressed and having lunch by the time Lottie arose from bed. Everyone was upset with the new Lottie. Millie, Julian, Buddy, and even Mrs. Whitfield had remarked to her about the change. Unable to effect a positive response from her, Julian began to make almost daily visits out of concern for Lottie and her children. When Millie tried to entice her to go shopping or have lunch with her, Lottie declined. Not one to give up on a friend, Millie stopped pressuring Lottie to engage in their past activities, but she visited her every day.

Lottie found herself lacking a desire to be bothered. She told herself that no one understood and couldn't see how much happier she was. She didn't neglect her children. She did not want to miss a moment of their lives. They already seemed to grow too fast for her mind to register. She always spent her afternoons with her children, either outside watching them play ball or on their swing set or running around the yard. Other times, they were inside watching their favorite cartoons. She read to them on occasions, not every night like she used to, and she helped Raphael with his homework. It befuddled her as to what people expected of her. She was not a neglectful parent! She loved her children more than anything.

When Julian or Millie was around, each felt it necessary to supervise her children. Did they think she would harm them or allow them to harm themselves? Lottie actually thought she had become a better person, more personable, and easier to be around. She no longer worried about every little thing. She was almost positive that

Spanky was no longer sharing her mother's bed. He came home most evenings. She had her man and her children. What more could she want?

One Saturday afternoon on an autumn day, Julian came by to take them all to the Japanese Tea Garden. He had brought Raphael a brand-new baseball glove and ball, which he promised to teach his nephew how to use. He had turned Lottie's son into a baseball junkie. They often went to see the White Sox play. It was Raphael and Julian's favorite team. Lottie and the kids had been outside as they waited for Julian to arrive.

When his uncle exited the car carrying the glove and ball, Raphael sprinted to him. "Oh, Uncle Julian!" he exclaimed as he seized his present from Julian's hand. "Wow! Look, Mama." He showed the ball and glove to Teddy and Vicky, who giggled about his excitement. Running back to Julian, Raphael grabbed his arm and pulled. "Come, Uncle Julian, let's play."

"Slow down, son," said Julian. "We can toss a few before we go."

Lottie, Teddy, and Vicky laughed shamelessly at Raphael, who was having trouble catching the balls Julian threw at him. Julian went to Raphael and showed him how to hold his glove for a better chance of catching the ball.

"It's okay," he said encouragingly to Raphael. "Hold your glove upward, and when I throw you the ball, keep your eyes on the ball and follow it. When you see the ball fall, run to it and let it fall inside of your glove."

Determined to get it right, Raphael followed his uncle's advice and caught his first baseball. They all shouted and jumped and hooted at his success. Raphael wanted to play more, but his uncle said they had to go because it was getting late. Julian promised they would play again soon.

The Japanese Tea Garden was a wonderful place to visit, especially at that time of year. The trees were bursting with colors: brown, gold, red, and orange, with green leaves that fought to make their presence known. The golden sun hung low, so low that one was tempted to reach out and touch it. Small bridges served as passages across the melodious brooks like music, with the rushing water that cascaded throughout the park. Purple and white lilies floated on top of the water like they had been tossed indiscriminately across the winding stream.

Lottie and Julian held the hands of the children as they ventured through the garden. They stopped when they reached the playground to allow the children to play on the swings and slides and to rest themselves. They sat down on a green wrought iron bench and watched the children play. Julian glanced at Lottie. She returned him a smile and grabbed her brother's hand. Her hands were warm and moist. In her eyes, he saw a glaze, a haziness, a detachment. He didn't know how she did it, how she could be so lovely and alluring and kind and how she made you feel like the most beloved person in the world when she was so obviously not there. They had grown very close. Their relationship had grown because of Julian's ability to accept her as she was and to not impose his standards and beliefs on her. It wasn't easy. He had learned that his will for Lottie would never be what she wanted for herself. Nonetheless, he decided to enter into that forbidden realm that Lottie had established for herself.

"When Buddy and Mama told me they were sending me to Jamaica for my graduation gift after I returned home from Howard, I was exceedingly happy and very, very afraid," he said and laughed about his own insecurities at the time. He stopped a moment to stop Vicky from climbing the stairs to the slide by herself. He sent her down a few times and met her at the bottom. After a while, he lifted her into his arms and brought the giggling five-year-old where he and Lottie were sitting. He held her securely on his lap.

"As I was saying, I had only been to a few places outside of Chicago in my entire life, and none of those were out of the country. When we landed in Montego Bay, I was disoriented by the men in khaki shorts who converged on us passengers like they had been sent by our relatives to escort us home. The choice of who I would ride with was not determined by me but rather the aggressiveness of the cabby. My bag was taken from me, and I was led to a cab. My driver was driving fast, and he kept turning his head around to ask me questions about the 'States.' I finally asked him to slow down. Needless to say, I was a nervous wreck. I calmed down long enough to take in the scenery of the beautiful countryside. It was the last week of June. I had never seen grass so green and flowers so vivid and bright. It was hot! Sweat poured down the driver's face and soaked his shirt. I began to sweat so effusively that it became difficult for me to see, because the salty fluids from my steaming head were rolling down my face into my eyes, irritating them.

"I could smell everything, Lottie, even the red soil. There were cascades of foliage. The fruit trees were brilliant with colors. Flowers of each color of the spectrum lined the roads and peeked from around trees and boldly dotted the hillside, painting a colorful landscape that incited envy in the hearts of artists. Everything appeared wild and free. The houses, from mansion to shanty, seemed to have sprung up from the ground. They were gloriously embedded in the scenery. If the hill sloped, so did the house. They were just that natural to the culture and environment. Yellow houses, blue-green house, white houses, red houses. The narrow, infinitesimal roads foretold of wonder and danger.

"Curves in the road were so deep that the cab, with our bodies in tow, traced them. The hills and dips in the road were so pronounced that they made my stomach laugh. On the roadside were beautiful people of all shades, ancient people in straw hats and bright clothing who sold fruit, jerk chicken, fish, and meats of all kinds and trinkets and bobbles and baskets and more to the tourist that stopped at the various stands. As I rode with the reckless driver, I wished that we all could have experienced the trip together. Lottie, you would have lost your senses in the brightness and gaiety of the days. Buddy would have had to be dragged back home," said Julian with a chuckle.

Julian's chuckle turned into a belly-bursting laugh when Lottie joined him with a hearty burst of giggles. They both could lovingly picture their brother with drink in hand while he talked up every woman he met.

"You've not been on a vacation, have you, Lottie?"

Lottie shook her head.

"We Wallaces have never really lived, Lottie," said Julian. "Our lives have been unnatural, yet we live our existence like this is the way it's supposed to be. I basically fell in love with a woman whom I met there. Who wouldn't fall in love or think you are in such a festive and warm place? Her name was Lorraine, a fellow American, but she moved and smelled like a native. Her voice was soft. She was demure as she looked me straight in my eyes as we talked. She was dark-skinned, and her complexion possessed a golden glow. Her body was thin and firm. I was mesmerized. I left the island before her. That was difficult! I wanted to ask her to come home with me, but I couldn't, wouldn't, because of my family. She lived in Dallas, so the logical excuse for never seeing each other again was, 'Long-distance relationships never last.' How do you tell an outsider about a family like ours?" he asked his sister.

Lottie could not answer her brother. She was pensive for a long time. For the first time, she really paid attention to the shame that Julian felt. She reflected on the wonderful place that Julian had described to her. Something inside of her wished that she could go there. She had never even thought of traveling or what the outside world might offer her. She could not afford to indulge in such fantasies or anything else that would take her away from Spanky. Somehow, she knew that Spanky would be reluctant to take her on a trip. She couldn't think of a reason why he should not; she just knew it would never happen.

Julian gathered his crew to go home. Vicky and Teddy hopped along hand in hand, singing, "Baa, Baa, Black Sheep," as they made their way to the parking lot, while Raphael, eager to get home to his glove and ball, jetted past everyone to be first at the car. Lottie and Julian, hand in hand, looked more like lovers than sister and brother. Lottie put her arm around Julian and took a deep breath, comforted by her brother's love.

When they arrived home, the children were tired. Julian carried sleepy Vicky into the house. Lottie carried Teddy, and reluctant Raphael lagged behind. Raphael had wanted to play ball with his uncle, but it was dark already, so he knew they would not be playing.

Mrs. Whitfield had set the table for dinner. She was waiting for them to return before she brought out the food. Lottie smiled at her and sat down at the table.

"I think dinner is going to have to wait for those three," Julian said to Lottie. "Are you hungry?" Lottie nodded. "Me too," said Julian. The two ate heartily. Julian had been starving. Lottie picked at her food but managed to get it all down.

Julian didn't want to talk to Lottie while they ate. He wanted her undivided attention. "You're using, aren't you, Lottie?" Lottie nodded and lowered her eyes. Julian was puzzled when she looked at him and smiled. "Can you tell me why?" he asked gently.

"Because, Julian, it makes everything around me lovelier. I don't want to hurt anymore. I used to hurt all of the time. Now instead of the pain, I feel bathed in love and sunshine, and there is beauty everywhere, all around me. I can giggle instead of cry," she said, wrapping her arms around herself in a hug.

"Lottie, the drugs are taking you away from your kids, from all of us," said Julian.

"What do you mean, Julian? I'm right here," said Lottie. "Listen, baby brother, this is between me and Spanky. This is our special thing. My indulging with Spanky has brought us closer together than ever. I'm more of what he wants now. He comes home almost always. I go to his club with him. I'm no longer a lonely woman who sits at home because her man is not with her. Sure, I may take a few hits on my own, but that's not a big deal. Sometimes I use a little so that I can escape and dream about how wonderful I am going to feel when he comes home. What am I going to wear? Is my hair just right? Do I have enough of his favorite perfume? Julian, he's mine. Finally, I don't have to worry about him being with Mama. He's with me."

"So this is who you are now, Spanky's little Barbie doll. You used to be your children's mother. They were the most important things in the world to you. Who takes care of them now, Lottie? Who bathes them, feeds them, gets them up in the morning? You know who? Mrs. Whitfield. While you stay in your bed and in your room obsessing over that creepy old man!" exclaimed Julian. "You may be around us, but you're far from being with us, a part of our lives. I grieve for those children upstairs, Lottie. It has gotten to the point that I no longer trust you to care for your own kids."

Grabbing her by the shoulders, Julian rattled Lottie in an attempt to physically wake her up, if not mentally. "Stop this, Lottie!" he said. "Stop before things get totally out of hand. Roger 'Spanky' Fielder is destroying you. Hell, what am I saying? He already has destroyed this whole family. From the moment he stepped his black ass through Mama's door, our family has lived under his will and power, his total disregard for you and Mama's feelings. I wish he were dead!"

A chill traveled down Julian's spine as he watched Spanky lying in his coffin. The tips of his ears burned with fire, and he gritted his teeth. The beating of his own heart sounded like thunder to him. Unconsciously, he covered his ears. He had made the same gesture the night his mother caught Spanky in Lottie's bed. He had used his hands and pillow to block out the sounds. He could not bear to listen. He had heard enough to know what had happened. He was torn between dashing out of his room to do something to help and not doing anything. He embedded himself in his mattress, covered his ears with pillows, and buried his entire self under the sheets and comforter on his bed. He struggled hard to bore himself through the gut of his mattress all the way through to oblivion. He cried and clawed and wrestled. So unbearable was the pain. He hated himself, he hated is life, he hated his mother, and he hated the most disgusting man he had ever known. He willed himself back through time, back through his mother's womb into nothingness. Nothingness and nowhere was where he stayed. He could no longer hear and no longer see. No one knew that he was blind and deaf; no one cared, for when the storm was over, they all had retreated to nothingness and nowhere.

Days came and went without either Lottie or Mamie or him encountering each other. When one of the three accidentally met in passage, he or she would step aside, because a brush of clothing, a contact with flesh could have led to contamination and, ultimately, death. His mother and his sister had finally succeeded in disgusting each other.

Julian was sixteen, a senior, for his skills exceeded that of the average student his age. He was in an accelerated program at Wendell Phillips High School. He would graduate early. He had always loved school, but he was grateful for it at that time. School was his refuge. He could eliminate bad thoughts out of his mind or focus on his classes and research and reading. Oh, how he read! He consumed books.

Each day after school, he would creep silently into the house and into his room. He trusted no one. His life was sordid, and he lived in constant fear that someone would discover its secrets, that someone would eventually see the dirt on him and frown on his diseased existence. Julian was not friendly at that time. He spoke to no one in or out of his family. He was an active student. He was safe about his choices. Sometimes he would offer his opinion during class discussions. He was a volunteer tutor and library helper. He basically did anything to keep himself busy and only academically involved with his peers. He did not go to the basketball games, football games, and parties. And if a girl approached him, he would almost wet himself. Julian was a forced and willing scholar.

His self-absorbed lifestyle was a waste. He was so handsome that the girls at his school assumed he must be interested in boys only, yet they never saw him with a boy or anyone else. His medium-brown complexion was flawless, his curly black hair was full, and his thin, six-foot-tall body moved gracefully and slow. The two years that Spanky stayed away was a blessing to Julian. When Spanky left, he was in his freshman year of high school. He had only two more years of high school and hell to endure. The day he graduated from high school was the happiest day of his life. Mamie, Buddy, and Lottie attended his graduation ceremony. They were proud of him. After all, he was the valedictorian of his three-hundred-plus class. He was sought by many high-ranking institutions, but he chose Howard University, where he would surely achieve his freedom.

Julian didn't want to tell his family about his summer plans. He told them he was going to take a road trip to see some of America. The truth was, he was going South to see his grandfather. In his estimation, Raymond Fielder Sr. was the only person alive who could help him understand his family.

Julian, like his mother, sister, and brother, was not a religious person. Inspired by Mrs. Bell, his language arts teacher, he delved into the philosophy of religion. She was a devout woman who used portions of the Bible to define parables, analogy, synonyms, and more—a somewhat justifiable method of teaching. She never discussed religion with the class, but she sure knew how to inspire one to want to know more. Inevitably, discussions lead to belief, but she only listened as they debated whether or not God existed. Most of his classmates believed. When asked what he believed, Julian said he didn't have the bases to say yes or no.

Julian stayed one day after class to speak to Mrs. Bell privately. After a brief exchange, he asked her if he could borrow a Bible. He admitted to her that his family did not own one. She didn't give out bibles to her classes because of the school's policy, which banned religion from the school curricula. However, she did have her personal Bible with her and told Julian that he could have it, since she had others. She was pleased to give Julian her Bible, and she encouraged him to read the entire book for his own edification.

Julian could not determine a true belief from what he read. The Bible was historical from his point of view, but the Bible had confirmed for him what he had always known—that both good and evil exist together, that there is a right way and a wrong way to live. It helped him to feel less guilty for feeling the way he did about his family, because he truly felt that Mamie and Spanky had made bad choices for themselves—choices that had a direct effect on all of them. All that was left for Julian to do was to find out for himself how and why his family was so different from everybody else. Only his grandfather could answer his questions. He had never met his grandfather or knew much about him. He just knew that his mother hated both of her parents.

When Julian got off the train in Jackson, Mississippi, he began to feel very ambivalent about his decision to go there. He was nervous and hot. He had written his grandfather to let him know that he was coming for a visit. He had included his graduation picture so his grandfather would recognize him. He had never even seen a picture of his grandfather; therefore, he didn't exactly know who he was looking for.

An elderly man, whom Julian perceived to be in his late seventies or early eighties, walked directly toward him. His hand was already extended, ready to shake Julian's hand. If the man approaching him could have walked faster or run to greet him, he would have done so as eager as he was to meet his grandson. He was smiling broadly. He carried in his hand a battered brown felt hat. He wore a brown-and-orange plaid shirt and brown slacks. Julian moved toward him, shortening the distance between them.

"Julian?" asked the old man. Julian nodded yes, and they embraced. "You is a Fielder all right," he said, looking intensely into Julian's eyes.

Julian thought to himself, *You's a Fielder all right too.*

Raymond's wrinkled face bore a striking resemblance to his son, Roger. His hair was wavy and completely gray. His eyes only showed a hint of their original light brown. Time had painted over them a fine coat of gray. The thick glasses in his grandfather's pocket told him that his grandfather suffered from severe cataract.

Julian was surprised to be led to a 1965 black-and-white Ford sedan. The car, though old, was impeccable.

"Ain't got no use for them new cars. This his a one run fine," said Raymond Sr. in his colloquial lingo. Julian could not suppress his laughter; neither could his grandfather.

They drove through the back roads of Jackson. His grandfather was, obviously, uneasy about driving on the expressway. The two men didn't say much to each other during the drive, not because either felt ill at ease but rather each was absorbed in thought. Julian was taking in the country. He discovered a great appreciation for country life. The dense woods and vast spaces of greenery was a novelty to him. Sprouts of corn, fields of cane, cotton, and wheat and other plants that he did not recognize or know blanketed the landscape. He saw a deer dash across the road in front of them and disappear into the woods. Squirrels raced one another up the trees and leaped from branch to branch.

His grandfather suddenly hit the brakes. Julian fell forward. He caught hold of himself just in time to not hit his head on the dashboard. When he got himself settled, he saw what was happening. The longest black snake possible of existing moved slowly across the road in front of them. Julian yelled out of pure horror. Raymond Sr. smacked his leg and Julian's back as he roared in laughter.

"Sorry to frightin' you, son! That wus a biggon!"

"Man, Granddad. I don't ever want to see a snake again!" said Julian.

"You will, son, and mo," replied Raymond.

Julian composed himself and was soon soothed by the sounds of birds and other sounds he dared not ask about. He saw farms, both large and small, with their stock fenced in or locked up in pens. Pigs and chickens roam freely. He saw teams of workers—blacks, Native Americans, whites—harvesting potatoes, beans, peas, and peanuts.

Some worked in the sugarcane fields. There were watermelon fields. The South was a productive place.

It took almost two hours for them to reach his grandfather's farm. A mangy dog barked and ran to meet the approaching car. A green house in need of paint stood before them. It had a drooping roof, and the front screen door almost hung off its hinges. The steps leading to the front door were worn and needed to be replaced. A red barn sat a few feet away. There was a pen encompassing three very fat pigs. Chickens and roasters pranced around the grounds. They were pecking in the red soil for corn and worms to eat. A chicken shack ended the features of the small farm.

Raymond pulled up to the barn, where they got out of the car. Inside of the barn, Julian saw a horse. He followed Raymond into the barn, where he led the horse into a stall without a gate. From where Julian stood, he could see clear through to the other end of the barn. Outside of the other end of the barn were two cows and a bull and two calves.

Raymond led Julian to the back of the house. Pushing another dog aside, he carefully led the way up the creaky back steps and inside. They entered through the kitchen. It was larger than what Julian expected. The house appeared smaller from the outside. The focus of the kitchen was the large gas stove. The sink faced a window, overlooking a vegetable garden that needed to be weeded badly. It occurred to Julian that the vegetables would surely be choked to death by those insidious intruders. There was a large white wooden kitchen table, which was rapidly shedding its coat of paint, sitting in the middle of the kitchen, facing a modest window, which streamed bright light into the room. The walls displayed evidence of the many meals that had been cooked and eaten there. The wooden floors creaked as they led them to a long hallway with two bedrooms on each side.

The last room, which was closest to the front of the house, was assigned to Julian. He knew without asking that it had been Spanky's room. The walls, which were initially white, had yellowed with time. The regular-sized bed was covered with a multicolored homemade quilt. Squares and triangles worked together to form its pattern. No pictures hung on the wall. A single brass light fixture had been placed on a bedside table. Next to it lay a baseball glove, almost rotting from neglect. Julian wanted to throw it away, but he knew he didn't have the right to do so. There was an empty brass candle holder with a white lace dolly beneath it on the dresser. The window faced the front corner of the property. Blue lace curtains, which had faded over time, hung at the window, offering the illusion of privacy.

Julian placed his suitcase on the bed and walked out of the room. He wanted to see the rest of the house before he unpacked. The living room was a nice size. A winter-green sofa, a round wooden coffee table, and a lounge chair were adequate for the space. A round gold rug covered the wooden floor. Traditional white lace curtains danced in front of the large window that faced the front of the house, allowing a cool breeze to enter the room. The front door led to a porch that was the length of the house. When Julian stepped outside, he noticed the hooks that once held a swing. The main focus of the room, however, was the fireplace, filled with fresh wood. The wood was not needed in the heat the South experienced that time of year.

On the mantel above was an old framed picture of a young attractive couple: a man in a dark suit who was tall and slim, with his arms draped around the shoulders of a pretty woman who wore her black hair in a bun. She was dressed in a black dress with white lace on the collar and sleeves. Julian recognized his grandfather and could tell that the woman at his side was his grandmother, Ester, because her daughter Mamie looked just like her. She was most beautiful, but her essence was coated with sadness and a hint of forlornness. The smile on her face was a ruse to make onlookers think that she was happy. Julian could feel her strength and her pride. Also on the mantel was a wooden cross and a vase of fake roses, dusty and fading.

Julian passed through the archway that introduced the dining room. Four large legs with claw-feet supported a square tabletop, which was covered by an embroidered tablecloth. Six chairs were covered with paisley material of the same green used on the sofa in the living room. Consistent with the living room were the familiar white lace curtains. There was a china chest on the main wall, which displayed his grandmother's special dishware.

Julian turned the corner into the kitchen, where his grandfather was warming up leftover collard greens, cornbread, corn, and fried chicken. The aroma induced Julian's appetite. Suddenly, he was starving. He and his grandfather sat opposite of each other and indulged in the meal with little to no conversation. They washed their meal down with fresh buttermilk. Julian had never had buttermilk before and was surprised by how tasteful it was. He decided to add it to his diet when he returned home.

Totally sated, neither moved to clear the table. Raymond pulled a couple of toothpicks from his pocket and offered his grandson one. Julian accepted one graciously. Leaning back in his chair, he gazed upon his grandfather, contemplating on how to approach the myriad of questions on his mind. Raymond sat with averted eyes, skillfully picking at his stained but healthy teeth.

Everything had been so pleasant that Julian decided his issues could wait. Instead, he and Raymond sat and drank coffee and talked about his trip there and school mostly. Raymond was both surprised and proud to discover that Julian had graduated school at such a young age. In fact, many things about his grandson were pleasing to him. He was a bright young man and sensitive. He was quiet and had a sense of humor that matched his own. Raymond saw success and a world of possibilities for Julian. Julian stood and stretched his arms. He was so tired. His grandfather showed him the bathroom and gave him fresh towels. He took a bath and tumbled into bed. He knew nothing until the next day.

Julian rose from bed and unpacked his suitcase. He put on a pair of jeans and a T-shirt and went in search of his grandfather. He went to the kitchen, but Raymond was not there. He heard Raymond whistling from outside. Julian went to greet him. Raymond was in the garden pulling up weeds.

"Hey, boy," he said to Julian.

"Good morning," bade Julian.

"Morning?" said Raymond as he laughed. "Boy, it's near 12:00 by now. Come on and let me feed you," said Raymond, still chuckling.

"I hadn't realized it was so late," said Julian. "Why didn't you wake me, Granddad? How long have you been up?"

"Oh, I gets up 'bout 5:30, ever day. Habit, you know," he said. "I done fed the chickens and the stock, milked the cows, and gathered eggs. Now I'm gonna use them eggs to make you breakfast. Come on."

Julian was amazed by his grandfather's energy. "So what are we going to do today, Granddad?"

"How's 'bout some fishing? There's a pond 'bout a mile down the road."

"Yes!" said Julian, excited by the prospect. "I was hoping we would fish while I'm down here."

"When we finish, I'll show you how to clean 'em, then we gonna do some hard work getting them weeds out the garden."

Julian laughed. "I figured we wouldn't be having fun all day."

As they strolled down the paved road, Julian kept a sharp eye out for snakes. He did not want to be surprised by one sneaking up on him. Raymond laughed out loud.

"If you leave them snakes alone, Julian, theys leave you alone."

Julian breathed a sigh of relief. Although still on guard, he was able to concentrate on other matters. "Grandfather, will you tell me about Mama and Spanky, how they grew up."

"'Tis been most twenty years since Ester died," he said. His pain was still obvious. "I been 'lone ever since. Don't get me wrong, son. I make out okay, but that's a lot of years for jest thinking, you know? What else can a man do wit his time? There been couple of women since Ester, nothing to speak of though, a widow here or there. I ain't want to settle down no more, so I jest keep a moving. Didn't seem right to marry no woman after Ester. I wuz her man, always wuz, always will be.

"There's times I think 'bout Mamie an Spanky, but it jest didn't feel right burden 'em with my loneness. After all, 'twas they mama and me that run 'em off. I ain't felt much like they daddy over the years. Spend most of my time trying to forgit 'bout them. They cause me and Ester a lot of pain, boy. Jest couldn't understand 'em two, where they git they notions, how the devil got in 'em like that when we wasn't looking. Thought 'bout that lots over the years too. I thank I kinda see how now looking back over my shoulders there. Hell, we ain't taught 'em nothing, me and Ester, not really. Not 'bout sex and life and all. We jest didn't see no reason. That's jest the nature of things. We know we'd marry 'em off someday."

Stopping for a moment to consider his grandson, Raymond peered between narrow eyes at Julian, a question forming on his face. "You knows 'bout 'em two, don't you, son?" Julian nodded with downcast eyes. He was too embarrassed to look his grandfather in the eyes. "Poor, poor boy. I kinda thought so. Kinda thought that may be the main reason for yo visit. I ain't gonna keep you in suspense. I owe you that much. Like I was saying, I hadda look closely after Ester when our olden boy got killed. She went real poorly in her mind and spirit after that. Took to the Lord fiercely to keep her mind straight. I follow alone wherever she went and whatever she did to keep an earthly eye on her. We kinda forgit 'bout Mamie and Spanky. Kinda left 'em alone to fend for theyself, so to speak. That there is where we went wrong. It was like Ester had run clear out of love. She didn't have none left to give to Mamie and Spanky, not even to me. I didn't care for me, 'cause I had enough love for both me and her. I jest didn't spread none of it to Mamie and Spanky."

They walked farther down the road, each in reflective thought. When they came to the foot of a small hill, Raymond led them up the hill and down again to the glistening water. It was hot, very hot. Julian wished he had worn a hat. Raymond sensed his discomfort and led the way to a willow tree, whose arms and hands stroked the top of the water.

"I usually git started fishing round 5:30 in the morning when it's cool or late at night."

The two old souls sat down on the bank and took out their gear and bait. Raymond showed Julian how to bait his fishing hook, then they started to fish.

"I know that's how things got started with 'em, but you couldna told me that at the time. All Ester and me saw was two low-down, dirty critters in there going at each other. I was so mad I wanted to beat the tar out 'em, but Ester wouldn't let me. She stopped me jest as I was 'bout to git started. She said, 'Raymond, 'ems the devil's young'uns. Let him have 'em. They ain't our chillin no mo.' Affa that, I open up the door to put Spanky out with jest the clothes on his back, and I told him, 'Don't come back here no mo.' Ester told 'em, 'You's trash, both of you, sinful, and the Lord ain't gonna deal kindly with neither of y'all.' I watched that boy tear outta dis house like lightning had struck him."

There was a tug on Julian's line. "Granddad, help!" he yelled, not knowing what to do.

"Boy, you done caught your first fish!" exclaimed Raymond. "Easy now. Pull back on the pole. Not hard. Pull slow, slow. Let the fish come to you."

"Woo! Woo!" said Julian once the five-pound catfish lay on the ground. "Look, Granddad!"

"I see," said Raymond. "I'm proud of you, son!"

His thoughts were consumed with the scenario that his grandfather had given him involving his parents. He didn't ask for more at that time, and Raymond did not offer him any more information. Julian baited his hook again and sat down to catch more fish. Soon both he and Raymond lay lazily on the ground. Raymond chewed on a toothpick, and Julian gazed at the clouds, which moved as slowly and peacefully as he felt. In fact, they lay in total peace. Once they became hungry, they walked back to the house, and Raymond showed Julian how to gut and clean fish. They had caught five nice-sized fish, which they prepared for dinner.

After dinner, they went outside to the garden. Raymond gave Julian a hoe and took a rake for himself. They worked around the bean poles and the squash and the greens and the watermelons and the peanuts, chopping and pulling out weeds. Raymond stopped a moment to rest and stretch his back. He looked up at the darkening sky and made the decision to quit work for the day. A grateful Julian leaned his hoe against the fence, as Raymond had with his rake, and went inside with his grandfather.

Raymond and Julian were two tired men. Julian went to shower, while Raymond made coffee for them. When Julian emerged from his room, he was wearing pajamas. He sat down to the rich aroma of the coffee.

"'Twas years 'fore I heard from Spanky 'gin. Wanna come home and visit. Called shortly after Ester die. I say to him no, sur. Jest find your sister and tell her 'bout y'all's mama. It was they sin that kilt

Ester so young. I blames myself too. I shouldn't had left 'em two alone together so much neither. Spend all my time at church or sniffin' after Ester." Raymond shook his head in regret.

Julian felt bad about bringing up the past and especially so when he noticed the tears in his grandfather's eyes and the pain that seized his being. Raymond was trapped by the past. Julian tried to imagine for himself how things were for his grandparents at that time. They were churchgoers, and the parents of two children who had mortified them. He recalled the hopeless woman in the picture on the mantel. Although she appeared strong, she did not have anything inside of her that could carry the burdens of losing a son to death and the spiritual death of her two remaining children. Ester had nothing to live for. So much of his grandmother had died with her firstborn son that there was little of her left, too little to care for the needs of her other children and her husband.

For some inexplicable reason, Julian became aware of the distance between his grandfather's isolated dwelling and the rest of the world. The irony of it all hit him hardest: that legacy of isolation had followed his daughter all the way to Chicago, where she perpetuated it in her children's lives as well. Julian felt like a little child lost in the forest. He had to find his way out. He realized that Mamie and Spanky had been the Hansel and Gretel of Hattiesburg, haunted by the wicked witches of ignorance and neglect. As with the storybook characters, they had turned to each other for security.

Julian remained silent. He had no words of comfort for his grandfather. How does one reclaim the spirit of the past and the hopes that faded before you while you yet lived? He was not angry with his grandparents. They were victims of Mamie and Spanky too. He refused to torture Raymond further by telling him that the affair between his children had not ended there but was still going on after all this time and that he was Roger "Spanky" Fielder's son by his sister.

Instead, he asked an innocuous question that he had not asked his parents, unwilling to show them an interest in the man who was, but never claimed to him to be, his father. "Grandfather, how did Roger get the name Spanky?"

Raymond lifted his head, reached into his pocket for a handkerchief, and blew his nose. He chuckled lightly at Julian's question. "Spanky had always been a rowdy young'un," said Raymond. "He gots so many whippings when was little that his olden brother Raymond Jr. started calling him Spanky as a tease, and it jest caught on. Julian, how's Mamie doing? Calvin wrote to me and say they had split up, but he didn't say why. You know she never wrote home. Not one word in all them years. Didn't hear from Spanky agin neither after I told him not to come home but tell his sista 'bout her mama dying. You's the onliest one I ever hear from."

Julian smiled half-heartedly and said, "Everyone is fine, Grandfather, just fine. I have a brother, Calvin Jr., whom we call Buddy, and a sister, Lottie. I'm the youngest, and Buddy is the oldest. Spanky owns a liquor store and nightclub in Chicago. He takes good care of his sister and her children. We don't want for anything, and so does our father, Calvin, by the way."

"I'm mighty glad to hear that!" said Raymond with sadness in his eyes. "When you gits home, son, you sneak and send me some pictures of everbody like you send me one of yo'self. I needs to see them 'fore I leave this earth."

"I will. I promise," said Julian, which was the last thing he remembered.

When he awakened, he was still sitting at the kitchen table. He smelled fresh coffee and heard the bathwater running. He fixed himself a cup of coffee as he waited for his grandfather to finish his grooming and dress.

"Well, good morning, sunshine," Raymond said to Julian.

"Why didn't you wake me?"

"Boy, you were snoring so hard that I wouldn't been able to wake you, so I jest went and got in my bed. Hungry?"

"Starving."

Julian stayed a full month with his grandfather. He had planned to only stay a week, but house and barn and hogpen repairs plus garden upkeep made his plans to leave very insignificant. They talked little more about their complicated family and more about Julian's future goals.

At the grave site, Julian looked around at his family and, inside of himself, felt Mamie and Lottie's pain. He took Lottie in his arms and held her to him. Julian led Lottie away from Spanky's grave. Buddy took the cue from his little brother and gently guided their mother to the limousine.

After Spanky's internment, Julian suggested that they all go back to Mamie's house. Once they arrived at home, each was exhausted from their emotional distress. Julian said he would make coffee and sandwiches for everyone, so he went immediately to the kitchen.

Mamie sat down wearily in her lounge chair and watched her children. Her eyes settled on Julian, who was serving coffee and sandwiches to them. She knew her baby boy was kindhearted, but she had not noticed before how confident he was. His smile was cordial and polite. Mamie felt sadder. When had he become this person? He was no longer the boy who used to hide out in his room. He was now assuming a leadership role in the family. She needed that. They all needed that assurance from him. With quick, shifting eyes, she looked at Buddy, who was uptight and nervous. He looked at no one directly, well, except for Julian. He, too, required his brother's attention. He was happy to not have to do or say anything. Turning slowly to face Lottie, who was sitting on the couch stiffly like a cardboard model, Mamie seemed less threatened by her, because she had already injured her to the core. Mamie had not spoken to or seen Lottie in over a year. Today at the funeral was the first time she had laid eyes on her, and the anger Mamie felt for Lottie had not subsided but rather intensified once she found out Lottie was responsible for murdering the love of her life.

Lottie stared back at Mamie but did not utter a word. She pretended to be busy stirring her coffee. Her daughter was thin and tired-looking. Her eyes sported dark circles underneath. Mamie read many things in her daughter's veneer. Most of Lottie's thoughts and feelings, she felt herself. Settling back in her chair, she said, "Lottie, how did you end up killing Spanky?"

Lottie stood up so fast that she dropped her cup of coffee from her lap. "Do you think I killed him on purpose?" she yelled at her mother. "Do you think I wanted my man and the father of my children dead? It was an accident, and that's all I have to say." Lottie was leaving the room to get a towel to clean up the mess she had made.

"I know you're being investigated for his murder. I know the police is going to put your ass in jail, which will suit me fine."

Lottie did not respond but instead continued walking into the kitchen. Standing in the doorway while Lottie grabbed a towel, Mamie blocked her exit and said, "What do we do now, Lottie? How do we go on from here? You and I totally depended on Spanky. He was our world. I won't pretend that loving Spanky has been easy for you or me. The past few years have been extremely difficult for me. Every day I could feel him slipping farther away from me. He had forsaken me in many ways, but as long as he was alive, there was always a chance . . . there was hope that he would one day be mine again."

Mamie flopped down in a kitchen chair and cried quiet, salty tears. Lottie brought her a towel and tried to put her arms around her mother, but Mamie pushed her away. "I have grown very bitter toward you, Lottie. I'm even more so now. I feel that you purposely stole my life from me. Spanky was the main vein to my heart. The last time I saw him, we argued viciously. I begged him to leave you, as I often have, but he wouldn't. He said you and the kids needed him more."

Lottie left her mother at the kitchen table and returned to the living room, where her brothers were talking to each other in low voices, obviously about her since they stopped talking when she entered the room.

"Is everything okay with you and Mama?" asked Julian. Lottie shook her head no, and the tears in her eyes rolled down her face into her clothing.

Julian decided not to comfort her. He understood that his sister and mother had a great deal to work out, even while in pain.

"I have to lie down," said Lottie.

Julian was going to follow her, but he was stopped by Mamie. "Let her rest, son," said Mamie on her way back into the living room. His love for his mother and sister overwhelmed him. He decided to go outside for fresh air.

Buddy was preoccupied with trying to figure how his sister had managed to get herself in trouble and how it would all end. The realization that Lottie could go to jail for killing Spanky scared him almost to death. How could this happen in his real life? Had Lottie been high and let things get out of control? It was no secret that Spanky had been verbally and physically abusive to Lottie in the past. His concerns led him to seek answers from his brother. He went outside where he found Julian sitting on the front steps.

"What's with the police and their investigation, man? I hadn't thought that Lottie could go to jail, especially since she said Spanky's death was an accident," said Buddy.

"Well, Buddy," said Julian, "she was alone, except for the children who were asleep, and Spanky was dead in the garage. She waited until I got there to call the police. That didn't look good. She briefly told me what had happened, that she had shot Spanky. Then I urged her to call the police. We didn't have much more time to talk, and she hasn't given me any details. She confessed to the police that she had accidentally killed Spanky. They searched the house for the weapon, but they couldn't find one. Lottie told them she couldn't remember what had happened to the gun. She said she didn't remember actually shooting Spanky. Her response sounded suspicious to them and me. It sounded like a cover-up. They took her to the station, where she gave a statement. They released her, pending an investigation. We'll know soon enough what the law will have to say. Buddy, I—"

Julian was interrupted by a scream and confusion inside the house. Buddy and Julian rushed into the house and heard the noise coming from Lottie's bedroom. Mamie was standing over Lottie, beating her with an umbrella. Julian grabbed Mamie and pulled her away, ending the assault. Lottie was balled up in a heap, still crying and looking at her mother incredulously.

"Mama," said Julian, "what are you doing?"

"Why does she get to lay up in my house and sleep like a baby? Who told her she could rest easily while I suffer? She killed Spanky, so she has to suffer too. Get her out of here, Julian! Get her out of my house!"

Julian didn't hesitate to do as his mother commanded. Buddy led his mother into the living room and tried to calm her down. He held her close to him as she sobbed and told her everything would be fine.

Julian took Lottie back to her house and settled her down. "Mama had every reason to go off on me, Julian, but I was not resting. I was having a nightmare. I dreamed about shooting Spanky. I saw myself pulling the trigger over and over and over. I was so angry with him because I caught him with Vicky in his lap and his hand underneath her dress. She was crying and asking him to stop. I was enraged. He wouldn't talk to me. He didn't answer me when I accused him of molesting my daughter. I went into the hallway closet and got his gun, then I met him in the garage. As he was about to get into his car, I shot him. I caught him with my baby girl, Julian! Please help me!"

BOOK II
LOTTIE'S CHILDREN

Raphael didn't hear the teacher when she called on him to read. He was back in time, remembering the day his mom went away. Lured back by Mrs. Robinson's faraway voice, he tried to refocus. He picked up his book to read, and there it was, the blood. He didn't want to appear alarmed, but his hands began to shake, and beads of perspiration formed on his brow. He excused himself and ran from the room.

He made it outside before anyone could stop him. Too embarrassed to return to class, he decided to go home instead. He was very happy to find no one home. He needed some time to himself. He went into the bedroom he shared with Teddy and closed the door. Drawn to the mirror by his own image, Raphael looked closely at his white shirt. He knew it would be there, and it was. The bloodstain formed a circle over his heart. It had been a while since he had last seen the blood. He thought it had gone away for good. He didn't try to wash it out, for he knew that wouldn't work. When he first started seeing the blood, he had scrubbed his hands raw trying to get rid of the stain. He asked his grandmother, Vicky, and Teddy if they could see the blood, but they saw nothing. His grandmother told him that he had an overactive imagination. Only he could see the blotch on his shirt. His uncle Julian had pretended to see it once, but he had to finally admit that he couldn't really see anything. However, Julian was concerned enough to take him to see a psychiatrist. What disturbed Raphael most was the fact that the blood only appeared when he wore white, which was a problem since his school uniform at the private school he attended required a white shirt.

Raphael tried to remember when the blood started appearing. It hadn't always been there. His psychiatrist suggested that he suffered from separation anxiety because his mother was away. Raphael believed that to be true when he thought about it. It had been around that time when he discovered the bloodstain. "Mama," he whispered.

Lottie's beautiful image formed in the mirror and spoke to him, *Remember, my darling, Raphael, I love you and will always be here for you.*

Five years is a long time, he thought. *When will you come home, Mama? I don't think I can wait.*

Spanky had left Mamie and Lottie with plenty of money and investments. Lottie had chosen to keep the liquor store and lounge open since they were in the hands of his business partner, Dewy, whom Lottie knew to be capable and fair, but she boarded up the house, not yet sure if she wanted to keep or sell it. She would be in prison for a long time. There was no rush to make that critical decision. Raphael, his sister, and his brother moved in with their grandmother, Mamie.

Raphael never understood how his mother could be convicted for second-degree murder, especially since the police never found the gun. She should have never confessed. He didn't mind living with his grandmother; however, he still felt like he and his siblings were alone in the world. They had not spent any time with their grandmother before. He was aware, from what he had gleaned from "grown-up conversations," that there was a riff between his grandmother and mother. All his relatives were there for them: his uncles Julian and Buddy and his grandmother. Even Millie and Mrs. Whitfield were constantly around. Julian and Mamie had argued over who would raise them in the beginning. Julian felt that he was the only one capable, plus he had been around the children their whole lives. Mamie, on the other hand, said that she needed to get to know her grandchildren, and she could provide them with a more stable home since she didn't work.

Mamie reminded Julian that he had his own life to live and that he resided in a two-bedroom condominium, which was not sufficient for three children. His grandmother won the debate, and they moved in with her. He had to share a bedroom with Teddy, but he didn't really mind that. Of course, Vicky got their mother's old room. Raphael's problem was that he just did not like his grandmother's house. It was too dark, not sunny and bright like their home was.

Their new life was an adjustment. Everything was different. First, they no longer went to public school. His uncle Julian had said the change in school was for privacy concerns—in other words, too many of the school's staff and students knew about his mother's plight; therefore, his uncle had enrolled them in private school. Raphael was sad about that because as an eighth grader, he had only one more year before he would be attending high school. He wanted to finish school with his classmates. Now he had to adjust to a new environment and new people.

Julian made sure that each of them received counseling. He did not know for sure how sound his grandmother's thinking was at the time. Mamie was livid about that decision. She did not want strangers delving into her family's life.

Raphael did not think his counseling was working. He didn't really know what made him start doing bad things. Most of the time, he couldn't remember doing them at all. He remembered when his grandmother had accused him of setting the kitchen garbage can on fire. He was not able to remember setting the fire. All of a sudden, it was there, and his grandmother was over him, screaming and fussing at him as she fought to put out the flames. There was also the time he had been playing in his grandmother's bedroom when her pink pearls went missing. They never found them. He didn't take the pearls. Once, he brought home a battery-powered race car. He swore he had purchased it with his own money, but his friend Terrence Coleman told the teacher that Raphael had stolen it from him. He never did find the twenty-dollar bill his grandmother gave him to buy milk and bread on his way home from school. Somewhere between the four blocks between the school and grocery store, the money had disappeared. Vicky still swore that he entered her bedroom one night and cut a plug out of her hair. He wondered why he could never remember doing those things.

Raphael sat on his bed heavily. Life was so overwhelming for him at that time. His mind inevitably wandered back to the day his mother left. Shortly after his father's funeral, she sat Vicky, Teddy, and himself down and told them that eventually she would have to go away for a while. It took over two years for that event to happen, but that was two years of absolute stress and worry. Every day for his siblings and him was the day she could leave. She told them she was being jailed for a few years because the court had decided that she must pay for the death of their father. Teddy, the bold one, asked how long she would be away.

"Teddy, it is going to seem like a long time, but it will go by fast. I'm leaving you guys in the care of your uncles and grandmother," said their mother. "It breaks my heart to leave you, but the family has decided that you will live with your grandmother until I get back, and I will be back," promised their mother.

Raphael hardly heard a word she said, for he and his siblings were crying so hard and loud. Lottie held them close until they were soothed. Afterward, she pulled Raphael aside and handed him a teddy bear that was holding his heart in his paws. She told Raphael the bear was special to her because his father had given it to her.

"Raphael, you're my big boy. You've got to be brave and strong. Whenever you feel lonely for me, I want you to hug this bear and remember that I am thinking of you all of the time. I love you, Raphael. Don't be afraid."

"I love you too, Mama, and I'm very afraid. What will happen to us without you?" expressed Raphael.

"You are going to be safe and loved, son, by me, your uncles, and grandmother," she responded. Lottie, who was already on her knees, whispered in Raphael's ear that he must never talk about the night that Spanky died. What she said puzzled him because he was asleep.

"How can I talk about that night, Mama? I was asleep. I don't know anything."

Lottie smiled and smashed Raphael and his teddy bear into her heart.

"I don't want you to go, Mama!" he protested. "Please don't leave us. Please."

CHAPTER 2

Vicky was glad the whispers and stares would finally stop. She was in fifth grade when they changed schools. Raphael had told her things would be better for them at the private school. Classes would be smaller, and they had strict rules about student behavior. And best of all, no one knew about their mother. Vicky understood that her mother had killed her father and was in jail for it. Raphael had told her and Teddy to not be embarrassed. All she really knew was that she felt really sad and afraid for their mother. She was also afraid for herself and her brothers after suddenly losing their father and mother. Vicky understood that her mother had to pay for what she had done. Nonetheless, she was angry with Lottie. It was not that she was being abused or neglected. Her grandmother was a comfort, and her uncles Julian and Buddy, Millie, and Mrs. Whitfield were always there for her and the boys, but her life had become unhinged.

Vicky gave the school a chance, but she still didn't like it. She had not made any friends, and the classes were boring. More so, she hated living with her grandmother. Why couldn't she stay with Millie? She had known Millie her entire life. Millie was familiar to her, and she was like a second mother. She had never really known her grandmother and had only seen her a few times. Her grandmother's house didn't feel like home. She longed for her old bedroom. She was yet to sleep well in her mother's old room. She kept having bad dreams about a big hand that was reaching for her. She would run, trying to get away. Nevertheless, the hand always caught her. When it caught her, it would grab her and smother her screams. The big hand would cover her entire face while a smaller hand tore at her clothes. She would be awakened by her own screams. Her pajamas would be soaked from perspiration. A few times, she had urinated in bed as well. Her grandmother always rushed into her room to soothe her and change her nightclothes and bedding. Eventually, with her grandmother's arms around her, she would fall back to sleep.

Vicky finally settled into her new life. She was branching out some and was learning to put her energies into things that she enjoyed and made her happy. She liked tennis. She would watch the tennis games on television. She decided to pursue it, and with her grandmother's help, she enrolled in tennis classes. She met a few girls whom she liked. They would go eat together after class, and sometimes she went with them to the movies. Nonetheless, her real best friend and mentor was Millie. Vicky spent as much time with Millie as possible, especially after school, during the longer days of spring and summer. They shopped together, and Millie took responsibility for Vicky's hairdresser appointments.

When Julian was too busy to entertain the children, Millie took over, taking them to the museums, zoo, parks, plays, and the library, where they read and took art classes. Lottie's children led full and rich lives, and it showed. All of them were in a better place. Vicky could talk to Millie about anything. If it had not been for Millie, she didn't know what she would have done the day she was raped. Vicky was not aware of how far she had walked or how long it had taken her to get from a few blocks from her school to Millie's house. Her mind was impaired from the assault. She walked without feelings in her legs. She walked in spite of the headache and the pain in her genitals and pelvic area. She walked in spite of the sticky residue between her thighs. She walked for help. Help came in the form of her surrogate mother, Millie. Millie opened her front door to a terror. Vicky stood there looking like she was barely alive. Her face was dirty and scratched.

Her hair was a hornet's nest on her head. Her blouse was torn and hung loosely about her shoulders, and blood streamed down her legs. Millie didn't have to wonder what had happened. She knew by the presentation of Lottie's thirteen-year-old daughter what had occurred.

Millie grabbed Vicky in her arms and literally dragged her inside the house. She helped her to the couch. "My poor, poor baby." Millie sighed. "You rest, honey. I'm going to call the police."

"No! No!" shouted Vicky. "Millie, you can't do that. Everybody will know then. Grandmother, Mama, no . . . Everybody will know."

Millie was abashed. She was surprised by Vicky's protest. Surely, the girl was not thinking straight. "You shouldn't care about who knows, Vicky. This was not your fault. You were assaulted! You didn't do anything to cause this! You are not thinking rationally. I have to do what I think is best in this situation. I won't call the police now. First, we're going to the hospital. They will call the police for us."

Vicky cried and moaned all the way to Christ Hospital, the closest to Millie's house. Once inside, they waited briefly to be seen. Millie held Vicky without pause. They followed the nurse into an examination room, where the doctor examined Vicky, and the nurse took a rape kit. While Vicky was occupied, Millie called Julian because he had power of attorney over Lottie's children. He arrived just as the police was ready to interview Vicky.

When Julian saw Vicky all bruised and swollen, he covered his mouth to keep from speaking what he was thinking, *Where is that motherfucker who did this?*

A policewoman started the interrogation. "Hello, young lady," she said. "Can you tell me your name?"

Vicky looked directly at her uncle Julian with tears welling in her eyes. Then she looked at Millie with longing. The policewoman recognized her reluctance to speak in front of her uncle. "We really only need one adult present to talk to Vicky," she said. "Perhaps, sir, you could wait outside and let us ladies have some privacy."

Julian understood and backed out of the room, his eyes on his niece. With a glance at Millie, he left.

"Vicky, I need to know what happened to you," said the officer.

Vicky lowered her eyes and said, "I was late for school this morning because I overslept. I was walking through the alley a few blocks from the school when I saw three boys coming toward me."

"About how old were these boys, Vicky?" asked the officer.

"They were older boys, really men, about eighteen or nineteen years old," responded Vicky.

"Continue, please," said the officer.

Vicky took a deep breath and continued, "I started to walk faster because I had a bad feeling about them. Before they even reached me, they were laughing and oohing and talking dirty about me. I looked down at the ground and tried to walk past them. 'Ooh, ooh! What do we have here,' one said. Another one grabbed me by the waist and slung me around. He carried me to the side of a garage and threw me on the ground. I was kicking and screaming and begging them to leave me alone, so one punched me in the face, but I still fought back. One slapped me and then put his hand over my mouth. The one who slapped me stuck his tongue down my throat, and I gagged. That made him more aroused, and he grabbed my breast and squeezed them until I screamed, so one of them decided to shut me up by shoving his penis down my mouth. They took turns raping and sodomizing me. They ran away and left me lying on the ground."

"Vicky actually walked from there to my house," added Millie.

"Can you describe these men?" the police asked.

"I could try," said Vicky. "I had my eyes closed most of the time."

"That's okay, Vicky. We're going to try anyway. We'll show you some pictures, and you can work with a sketch artist to render a portrait of them. You get some rest, young lady. We'll be in touch."

"Do you think the police will catch them, Millie?"

"We can hope, sweetheart."

"Got what?" Mamie asked.

"My new *Raw* video by Eddie Murphy," said Teddy as he searched beneath his bed. "I found it!" he hollered to his grandmother. "Wanna watch it with me, Nana?"

"Okay, Teddy. Let's see what Mr. Murphy is talking about," said Mamie with a chuckle.

The two of them watched Eddie Murphy give one of the most vulgar presentations that Mamie had ever seen, definitely not the sort of language befitting her young grandson. Nonetheless, she and Teddy roared at Murphy's satirical jibes at every subject, from women to politics to being black.

"I'm going to be just like him!" proclaimed Teddy. "I have already finished my act for the school's talent show. Wanna hear it, Nana?" Teddy was the only grandchild to call his grandmother Nana. Teddy, rambunctious and impatient as usual, did not wait for his grandmother to respond. He lunged into his rendition of young Eddie Murphy.

"Something strange happened to me on the way to school today. I was walking along when I ran into old Sharks. Ya'll know Sharks. Anyway, he said, 'Hey, boy, they teaching you anything at that school?'

"'Of course,' I said.

"'What's two plus two then?' he asked.

"'Four.'

"'What's six times six?'

"'Thirty six.'

"'Okay,' he said, 'if I give you this dollar, boy, and tell you to go to the store and buy me a $0.50 pop, how much change you gonna bring me back?'

"I smiled and said, 'None.' Then I grabbed the dollar and ran.

"He laughed hard and said, 'They teaching you all right, teaching you to be a smart-ass. That's what they teaching yo' black ass.'"

With the timing of a professional comic, Teddy continued, "Man, I was very excited about going into junior high this year. I just knew I was going to meet some babes. The first day I walked into Mrs. Cochran's classroom, sporting my best wears and walking hip, she stopped me at the door. 'Name?' she asked.

"'Theodore Fielder,' I said.

"'Take the fourth seat in the second row,' she said.

"So I strutted over to my seat and sat down. Out of the corner of my eye, I saw this beauty. Man, I was certain I was about to score. I leaned over smooth like to put something in her ear when I had the big one. That gas came out of nowhere and without warning! Man, it was so rotten that the whole class smelled it. Needless to say, the girl was repulsed and raised her hand and asked Mrs. Cochran if she could move away from me because I had 'bad manners.' 'Damn!' I said as I slithered down in my seat. If the class didn't know who had farted, they knew then.

"Do you know what the worst part of school is? I'll tell you, it's lunch. Man, they fry everything. They even fry the pizza. I got mad about this fried shit last week and threw my pizza on the floor. The last I heard, that sucker was sliding down Michigan Avenue. [By the way, you have not seen me at basketball practice 'cause I've been in detention every day since.] On that note, I'd like to thank my fellow slime for your attention." Teddy finished with a bow and a grin.

"That was funny and good, Teddy, but try not to curse."

"Nana," said Teddy, "I have already cleaned it up. At first, every other word was a curse word!"

Teddy was frustrated with his grandmother. She had not laughed enough, and she criticized his use of one—one, mind you—curse word. She was just old; that was why she couldn't get on board. He was sure his classmates would love it! Anyway, she had not learned anything from Eddie Murphy. It was the cursing that made a joke funny. He was certain that his mother would not have objected to him using a few curse words. She had always let him do things his way. Sure, he was younger when she left, but he remembered that much about her. When he wanted Vicky and Raphael to turn off the television and watch him dance or listen to him sing, his mom always made them do as he asked. If he wanted to watch his cartoons instead of what they were watching, she always made them turn the channel. He missed his mother very much. Sometimes it was hard for him to remember how she looked. At those times, he would pull her picture from his wallet and gaze at her. She was the most beautiful woman in the world to him. He had not minded losing his father because they never had a relationship. He didn't know him very well anyway, but it broke his heart when his mother had to leave. Five years was forever!

Pretending to stroke her hair in the picture, Teddy lay across the bed and tried to remember the last time he saw her, the day she left, but he couldn't recall much. His vision of that day had faded with the pain. He didn't really want to remember. He had experienced immeasurable pain and loss. He had to get rid of those feelings, so he threw himself into his art and his friends. Teddy was an extrovert. He had more friends and activities than his brother and sister put together. He stopped reading the letters from Stateville prison. They made him sick. He stopped counting the months and years because he became depressed by the slow movement of time. He wanted to be happy, so he indulged in the things that made him happy, which, according to Mamie, was everything. Teddy loved life. He gave his grandmother love and much joy.

CHAPTER 4

errence Coleman could not believe it when Raphael told him that he had never dated a girl before. After acquiring this knowledge, he felt better about his own lack of experience. Terrence admitted to Raphael that he had never had a girlfriend either, which endeared Raphael to him even more. As time went by and their friendship grew, Terrence thought that it would be a good time to hook Raphael up with his sister Denise. He had noticed how Raphael looked at her when she was around. He was definitely attracted to her. Terrence was motivated by his need to introduce his overly popular sister to a nice boy. He did not like the riffraff she dated. The fact that Raphael did not know about Denise's less-than-respectful reputation was a further inducement.

Raphael was a wreck. He had put Terrence off during the school year, citing his heavy class load as an excuse for not asking Denise out on a date. With school out, he could not find a reason to say no. There he stood, casually dressed and ready for his first date. His hands were sweaty, and perspiration beaded on his shiny forehead. Raphael imagined that most people went to a movie and a burger on their first date. He wished he had done this sooner, but he had never really taken the time to even look at a girl, except for Rochelle Boone, who sat next to him in chemistry and was often his lab partner. He had liked her a lot; however, he never acted on his impulse to talk to her in casual conversation.

Raphael couldn't drive, and his grandmother wouldn't allow him to be out at night on public transportation, so he decided to take Denise to a matinee. He was very impressed when Denise came to the door. She had on a blue-flowered sundress and blue sandals. Her hair lay limp on her shoulders and framed her face. She was not a pretty, pretty girl but rather a very attractive one. She was sixteen at the time and going into her senior year that fall. He grew lighthearted as she smiled broadly at him and invited him into the house. Raphael was not prone to make idle conversation; therefore, he sat quietly on the couch. He tried to appear enthusiastic as Denise told him how happy she was that Raphael had asked her on a date. He did not want to seem boring. Things seemed to be going well, so he relaxed himself. Denise was more than capable of keeping a conversation going on all by herself.

Denise sat close to Raphael on the bus and even boldly held his hands during the movie. He fought hard to control the tremors that registered throughout his body. He tried to ignore Denise's warmth and softness and the smell of musk permeating his nostrils. For one moment, he was sure he would throw up from nerves. His stomach was in knots.

Raphael didn't really feel like eating, but he had told Denise that they would stop to eat. He was certain that he could not keep any food down. They walked to a McDonald's restaurant. Denise ordered a Big Mac, fries, and pop. He, on the other hand, ordered a hamburger and pop. He watched Denise attack her food with bravado. She realized eventually that Raphael was staring at her. The expression on her face was comical, so he started to laugh at her, and she joined him in a nice belly roll.

"I'm sorry," he said through bouts of laughs. "Do you eat like that all of the time, or are you really hungry?"

"I guess a little of both," she answered. "I've always been a big eater. My dad teases me about eating so much without gaining weight. I want to thank you for the movie, Raphael. I had heard that *The Third Encounter* was a good movie. I certainly enjoyed it. Did you?"

"I love anything that is science fiction. It was a great movie! I have enjoyed being out with you too, Denise. I hope we can go out again."

"I'd like that," said Denise, "and I am glad I didn't have to ask you."

When they reached Denise's front door, Raphael thanked her for the good time he had and turned to walk away, but he was besieged by Denise, who kissed him long and hard on the lips. He gasped for breath and fought to hide his irritation. Denise had gotten too close too soon for his liking. He ran down the steps to the safety of the street.

Once home, Raphael refused to answer any questions from his family about his date. He was sure Teddy and Vicky would ask if he had kissed Denise good night. That kiss, which he had not initiated, had taken some of the pleasure out of his first experience at dating. Denise left him no doubt about his manhood, but he did not understand why he was repelled by her kissing him. Perhaps it was the manner in which she had done it. Perhaps he felt robbed of the opportunity to kiss her first and when he wanted to do so.

Raphael did not call Denise again for a few days; however, she did call him. When she asked him to go out with her, he declined but promised Denise that he would call her soon. He told her that his baseball coach was having extra practices to prepare them for the end-of-season games, which was the truth, but not the reason. He simply didn't feel like going out with her at that moment.

When Raphael finally called Denise again, he was ready for whatever might happen. All went well on their second date. They had gone to the Parkway Theater to see Teddy perform. Teddy had joined an arts production group, which had originated at his school. This event was the group's first performance out of the school. Instead of telling jokes, Teddy had gotten the lead in a homespun play that the group had written. Afterward, he, Denise, Teddy went out to eat. When they finished eating, Raphael took Denise home. He was happy that Denise had not made any overt moves on him.

Denise invited Raphael inside at the doorway of her house. He sat on the couch and watched *Soul Train*, while Denise went to get them sodas to drink. He had barely taken his first sip when Denise threw her arms around him and started kissing him passionately. Raphael choked and went into a coughing spell, spilling his drink on his best pair of jeans.

Denise laughed and grabbed Raphael again and enfolded him in a tight hold. Her hand explored his body; she went under his shirt and caressed his bare chest and let her hand roam until she reached his penis, all the time smothering him with a prolonged kiss. Raphael leaped from the couch. He looked at Denise in utter disbelief.

"What is wrong with you, girl? Why do you keep throwing yourself at me? Are you a sex maniac?" he asked as he fixed his clothes.

"Lighten up, Raphael," she said. "Most boys enjoy having a girl move on them. It takes the guessing out of the game. They know where I am coming from."

"Well, I certainly don't know where you're coming from. I like the game in which the boy makes the first move." Raphael was moving toward the front door as he stated this proclamation. He opened the door and escaped Denise's romantic lair.

Denise called the following day, but Raphael refused to take her call. She called twice more; he did not take those calls either. His grandmother was concerned after Denise had called and Raphael had declined to talk to her. She wanted to allow Raphael some privacy, but she also wanted to know if there was a problem.

"Raphael," she said, "why won't you take Denise's calls? Don't you like her?"

"Not really," said Raphael. "She is too pushy!"

"Son, I was hoping you were having fun, since you took her out twice."

"Too pushy, Grandmother. Plus, I really don't have the time to date."

"You have the time, Raphael," said Mamie. "All I see you do is play baseball and mope around the house."

"That's not true, Grandmother," responded Raphael. "I hang out with my friends. We do lots of things together."

"Girls are more fun," said Mamie with a laugh, which angered Raphael.

"This is what I'm talking about—women, girls, whatever. You are all weird."

Raphael did not want to argue with his grandmother. He walked out of the house, not knowing where he was going or what he was going to do. He wanted to get away from his grandmother. He couldn't talk to her about his personal feelings. He wandered to the park and sat down on a bench. He really did not know how to loaf around. He preferred the comfort and security of the house. So much of his time was spent studying, listening to music, and reading. When he hung out, it was with Terrence, whom he had pulled away from to keep from talking about or dealing with Denise, or his brother and sister.

As he sat in the park alone, watching the myriad of people outside enjoying the beautiful summer day, his mind went back to another time and place when his mother, Lottie, could not keep him in the house. He would come in every afternoon laced with dirt from playing baseball and having adventures outside with his friends and siblings. He also remembered the time when he decided to go to a White Sox game by himself. His uncle Julian had not been free to go. He was twelve years old, but he and his uncle had taken the train or bus many times to avoid the heavy traffic. He knew well how to get there.

Raphael arrived during the second ending of a game between the Sox and Baltimore Orioles. The passion he felt for the sport was more so then. He boldly rooted for the Sox and cursed with the mightiest of fans when his team faltered. He ate hot dogs until his stomach swelled.

He felt alive and free. It was wonderful! That was the day that he knew for sure that he wanted to be a professional baseball player.

The memory of that experience prompted Raphael to go to a game that afternoon. He was on a glorious high when he exited the bus two blocks from his house. He hummed softly and walked with a skip. When he spotted Terrence walking with two other guys a little distance away, his belly dropped. He had not talked to him or seen him since dropping Denise. He could only hope that Terrence would be civilized about the whole situation.

"Hey, Terrence," he said as enthusiastically as possible. Raphael increased his speed. He realized that he had missed his friend and hoped to reconnect with him. Raphael was so excited about seeing Terrence that he smiled broadly as he reached out his hand to embrace him. Raphael grew terrified as he noticed the less-than-friendly expression on Terrence's face. He looked at his two companions' faces and saw similar expressions.

"You fag!" said Terrence. "I gave you a chance to show me your manhood when I introduced you to my sister, and you dropped her over a kiss. A kiss, man, what straight man does that?"

Raphael was astonished! "Man, where do you get off calling me gay?"

"Denise told me how you fessed up when she put her moves on you. When I asked her why she wasn't seeing you, she told me it was because you are a gay boy. I know she's telling the truth."

"No, Terrence," said Raphael. "I stopped seeing Denise because she is too aggressive—kissing on me, messing with my clothes, touching my penis. You don't do those things to a man you just met. She didn't give me a chance to choose what happens on my date."

"So you're calling my sister a whore?"

"Raphael, my child, who did this to you?" asked Mamie. "I got to take you to a doctor. You are hurt bad, boy."

Although his pain was excruciating, he refused to go to the doctor. "I'll be all right, Grandma. I don't want to go to the doctor. Just fix me up the best you can and let me go to bed."

"I'm going to try your way for now, Raphael, but if you start to look worse, the doctor is where we're going with no arguments to the contrary. Vicky, bring me some pain medicine and my medical case."

His grandmother could help with his wounded body, but no one could help with his wounded heart. As Mamie attended to him and Vicky and Teddy stood about, Raphael told them how he was hurt.

"Denise lied on me, Grandmother. Just because I didn't want to see her anymore, she told Terrence I confessed to being gay and wasn't interested in her as a girl. That's not true, Grandmother. She was too aggressive and only thought about sex. Nonetheless, when I told Terrence about what really went down, he accused me of calling his sister a whore, then he and his two friends jumped me."

Beyond baseball and family outings, Raphael did not venture much outside for the remainder of the summer, preferring to stay far away from Terrence and his friends and the slander and fabrications that were going around about him—some of which he had to endure on the baseball field.

icky hated Terrence Coleman. She was too furious with him to say anything when she noticed him gawking at her. She would stick her nose in the air and sweep her hair in front of him, actions which only enticed him more. Wherever she went, he was there. When she went to the store, he would be standing outside when she exited. When she went to the movie, he just happened to be seeing the same movie. She thought the incidents were contrived by Terrence to make Raphael angry enough to come out and confront him. For this reason, she decided to not say anything to her family about him stalking her.

One day, on her way from Millie's house, Terrence accidentally bumped into Vicky, at least he said it was an accident. She scolded him with an expression of abhorrence, still refusing to acknowledge him by any means, especially talking to him. She turned from him and walked away.

"I'm sorry, Vicky!" he yelled. "I wasn't watching where I was going."

"So that's your excuse? What about all of the times you have been following me everywhere I go? I'm wise to you, Terrence. Just stay away from me!" said Vicky as she turned to walk away.

"It's true," said Terrence, walking fast to keep abreast of Vicky's fast pace. "Vicky, I really have been wanting to ask you something. I've been waiting for the right moment to approach you. I just didn't have the nerves before," said Terrence as he looked down on the sidewalk to keep from facing Vicky. "Will you go out with me sometime, to the show or something like that?"

Vicky knew he was insane then. She glared at Terrence through the tight slits in her eyes. Unable to contain the absurdity of it all, she burst out laughing. "You sleazeball," she said. "Do you really think I'd go anywhere with you? You beat the crap out my brother, then you turn around and ask me for a date. Who's the fool here, Terrence? Get a life, asshole!" Giving her svelte body all the allure she could, Vicky swaggered away. "You can't touch this," she said to Terrence over her shoulder.

Vicky lay across her bed and tried to calm her beating heart. She was indeed angry, but she was also intrigued by Terrence. Feeling guilty, she shouted to no one, "Who does that rodent think he is? How dare he ask me, of all people, for a date! Did he think what he did to Raphael would mean so little to me? The dog. Well, he can just go barking up some other tree. Dog face!" Vicky got up. She was restless. Summer was almost over, and she did not plan to spend the rest of it lying in bed.

The next day, Vicky pleaded with Raphael to go with her to the mall. He wasn't having any of it. Teddy was so focused on his next performance that he couldn't be budged. Having only a couple of hang-out-with-me friends who were out of town for the summer, it was second nature for Vicky to go by herself, as long as the sun was not going down. She had to be home by then. She left the house and caught a bus to Evergreen Plaza, the mall where she usually went shopping.

Vicky narrowed her list to a beautiful maroon-and-black sweater and a black leather skirt. She would go with Millie later to pick up more school clothes. She decided to stop for a bite to eat. Munching on pizza, Vicky did not see Terrence approaching her.

"Vicky, I know you're angry with me about Raphael. I admit I was wrong for firing on him, but what's a guy to do? I had to stand up for my sister."

"Your sister is a fucking liar," spat Vicky.

"Are you telling me Raphael is not gay for real, or are you just saying that to protect him?"

"Does it matter? The fact of the matter is, you beat up my brother, and I hate your guts for it," retorted Vicky.

"Listen, Vicky, I was wrong. Give a guy a chance. I'm crazy about you. I can't get you out of my head. Please say you'll go out with me. We can go see a movie right now, or I can sit down and eat with you. What do you say, Vicky? Will you give me a chance to prove to you that I am not so bad?"

Vicky looked at Terrence a long time. He was tall and thin. His eyes were brown, and thick eyebrows hooded them. His smile was wide and warm. His lips curled upward, his walnut-brown skin was radiant from a summer tan, and he smelled good, like spice and musk. She hated herself for being attracted to him. She hadn't even paid attention to him before he attacked Raphael. He was just her brother's friend, or so she thought. How could she be persuaded by such a creep? More than anything, she wanted to go out with him. How could she ever explain herself to her family? Her grandmother would surely say no, but she was more concerned about Raphael feeling betrayed by Terrence and her.

Seeming to read her mind, Terrence said, "Look, if you are worried about what your family will say, we can keep our relationship a secret, Vicky. They don't have to know that we're seeing each other. Raphael will be leaving for college soon anyway. Please say yes, Vicky."

Vicky contemplated the idea for what seemed to Terrence hours. She finally said yes. That weekend, they got together for the first time. Afterward, she floated home. Nothing else in life could matter to her after spending most of the day with Terrence. They held hands all the way back home. They separated a small distance from Vicky's house, not wanting to be seen together.

Vicky stayed in the house most of the next day waiting for Terrence to call. He had practice and wouldn't be calling her until later in the day, but she was worried that someone else in the house would answer his call before she could. She was not ready to let her grandmother or siblings to know that she was seeing a boy, especially Terrence. The only other person in the house who could recognize his voice was Raphael. She knew that Raphael and Terrence still practiced together; however, she was not apprised of any reconciliation between the two. Therefore, Vicky was cautious. Anyway, she really didn't have to be so concerned about Raphael answering the phone because he had been phone shy ever since those streams of prank calls he had received after ditching Denise. Even though the calls had stopped, Raphael was still intimidated by the telephone.

Vicky was reading when the phone rang. She was so engrossed in her book that when the phone rang, it startled her. She laughed at herself. "Hello," she said. "I'm up to it. Yes, I can get away for a while. I'll meet you there. In an hour? Okay." Vicky hung up the phone and dashed to her room to change clothes. She was going to meet Terrence at McDonald's. She put on a pink- and blue-flowered short set, pulled her long hair into a ponytail, grabbed her bag, told her grandmother where she was going, then sprinted for the door.

She sucked in the heavy summer air and hummed as she walked. She entered the restaurant and spotted Terrence immediately. He was sitting at a table near the window. When he saw Vicky, he stood while she seated herself. Terrence smiled and sat down. He could barely speak at first because Vicky looked so beautiful. He was smitten, and so was Vicky. She blushed as Terrence took hold of her hands and just held them as he looked intensely into her eyes. Vicky ached all over. It was agonizing for her to sit there so raw in front of Terrence. Terrence, who had never dated anyone before, tried his best to act sophisticated. His greatest fear was that he would eventually make a fool out of himself in front of this wonderful and beautiful girl.

He broke the spell with an inquiry about Vicky's day. He spoke so low that Vicky had to lean forward to hear him. His spicy smell was seductive, and it made Vicky want to be nearer to him, so she asked him to come sit next to her. No etiquette applied as they talked while eating greasy hamburgers and fries. When they finished eating, Terrence grabbed their soda cups and followed Vicky outside.

The humidity and heat smacked them in their face when they walked outside.

"It's just too hot out here for human beings," she said, and the both of them laughed.

"Yea! The heat index is 103 degrees," said Terrence.

"It is definitely too hot to hang outside," said Vicky.

"Let's just go to my house and watch television. It'll be cool there," said Terrence.

Upon entering Terrence's house, they felt instant relief. It was cool and nice inside. Both of Terrence's parents worked, so they were alone, with the exception of Denise, who did not come out from her room. Terrence offered Vicky a seat on the couch while he went to the kitchen to get them cold sodas to drink. When he returned to the living room, he handed Vicky her drink and took a seat for himself on the floor next to her. Vicky gently stroked his wool hair and played with his ear. Unable to endure the touch of her soft hands, Terrence took her hand in his and kissed it and calmed it.

As the shadows of early evening fell over the living room area, Vicky knew it was time to leave. Terrence walked her home. They stopped as they grew near to Vicky's house and kissed. It was the first kiss for both of them. They kissed and lingered in their embrace until Vicky pulled them apart.

"This is far enough, Terrence," said Vicky, pressing her hand on his chest, pushing him away or herself away from him.

"Good night, Terrence," she said.

"I had a great time," said Terrence. "You have a good night, Vicky. I'll call you tomorrow."

Terrence was leaving for Northwestern University in two weeks. Although he was attending the Chicago campus, he had decided to reside in the dorm. The summer had gone by too fast for Vicky. Soon they both would be bogged down in schoolwork and activities. Yesterday, when they discussed the fact, it became a hard dose of reality.

"Terrence, I think I love you already," said Vicky. "What will happen to our relationship now?"

"Vicky," said Terrence, "I have loved you since I first laid eyes on you. I'm never going to be away from you. We will see each other as often as possible. You have got to do something for me."

"What, Terrence? I'll do anything for you."

"Then tell your family, including Raphael, that we are dating."

Vicky chilled at the thought, but she was willing to talk to her family. "I will," she told Terrence.

eddy couldn't believe his luck! He had secured an audition to open for Marsha Warfield, a famous comedian and actress, when she performs at Park West theater in the next few weeks and was awaiting the producer's decision. Teddy's summer was almost over. It had been a productive three months. His theater group had prospered with three productions. Although he had not had time to do comedy, he had used his spare time writing and discarding jokes. He didn't dare test them out on his grandmother again, for his jokes were laced with profanity. He wished Raphael had not been in such a foul mood. He didn't trust Raphael's opinion or his ability to rise to a proper level of levity. He considered Vicky, but she had been weird lately that he didn't think she could sit still long enough to listen to an entire performance. He decided to be his own judge. Teddy inly felt slightly ambivalent about his work. He felt he could trust himself to know when he had a good joke or a bad one.

The days were long. Teddy couldn't contain his anxiety. He decided to get out of the house. He chose the mall. He wanted to play video games or perhaps see a movie. Teddy could have called a number of friends to go with him, but he wanted to be alone. He didn't want to be on stage for them, so to speak. He didn't feel like it. He wanted to tone down his energy level. For once in his life, he felt very serious.

Teddy used most of his money on video games. His concentration was so bad that he was beaten at every turn. He was hungry and hoped that he had reserved enough money for a burger at least. He went to the first restaurant in the mall that he could find, a McDonald's. He sat down at a small round table and started eating when he saw Vicky sitting in the same restaurant. He was about to call out to her when he saw Terrence Coleman approach her. Teddy's interest was piqued. He could not hear what they were saying, but he could tell by the expression on Vicky's face that she was giving Terrence her best allure. He was surprised, to say the least, when the two of them left together. Instinctively, Teddy grabbed the remainder of his burger and followed them. They went to see a movie. Teddy realized that he barely had enough money to catch the bus home, much less pay for a movie. He strolled through the mall and waited until the movie ended.

He did not want his presence detected, so he discretely made his way to the awaiting bus before Terrence and Vicky got there. He sat at the back of the bus and concealed himself by slouching down in his seat and covering his face with his baseball hat. Fortunately for him, the couple sat up front. Teddy did not exit the bus when the couple did. Instead, he got off the bus at the next stop and doubled back. Teddy lollygagged around until he felt it was safe to go home.

When Teddy arrived home, Vicky was already there, as he had hoped. She was watching television and appeared very happy. A smile was plastered across her face. Teddy wanted to confront her then and there but decided against it. He would indeed keep an eye on his sister. He vaguely remembered her asking him to go to the mall with her earlier. He had been so possessed by his writing that he didn't even acknowledge her. He wished then that he had gone with her. *Vicky and Terrence? Impossible,* he thought. He shrugged his shoulders and walked away with the image of Vicky and Terrence together nagging his mind.

Three whole days passed before the producers of Martha Winfield's show notified Teddy that he had been chosen for the opening. Ms. Winfield had vouched for him because he was a Chicago native and an unknown artist. She had been impressed by his talent and age. He let everybody in the house know by screaming to the top of his voice, "I got it! I got the opening position for the show!" Even Raphael came out to congratulate him.

"Nana, I can't believe how lucky I am!"

"Luck had nothing to do with it, Teddy," his grandmother said. "You are a very talented young man, and you work real hard for what you want. I'm proud of you, son! Just don't go on that stage cursing like you haven't had any home training."

Teddy laughed. Little did his grandmother know.

Teddy paced back and forth in his room. He had rehearsed his skit so much so that when he suddenly couldn't remember some of his lines, he panicked.

Raphael knocked on his door, and he was relieved. The distraction would be good. Teddy knew that he was forgetting his lines because he was anxious.

"Hey, little brother," said Raphael. "Ready for the big night?"

"I'm nervous, man. I can't remember my lines!" said Teddy with his voice quavering.

"You'll be okay, Teddy. You just have to relax," said Raphael assuredly.

"Raphael, I wish you were coming with us," said Teddy as he whimpered like a little puppy.

Although he had laughed at Teddy, Raphael felt very bad. He had been at only one of Teddy's performances during the summer. He realized how important it was for his brother to have his family there supporting him. Raphael decided to put his own troubles aside and be there for his brother. "I'll go, Teddy," he said. "Is everybody else going?"

"Oh, thank you, Raphael!" said Teddy, throwing his arms around his big brother. "Vicky is going too. Thankfully, Nana's not going. A limousine from the producer is picking us up, so she felt we would be safe. I got too much profanity going on for her to be there."

"I'll get dressed," said Raphael, "and meet you and Vicky in the living room."

Teddy remembered that he needed to dress as well. He took his black suit out of its garment bag and smoothed it down. The gold-beaded star on the left side of the black velvet jacket, paired with his black dress pants, was as spectacular as he had hoped it would be. When Teddy entered the living room and saw his siblings, he was speechless. There stood his sister dressed in a black satin dress with a maroon bodice; her hair was captured in a french bun and adorned with jeweled maroon combs on each side. Raphael was wearing gray slacks and a maroon jacket. He was so proud of the efforts they had put into looking good for his debut.

When the announcer introduced Teddy as the youngest comic to ever perform at Park West, he received thunders of applause. Teddy was so nervous that he thought he would faint.

"What if I bomb?"

His other self said, "Man, get out there!"

Teddy walked out on stage grinning hard. He stood for a moment or so just grinning. The audience laughed hard at him.

"I'm really not that young at all," he said. "All of the Fielders are short. I'm really twenty-one." The audience laughed. "I can prove it. See." Teddy pulled a small magnifying glass from his jacket pocket. "See that mustache?" Teddy held the glass above his upper lip and ran his finger across the hairless spot. "You have to look closely now," he said. The audience roared.

"I hate being young," said Teddy. "You can't do shit! Nobody believes shit you say. One night, when I was about ten, I told my brother that my dick was hard, which it was. We share a bedroom, you see. Don't you look at me like that," he admonished the crowd. "We weren't up to no funny business. I just wanted him to know that I was a man. So I pulled my pajama bottom down and showed him my stiff

144

prick. He doubled over laughing at me. He said, 'Man, that ain't no hard-on, your ass just needs to go somewhere and piss.'

"I said, 'Oh yea!' And I pissed all over his monkey behind. I showered his ass." Teddy grabbed his crotch and pretended to spray the audience.

"What I hate most about being young is how the babes treat you. If they are more than two hours older than you, you can kiss it off. I had this little, bitty, tansy, tiny girl tell me to call her when I grew some hair down there. One time, I grabbed this babe's buns from behind, and she turned around and looked high and low. Pretending to not see me, she said, 'Huh! Must have been a mosquito.'" The audience whistled and laughed.

"They tell me a man shouldn't weigh himself by such trivial things, but when you're tipping the scale at 85 pounds and only four point nine inches, you have got to weigh something. You know what, guys, on that great day when I wake up and I am tall and big, I'm going to whip the shit out of the first bitch that speaks to me." Teddy pretended to whip someone. "Get away from me, bitch. You wouldn't have my ass before I grew this ten-inch dick. You guys have been wonderful!" he said to the still roaring crowd. "Thank you very much."

⌒⫘⌒

The summer had not gone by fast enough for Raphael. He was glad to be leaving for college. He looked forward to the change. He was finally going to be on his own. He could be his own person without the pressure, the expectations. His uncle Julian had been disappointed with his choice of schools, but Raphael was glad he had chosen for himself. Vanderbilt was where he wanted to be. He wanted to be where it was warm and friendly. He wanted to be a part of an open society, where uniqueness prevailed. From what he knew of the university, Vanderbilt would be perfect! He finished packing and looked over his shoulders. He felt like he was forgetting something. There it sat on the dresser, the bear his mother had given him. He went and retrieved the precious object.

Nashville was wonderful! It was everything Raphael had hoped it would be. Although they were few in numbers, he was surprised to see how many different races were on campus. He had always thought that Vanderbilt would be less diverse. There was a lot of Caucasian students, but he could see himself represented too. When he checked into his dorm room, he was greeted by his new roommate, Michael Whitsley. Michael was an affable young black man. He was from Jackson, Mississippi, and the epitome of Southern charm. Raphael was quickly swept into Michael's saga. Sensing that he would be talked to death regardless of what he did, Raphael endeavored to unpack. Michael followed Raphael throughout the tiny room, talking about himself and his family of eight children. Raphael had hoped for friendliness, but he had not expected to be overwhelmed by the experience.

Surveying their new dwellings, Raphael and Michael walked the massive campus. Michael introduced himself to every female they passed. Raphael retreated into himself, preferring to not have to tackle the dating scene so soon. They discovered the popular places and the not-so-cool-to-be-here ones as well. Neither felt himself to be the first type to hang in the popular places. No one in that group even noticed them. They learned quickly to avoid the upperclassmen; although, sometimes hiding didn't work. Those guys spent a lot of time and effort seeking out the neophytes. Initiation into campus life was swift and cruel.

Raphael felt outside of himself for the first time in his life. He was invincible! He had taken to strolling alone on occasions, needing desperately to be away from Michael's nonstop conversations. He liked to study outdoors sometimes, stopping intermittently to lay back on the cool grass and fashion familiar objects out of the clouds that floated by. It was during such a mental break that she came and stood over him, towering between him and the sky above. He half raised himself to get a better look at her. She lowered herself to the ground, saving him the strain.

"Hi, I am Eloise Jordan," she said.

Raphael would have introduced himself, but nothing escaped through the narrow passage in his throat that housed his vocal cord. He coughed to clear his throat.

"I've seen you around," Eloise said, not intimated by his silence. "We have botany together. What's your name?" she asked.

"Raphael Fielder," he managed to say.

"So, Raphael, how do you like Vanderbilt?"

"I like it," he replied.

The silence grew between them like shrubbery. Eloise settled back on her elbows and gazed into the scenery before her. She offered no conversation. Raphael looked at her when he thought she wasn't looking. She had long tanned legs, and she was thin. Her body was that of an athlete. Her hair was cut short, which allowed one to fully appreciate her beautiful face. Her brown eyes displayed a bit of mirth.

Raphael became less tensed. He lay back down and continued with his cloud watching. "I enjoy doing this," he said too quickly to regret it. Eloise lay back and did the same. "What shapes can you see?" Raphael asked.

"Oh, wow!" exclaimed Eloise. "Look over there. It's a rabbit!"

Raphael laughed. "I see it too. Can you find the baby's face?"

Laughing with utter joy, Eloise said, "Yes, I see it. There's a pony, Raphael!"

They laughed heartily. Raphael and Eloise lay, smiling up at creation. Shortly, Eloise rose to go. "It's been nice, Raphael. I hope to see you again soon."

She extended her hand, and Raphael stood and took her hand in his. "I'm sure we will, Eloise. I'll look for you in science."

Raphael watched her walk away. Her steps were light, and sometimes it looked like she was skipping as she walked. He missed her. A pang hit his heart and made him want to run after her. He held back, remembering his last encounter with a girl. He did not want a repeat of Denise. He thought it wise to get to know this girl better. He felt things would be different with Eloise; it already had been.

It was difficult for Raphael to concentrate on his studies. Eloise's face blotted out all else. He had been at the library for hours. His first exam in psychology was two days away, and he wanted to be more than prepared. Raphael was exhausted when he entered the dorm room. Initially, he did not hear the soft moans and rumbling of sheets. His eyes followed the sounds. As his eyes began to adjust in the dark, he could see the outlines of Michael and a female engaged in intercourse. Raphael backed out of the room unnoticed. He was embarrassed by what he had seen. Anger followed as he sought a place to rest. He was tired and needed sleep badly.

He went downstairs to the student lounge and plopped down on the couch. A few night owls were there, but that didn't bother him. He sat on the couch and allowed his head to fall backward. The image of Michael and his lady friend kept popping up in his mind. He had never seen two people having sex before. He felt flustered and excited. He had felt this way before. An urge, which made his heart race, traveled from his stomach downward. His imagination swept the image of Michael and his lover away and replaced them with Eloise and himself in their place. His penis swelled, and his temple began to throb. He couldn't go to sleep; therefore, his headache intensified.

Raphael stood abruptly. He was too restless to sit still. He wondered out into the night, needing fresh air desperately to clear his head. He strolled aimlessly until he came to the spot where he had met Eloise. He was ashamed of himself for having such thoughts about himself and a girl he didn't even know. They had waved at each other in class, but neither had made a move toward intimacy. He envisioned himself there with her making love. He knew then that he would definitely have to do something to get to know Eloise better.

"I couldn't sleep either," she said from behind him. "It must be stress. Do you think it's stress, Raphael?"

Raphael was caught totally off guard. He did not turn to face her right away. He was too shocked, and he did not want her to see the state he was in. The darkness was not widespread enough to hid his feelings. "You're not afraid to be out here alone?" he asked her, talking into the darkness before him.

Coming face-to-face with him, Eloise said, "I was here this afternoon waiting for you."

"After classes, I spent the rest of the day in the library," said Raphael, turning his body away from her. He did not yet have the courage to look her in her eyes. Eloise clasped his hand in hers and stared out into the darkness with him.

Raphael was over the moon. He had to tell somebody about this beautiful girl. He decided to call Vicky. Of course, she would be the last one of his family that he got to speak to and the only one he talked to about Eloise. The two siblings tossed back and forth about school and family business. It took Raphael a while to get to his real reason for calling—to gush about Eloise. Vicky was happy for him and very pleased to hear that he was dating. She told Raphael that she thought he might never date again after his encounter with Denise. He admitted to Vicky that Eloise was indeed forward, but not in the same way that Denise had been. He welcomed Eloise's advancements because she was mature and willing to really get to know him.

Raphael and Eloise met every day after that night. They quickly became an item. It did not take him long to be totally at ease with

Eloise. He dreamed of the day that they would become lovers; however, he made no attempts to make his dream come true. It was good that they were taking it slow. He was having fun without the complications of sex.

They sat on his bed in his dorm room, studying. Michael was out for the evening. He had let Raphael know in advance that he and Eloise would not be disturbed. Raphael was always glad for the opportunity to be alone with Eloise. When they studied together, each respected each other's need for quiet, so they didn't talk much during those times. Good grades were important to both of them. Raphael was fairly sure that he wanted to be a biochemist, but he had a while before he had to declare a major. Eloise was definite that she wanted to be a pediatric doctor. Children were precious to her.

Raphael laughed when Eloise blew her warm breath on his neck; it tickled. He turned around and kissed her. Eloise returned the kiss. She kissed him long, hard, and deep. He instantly became light-headed, and his body began to respond. They embraced and sealed their lips together. Eloise rolled on top of him, and their passion for each other took control. She unbuttoned his shirt and stroked his chest. He pulled up her blouse and reached beneath her bra. He cupped her breasts in his hands and gently massaged them. He moved his tongue inside of her mouth, and she moaned. He pulled himself away from her and helped her undress. Her body was amazing to him. He stopped to admire her beauty. She urged him on by unzipping his pants and reaching down to pull them off. Raphael removed his shirt and lay next to her. They held each other close. Although Raphael was a virgin and nervous as could be, he willingly abandoned himself with Eloise. His hands moved between her legs until he found the spot to embed himself. His manhood found its entry, and he pushed himself hard and deep inside of her. Her hips rose to meet him, and she moved rhythmically against his body. Raphael fought the urge to scream but couldn't stop himself when he reached his moment of release. Eloise, who reached a climax at the same time, groaned her gratification.

They lay in silence and just enjoyed the moment. Finally, Eloise asked the question, "Were you a virgin?"

Raphael mumbled a painful yes. "Was I that bad?" he asked.

"No. Not at all," said Eloise. "I really couldn't tell. It was perfect, Raphael. You please me very much. I've only had sex once before with my high school boyfriend before we broke up. I thought having sex with him would keep me from losing him. I learned from that to save myself for the man who would respect me and not push me to go to bed with him."

"I'm glad that you waited for me," Raphael said.

They laughed and went for round 2.

Raphael felt like he was floating outside of himself. He was exhausted. He wasn't sleeping well at night. He was existing on one to two hours of sleep. He would stay up to midnight studying. He ate very little and had limited the time he spent with Eloise. Some days he did not see her at all. After studying, he would get in bed knowing what to expect. It was the same every night. Instead of sleeping, he would stare at the ceiling. Enabled by the streetlight that filtered into his dorm room, he saw a panorama of events and the people in his life, especially his family. His mother had been gone for almost five years, so he missed her the most. In the ceiling, he saw her at her dressing table, combing then brushing her long ebony hair. He saw Teddy and Vicky and him at the breakfast table in the morning eating their breakfast when their mother would come into the kitchen and kiss each one of them warmly. He remembered when she would spend the day entertaining them and reading to them bedtime stories at night. He also remembered when it changed. The change seemed to be caused by his father. It was strange to him that he couldn't see his father's face. He had totally forgotten how he looked. Sometime during the evening, he would drift off to sleep, only to be startled awake by his alarm clock at six o'clock each morning. Each morning, he was presented with another long day with no rest.

The end of his first semester was approaching. The entire campus was abuzz. Everyone's head was bowed down in a book or over a notebook or to a pen and paper. Anxiety rose like a cloud before a storm. Raphael was especially weary. His grades had slipped from the honor roll to average to barely making it. He had started studying in the library instead of hooking up with Eloise in his dorm. She took the change well, considering the fact that she was crunched down in preparing for final examinations as well.

Before long, Eloise started coming to the library to study with Raphael. Eventually, the tension from all the hard work got the best of them. Eloise wanted a break from it all, and so did Raphael.

Eloise touched Raphael lightly on the arm. "Let's get out of here, Raphael," she whispered. "Let's take a walk and get something to eat. We've been in here all day."

"That sounds great!" said Raphael. "I am starving."

They wrapped their arms around each other as they walked to a restaurant just off campus. After eating, the two of them went to their "spot" and sat and chatted for a while. The cool air was pleasant. They stopped talking and gazed at the stars. Holding on to each other, their lips met in a passionate kiss. They stopped to move to a more private place; they went to Raphael's room. Luckily, when they entered the room, it was vacant. Michael had not yet returned.

Greedily they pulled at each other's clothing until they were bare. Raphael took Eloise in his arms, and they fell on the bed, unified. Their lovemaking was wonderful as usual, until Raphael lost control and came too soon.

"What was that?" asked Eloise.

"I'm sorry, Eloise. It just happened."

"It never happened before," she said, looking at Raphael incredulously.

"I know, babe, I know," he said." I think I may be overly stressed. Do you want to try again?"

Eloise appeared reluctant, but she acquiesced. She told Raphael to concentrate on something else or stop and pull away before he allowed himself any satisfaction. When the same thing happened the second time around, Eloise became more frustrated, and Raphael was mortified. He sat quietly on the bed and watched her dress. She was angry.

"I can't abide with a selfish lover, Raphael. Not right now."

"You act like I came on purpose. It just happened. Before I knew it or could stop it, I exploded! Don't you know it hurts me too? I want to bring you pleasure. This is embarrassing!"

"I hate to make such a big deal out of this, Raphael. Maybe I'm stressed as well. We need to take a break until after finals, then our minds will be clear. We'll be better able to deal with this. Good night, Raphael," said Eloise before exiting the room.

Raphael's poor demeanor had not gone unnoticed by Michael. He knew almost immediately that something was wrong with his friend. He was also aware that Eloise had not been around lately.

"Hey, man, what's up with you and Eloise? You guys having problems? I noticed that she hasn't been around lately," said Michael.

"I don't want to talk about that, Michael. It's private," responded Raphael.

"I don't mean to intrude," said Michael. "I just thought maybe I could help if there was a problem."

"Listen, Michael," said Raphael, slightly raising his voice. "I know you're the stud on campus, and you got your way with girls, but I don't need your fucking advice. Just lay off me!"

Raphael stormed out of the room, leaving a perplexed Michael behind. He had begged and pleaded with Eloise to give him another chance, but she wasn't interested. She told him it was best that they stay away from each other for a while. One evening, as he walked the campus, he saw Eloise coming out of her dorm with another male student, and he almost died. Since they had not seen him, Raphael stood there and watched them walk away together, holding hands and leaning into each other as they talked. Tears flowed from his eyes. His heart ached and broke. He walked back to his dorm and tried to bury himself in his studies. He couldn't concentrate.

Raphael dressed hurriedly for class. He had a Western history exam that morning and could not afford to be late. He was reaching for his toothbrush when he saw it. It was back! He trembled and leaned into the mirror to get a closer look. The red blotch on his white shirt became more apparent. He had not seen the blood in ages. In fact, he had forgotten about it altogether. Raphael was so disconcerted that he couldn't function. He sat down gingerly on his bed to keep from fainting, then he remembered the exam. Forgetting to brush his teeth, he loaded his arms with his books and left the room. He started out partially running, then he slowed down his pace. He was too tired to keep up a vigorous stride. He got lost in his thoughts of Eloise with someone else, unaware of the time and his surroundings. He saw a group of students approaching him and huddled his books to his chest to conceal what only his eyes could see.

Raphael was frightened. His life was unraveling before him, and he didn't know if he could deal with it. He sat staring at his test paper. The girl across from him had finished with her test. She closed her booklet and placed her pencil on her desk. Raphael rushed through the exam but did not finish. He knew he had done poorly on his final exam in history.

When the students got their test scores, Raphael had only received a D. He crumpled the test results in his hand and made a paper ball, which he tossed into the trash can. Although it was only afternoon, he had already used up all his energy. He had taken his American literature exam that morning, as well as his biology test. All he wanted to do was go back to the dorm and climb into bed.

Raphael, who was fully clothed, fell asleep immediately. He drifted into another time, another place. There in a dim room stood a young child holding a gun that was much too big for him to handle with just one hand, so he gripped it with both hands. The child screamed, "I hate you! I hate you!" It was a boy shouting those angry words. The boy pulled the trigger three times. The fear that the dream had generated in Raphael caused him to awaken, wet with sweat and shaking uncontrollably. The dream had been so real to him.

Raphael sat in class several days later, not following instructions because he was too busy brushing the red spot on his shirt. He had taken to wearing white shirts all the time. He no longer tried to disguise the blood by wearing different-colored shirts. He often strolled the campus by himself, purposely avoiding his once favorite spot. Cloud watching was a thing of the past. Because of his tight exam schedule, he had not run into Eloise since the night he had spotted her with someone else. He felt morose.

Whenever Michael was in the room, Raphael tried to stay away to keep from being bombarded with questions about his personal life. All Michael talked about was getting him and Eloise reconciled. Raphael understood without a doubt that he and Eloise would never be together again. Michael could do nothing to improve Raphael's low spirit, and Raphael wouldn't tell Michael the details of his nightmares, which, according to Michael, always ended with Raphael tossing and turning in his sleep and mumbling, "I hate you, Spanky!"

One morning, when Raphael awakened, Michael was sitting in the chair at their desk just watching him. Raphael felt naked and embarrassed.

"Who is this Spanky dude, man? You really got a thing about him. You keeping saying over and over in your sleep that you hate him."

Raphael did not answer Michael or looked him in the face. He went into the bathroom and closed the door. After his shower, he opened the door and was glad that Michael wasn't there anymore. He looked out of the window and saw that it was a nice, sun-filled Sunday morning. As beautiful as it was outside, he could not appreciate it. He got dressed and lay across his bed to read. He opened *Sports Illustrated* and searched for an article that would interest him. After browsing for a while, he got bored. He climbed out of bed, grabbed his jacket, and left the room.

Not going anywhere in particular, Raphael walked and walked, circling around the hill until it drew him to it—"the spot." He slumped down on the ground, and as if lightning had struck, he remembered what had happened that fateful morning. He started crying. He cried until he retched. He gave no thought to others who were strolling the campus at that time.

"I remember, Mama," he said aloud. "You went to jail for something that I did. I am so sorry. All those years that you have been away was wasted time," he said, pounding his fist into the earth. "I'm the one who should have been put away. Me, not you, Mama!" he said with salty tears burning his eyes.

As he walked back to his room, the picture of that fateful day played over and over in his head. He had yet to remember why he shot his father to death. All the details of that day had not manifested. The first thing that he did when he entered the room was to look in the mirror at his shirt. The blood was still there, but he knew for the first time why he was seeing it. He was a murderer; his father's blood was on his hands. He attacked his mirror with a book. Still not appeased, he looked for something else to throw. He spotted the panda that his mother had given him.

"Mama, you gave this bear to me because you loved me, so I would remember you, you said. Oh, Mama, why didn't you tell the police it was me?"

With his anger directed at his mother, Raphael ripped the panda apart and slung it in the corner. Under the impact, a gun fell out and lay exposed in front of his eyes. He leaned down slowly and picked it up. The gun was heavy and cold, the same way it had felt that night when he shot Spanky. Events unfolded in Raphael's mind, and he saw himself moving cautiously across the dark living room. He followed his father as he went to his car. His father and his mother had been arguing. Spanky had spoken viciously to his mother before he hit her across the face. His mother was upset with his father because she had caught him touching Vicky inappropriately, in a bad way—the same way Raphael had seen his father hold Vicky, with his hand beneath her dress, while she squirmed and cried. Raphael could not endure his father any longer. Blinded by rage, he went to the closet in the hallway and took the silver box that held his father's gun off the shelf and grabbed it. He followed Spanky to the garage. His father didn't know he was there until Raphael shouted, "I hate you, Spanky!" However, it was too late by then. Holding the gun with two hands, Raphael shot three times. Afterward, everything went black for Raphael, and he did not remember a thing.

Raphael sat calmly at the desk and wrote his mother a short and sweet note:

My lovely mother,

How very sorry I am to have caused you to suffer all of these years. I remember, Mama, and I know your sacrifice. Well, you'll suffer no more because of me. I, Raphael Fielder, hereby confess to the murder of Raymond "Spanky" Fielder.

Goodbye, Mama. I love you.
Raphael Fielder

Raphael stood before the mirror. The red blotch was there as he hoped it would be. He finally understood the reason for the stain's presence and made peace with it. Raphael put a bullet through the unrelenting stain.

CHAPTER 7

t was almost Thanksgiving, and Vicky had not heard from Terrence since early October. She held on to the promise he had made to her before moving on campus. He had assured her that their relationship would not change, that he loved her, and they would always be together no matter what happened. She did not have his address or phone number; she always waited for Terrence to call her, which he did most weekends. With this change in his communication routine with her, Vicky began to feel isolated from him. She was busy herself, which cut into the time she spent thinking about him, but she was not so busy that she hadn't noticed his absence or felt lonely for Terrence.

Vicky was glad to begin her senior year of school. Over the past three years, she had gained a couple of good girlfriends with whom she hung out, and being on the tennis team had brought her in contact with a different set of girls, who were also her friends. Since her freshman year at Phillips High School, she had been popular with the boys. She felt confident and self-assured around them. She enjoyed teasing them. The guys had learned from experience that the pretty girl was a flirt and not really interested in going out with any of them.

Pining for Terrence, Vicky began to feel that there was something wrong. She began to wonder and worry about why Terrence was not calling her. She had hoped that he would be coming home for Thanksgiving. A darkness fell on her being, and she needed some answers. She finally broke down and called Terrence's sister Denise and asked her for Terrence's telephone number.

"Hello, Terrence, it's Vicky." The silence on the other end of the phone was so loud that it caused her heart to palpitate and her stomach to turn upside down. "Hello?" she said again.

"Hi, Vicky. I'm here," responded Terrence finally. "I was typing an essay and wanted to type the last few words before I forgot. I'm surprised to hear from you, babe. What's up?"

"Well, I hadn't heard from you, Terrence, so I got your number from Denise. I hope you don't mind because you never did give me your contact information."

"No, not at all," he said.

"You seem shocked that I called you. Was I not supposed to?" asked Vicky.

"Baby, it is more than okay that you called me. College is a lot different from what I thought it would be. I've always been a high achiever in school. It was almost effortless for me to make good grades. Right now, though, I don't feel so smart. It is taking a lot more diligence for me to stay on top of my studies. That is the reason that you have not heard from me. Time gets away from me."

"Do you still love me, Terrence?" Vicky asked, still not totally convinced that studying hard was the only reason Terrence hadn't called her.

"Do not go there, Vicky. Loving you sustains me because I know you're there waiting for me."

"What about Thanksgiving? Are you coming home?"

"With bells on," he said with a hardy laugh. "Have you told your family about us?"

"Not exactly. But I think Teddy knows, and Raphael is away at Vanderbilt. When you come home, we'll tell them together. Okay?"

"I'm frightened about how they will react, but I don't want to hide how I feel about you from anyone, and I want to be with you out loud."

"I can't wait to see you, Terrence."

"Same here, babe. Listen, Vicky, don't worry if you don't hear from me sometimes. I am still madly in love with you. I'll call as often as possible, and if you miss me or need to talk, call. If I don't answer, I'll call you back when I can. Say goodbye, baby."

"Goodbye, baby," she said, and they laughed together before hanging up their phones.

Vicky was elated. Terrence had given her all the reassurance that she needed. Nonetheless, in the ensuing days, a spirit of doom seemed to be lurking over her, and she didn't know why. She tried to toss it off by thinking about Terrence, but that wasn't working. Suddenly, she felt compelled to talk to her brother Raphael. The family had not heard from him in a while. The last time she had talked to him, he was over the moon about this girl Eloise, whom he had just started dating.

They had talked for a couple of hours about his roommate Michael, his class load, the weather, and more. He was in such a good mood that she didn't dare bring up Terrence, because she did not want to spoil things. Since he was so jovial, she decided she would tell him soon. Perhaps he would be receptive to her relationship with Terrence after all. This time, however, she wanted to write her brother a letter instead of calling him.

Vicky's letter to Raphael was long. She told him about school and how exciting her senior year had been so far. She talked about her interest in literature, especially the books she was reading; how well the tennis team was doing; her friends, dwelling on some of the events they had shared together; and the teachers whom she admired. She wrote endlessly about Teddy, their grandmother Mamie, and their uncle Julian. Vicky wrote about a letter that Julian had shared with their grandmother from a woman in the South who had been their great-grandfather's companion. The letter informed Julian that

Raymond Sr. had died. She told Raphael about her concern for their grandmother. Mamie seemed calm, but she had detected a sadness in their grandmother, not the kind that Mamie had exhibited when their father died and their mother went away but rather forlorn, coupled with something Vicky couldn't explain or understand. She had not turned to her grandchildren for comfort this time. Instead, she had retreated into herself, and as far as Vicky could tell, their grandmother was staying there. Nothing she or Teddy had done or said cheered her up.

Vicky waited weeks for a reply from Raphael; however, no response came. She felt abandoned by her brother. Terrence was physically unavailable, her brother was away at school, her grandmother was in a stupor, and Teddy was totally lost in school and his career. Vicky felt she would go crazy if she didn't do something among the living. She started hanging out more with her friends, even the boys. She filled her weekends and spare time with football games and movies. She was secure in her attractiveness and popularity. She found that she could easily garner the attention and affection of any male she chose. Vicky liked the ease of "playing the field." She grew accustomed to the reactions she inspired in others. She never forgot her limit with boys because she was totally committed to Terrence. Her friends grew in number, both male and female. She was voted homecoming queen and given the leading role in the school's production of *Romeo and Juliet*. Vicky was happy!

With glory came pain. It was Vicky who answered a long-distance call from Tennessee. "Hello, my name is Dean Parker. I am calling from Vanderbilt. May I speak to Mrs. Wallace?" he asked.

"I am sorry, but she is not available at this time. I am Vicky, her granddaughter. May I help you?"

"I really need to speak to Mrs. Wallace because she is your brother Raphael's legal guardian."

"My grandmother is not well, sir, but our uncle Julian is also responsible for our care. I can give you his telephone number if you wish."

"That won't be necessary, Ms. Vicky. I have your uncle's phone number on file as well. I'll give him a call."

"Wait a minute, Dean Parker! Can I ask you what this is about? Is my brother Raphael in trouble?"

"I'm sorry, Ms. Vicky. I can't say. I need to talk to your uncle about this matter. Thanks for your help. Goodbye."

Vicky was too anxious to wait to hear from her uncle Julian. She decided to call Raphael directly. The phone rang, and Michael Whitsley, Raphael's roommate, answered, "Hello."

"Hello," said Vicky. "May I speak to Raphael?"

"Who's calling?" the voice asked.

"My name is Vicky, and I am Raphael's sister."

"Oh my goodness! I am Michael, Raphael's roommate."

"I don't mean to be unpleasant," said Vicky with a sense of urgency, "but may I please speak to my brother? It's important that I talk to him now." There was an obvious pause on the other end of the phone. "Hello, can you hear me? Are you there?"

"Yes, I'm still here," said Michael. "Didn't Dean Parker call your family?"

"Yes, he did," said Vicki, irritated. "But he would not tell me what was wrong."

"I'm sorry, Vicky, but I am not the one you should be talking to. Dean Parker is the only one who can speak to your family about Raphael. I have to go," said Michael and hung up the phone.

Vicky slammed the phone on the receiver and dropped to her knees. Her stomach turned upside down, and a sound like bees hummed in her head. She ran to the washroom and threw up in the toilet. She sat there on the floor as sweat ran down her face.

When Julian entered the house, Vicky was even more sure that something bad had happened. Her uncle looked like he had been crying, his shoulders hung low, and his face was unnaturally drained of color. He didn't say hello and didn't look at her when he asked if Teddy was home. She told him Teddy was out and that she did not know where he was. She said her grandmother was in her room, where she had been since she learned that their great-grandfather had passed.

Julian told Vicky about her brother's suicide. She felt ill again and ran into the bathroom and threw up. She was crying so profusely that she almost choked on her own vomit. She lay on the cool floor tiles, waiting for the room to stop spinning. Julian came and gently lifted her into his arms and held her. They cried inconsolably until each was drained of any feelings at all.

Julian took Vicky with him to Mamie's room. He ceremoniously knocked at Mamie's bedroom door; however, his mother did not answer. He opened the door, and he and Vicky walked inside. Mamie lay on her bed, staring at the ceiling. She did not acknowledge him and Vicky.

"Mama, I need to talk to you." Julian waited for a response, but his mother had not even looked at him. "Do you hear me, Mama? Julian asked, and Mamie nodded. Julian sat on his mother's bed and gestured for Vicky to sit down as well. She sat on the opposite side of the bed.

"Sit up, Mama," said Julian as he carefully lifted up his mother and propped her against a pillow. "Look at me, Mama." Mamie slowly turned her eyes to meet his. "Can you tell me what has been bothering you? I want to understand what is wrong."

Mamie's eyes glazed over, and she seemed to be looking through her son rather than at him. A pang hit Julian's heart. His mother's sad beauty touched him, and he wondered if he was doing the right thing to tell her about Raphael's death. Mamie appeared to have aged in the few days since he had last seen her. Her single lock of gray hair fell forward in her face. She did not reach to brush it back. Her lovely skin, once so smooth, was dry and etched with fine lines. Julian fought the urge to cry. He had to stay strong; his family needed him more than ever. Vicky looked at him sympathetically, because she, too, was sensitive to the change in her grandmother within such a very short span of time.

Julian continued, "Mama, Vicky and I have received bad news about Raphael." Julian thought he had witnessed a moment of awareness in Mamie at the mention of Raphael's name, but it was only momentarily, for before him sat a distant figure. "Raphael is dead, Mama."

Vicky gasped and fell across her grandmother's lap. She sobbed uncontrollably. Tears flowed heavily from Mamie's eyes, though she spoke not a word. She just literally crashed into a deeper form of disassociation.

"I called Buddy, and he's going to come here and stay with you and the kids until I get back. I have to go to Nashville to find out what happened and take care of Raphael. I'll wait for Teddy to come home, then I am on my way." Julian left the room, and Vicky followed him.

"How could this happen, Uncle Julian?" she asked. "Was he that tormented? And by what?" asked Vicky, straining to understand.

Julian wrapped Vicky in his arms and smothered her in his chest. His tears fell on her sweet-smelling hair, and he said, "I don't know, honey. Dean Parker did not share any details with me. He said he would discuss everything with me when I get there. Perhaps he can explain the reasons to me then. We just have to wait to know for sure. There is a lot to be explained, Vicky. I don't have all of the details just yet. When I come back from Nashville, I'll have a better perspective."

"I'll sit with Grandma while we wait for the others. Does Mama know, Uncle Julian?"

"Yes, Vicky. She is very upset. We will all have our answer soon. Dean Parker would only reveal so much over the phone."

Vicky went back to her grandmother and held her in her arms. Mamie sat rigidly in her granddaughter's embrace. "Oh, Grandmother, how can I help you? What can I do to stop the pain?"

Mamie gently squeezed Vicky's hand.

CHAPTER 8

Teddy was very preoccupied. Between school and the activities he participated in and his weekend gig at Park West, he was all consumed. He was home just long enough to do his homework, eat, rehearse, and sleep. School was very important to him because he had to earn good grades to keep his weekend job—his grandmother had insisted upon no less.

Teddy felt badly about neglecting his family, especially since his grandmother had been acting so strangely. He worried about her more than she could possibly know. He wasn't worried about Vicky since Terrence went away to school. He just knew Terrence would eventually move on, being a college man and all. Plus, Vicky seemed happy enough without him. He had not spoken to Raphael since his last call home, and even then, Teddy didn't hold a true conversation with his brother because he was rushing out of the door. Teddy only hoped that being away at school would do his brother some good, perhaps even open him up a little and definitely give Raphael the opportunity to date. Teddy had assessed his brother to be totally at a loss when it came to girls. His experience with Denise had been a disaster.

Because he loved his grandmother so much, it depressed him to see the state she was in. At times, he wished he could avoid going home at all. He always hoped that when he walked into his home, he would find things back to normal, and his grandmother would be in the kitchen cooking something delectable. He was tired of Vicky's fish-sticks-and-fries dinners and delivery pizza and salads and burgers. He had talked to Vicky and his uncles about his grandmother, but no one could explain to him, to his satisfaction, what was exactly wrong with his grandmother. His uncle Julian had said she was suffering from "deep depression." Caused by what? Teddy still didn't know. He had watched his grandmother go through difficult times with the loss of his father and his mother's imprisonment, and neither of those had affected her this way. He just couldn't understand why the death of her father, whom she never spoke to or visited, could affect his grandmother so adversely. She wouldn't even laugh at his best jokes. She always laughed at his jokes, good and bad, even when she objected to their obscenity.

That afternoon, Teddy rounded the corner of his house and was seized with dread. He stood contemplating whether or not to go inside. He walked past his house then turned back around and went into the house. He tossed his book bag on the sofa and noticed something odd. There was no activity, no movement. He went to Vicky's room and found it empty. Out of curiosity, he went to his grandmother's room and knocked on the door. Vicky answered and told him to come in. His grandmother was in her bed, propped up by pillows. Vicky went and sat next to their grandmother and grabbed her hand. They both looked like they had been crying. Teddy observed his grandmother's tear-streaked face and the moistness of her eyes. He knew something was wrong and that he would rather not hear about, whatever it was. He walked slowly over to the bed and sat down with the two of them. He lowered his eyes and played with the designs on the Chanel bed cover. The three of them sat that way for a while until Mamie drifted off to sleep.

Outside of their grandmother's room, Teddy asked Vicky what was going on. He was more anxious than ever. He followed her into the living room. She sat on the couch, and he sat in his grandmother's chair. As Vicky was about to tell Teddy what had happened, their uncle Julian emerged from Raphael and Teddy's room.

"I am just going to say this, Teddy, and it's not good news. In fact, it's awful," said Julian, with her voice quavering. Julian paused briefly to collect himself.

"You're scaring the shit out of me, Uncle Julian! Get on with it," said Teddy.

"It's Raphael, Teddy," he said. "He's dead."

"Dead!" exclaimed Teddy. "Dead how? I mean, how can Raphael be dead?"

"All that we know right now, Teddy, is that he shot himself to death." Teddy gasped! Julian continued, "I am flying down to Memphis to find out what happened and to arrange for Raphael to be brought home."

Teddy folded into a ball and rocked himself back and forth. He moaned and cried like a wretch. Vicky went to him and held him. They cried themselves sick. Neither had ever experienced such loss and pain, not even when their mother went away.

Julian thought about his conversation with Buddy. He knew that his brother did not fare well amid family conflict and chaos, but he hoped that Buddy had made it to Mamie's house by now.

"Listen up, Buddy," said Julian. "Something dreadful has happened. Raphael is dead, man. He killed himself."

"Oh, Jules, not Raphael, not him, man. Why? Why would he kill himself?" asked Buddy with a shaky voice. "He had everything to live for."

"I'm short on details, Buddy. I'm on my way to Nashville to take care of things. Listen, man. I don't know whether you have been over to the house lately, but Mama is in a bad way."

"Because of Raphael?" asked Buddy.

"Well, that and another matter. I know you hate that house and are upset with Mama, but I can't leave those kids alone with her, especially under the circumstances. Can you go and stay with them while I'm away? I may be gone a couple of days, Buddy."

Buddy sighed in the phone. Pains long ago buried resurfaced and bruised his heart. "That's the least I can do, Jules. Don't worry about the home front. I got it. Has Lottie been told?" Buddy asked.

"Yes, and I am crazy worried about her. She is torn apart by the news, Buddy."

"I figured she would be. Things will work out, man. We Wallaces are a strong family, Jules. We will make it."

Julian sat on the plane feeling a little more at ease since he didn't have to worry about his family being alone during this horrible, inconceivable time. He knew he could count on Buddy. He wouldn't have said he would stay at the house if he didn't mean it. However, he also knew how difficult it would be for Buddy to be there. He allowed his mind to focus on Raphael, whose death he still could not fathom. He thought about Lottie and what this great loss would eventually do to her. He had written to Lottie about their mother's declining state. She called him after she had receive the letter to talk about Mamie. Her ultimate conclusion was that their mother suffered from overwhelming guilt. They agreed that Mamie's condition was tragic. Because they loved their mother, they were both in pain and did not know what to do about it.

Julian knew Raphael better than any of his family, with the exception of Lottie. The fact that this sensitive and brilliant young man had taken his own life astounded Julian. He had only spoken to Raphael once since he had been away, and that was shortly after his nephew had arrived at school. Raphael had seemed excited and happy about being at Vanderbilt. What could have possibly happened to change all that? Julian was not totally unaware. He realized that Raphael had problems, but the two of them had always been able to talk, and with his counselor's help, they had worked through his situations. Were there circumstances in Raphael's life that he did not or could not discuss with him? It was true that they had not been around each other as much during his junior and senior year of high school. Raphael had his teenager's activities and friends, and Julian had been dealing with his relationship with Christine and growing business responsibilities, not even counting his obligations to Mamie and Lottie's children. Perhaps he had not given Raphael enough attention. Maybe he had left him on his own too soon.

When Julian arrived on campus, he went straight to Dean Parker's office. The dean had been expecting him and was prepared to give Julian all the details he had about Raphael's death. He asked Julian if he would mind having Raphael's roommate, Michael, join them to provide insight into Raphael's behavior and frame of mind as of late. Julian did not object but rather welcomed any information that would help him understand why, why his nephew took his own life.

"We at Vanderbilt are very sorry about your family's loss, Mr. Wallace. The circumstances of your nephew's suicide are complex, to say the least. It seems that Raphael had suffered a mental breakdown after breaking up with his girlfriend. They had been close for a few months. According to Michael here, Raphael had also started having bad dreams, so he wasn't sleeping well. The dreams appear to have been reoccurring. I am going to let Michael tell you what he observed."

"Well, Mr. Wallace, Raphael would toss and turn and talk in his sleep. He would shout out, 'I hate you, Spanky!' When I asked him about his dreams and this Spanky, he would go off on me. His grades suffered because he couldn't concentrate on his studies, and he was tired all of the time. I came in from class yesterday afternoon and found him lying on the floor, bleeding. He was dead. There lay a gun near his body, and his teddy bear was on the floor. All of the stuffing had been pulled out of it. There was a letter addressed to his mother on the bed. I didn't open the letter. I simply gave it to Dean Parker."

"Letter? May I see it, sir?"

The dean turned to Michael and said, "That will be all, Michael. Thank you very much."

Julian stood up and shook Michael's hand. "Thank you, Michael. Thanks for being Raphael's friend. I'm sorry that you had to be the one to find my nephew."

"It was shocking, Mr. Wallace. Raphael and I were good friends. I'm going to miss him. If you and your family ever need me, I am available to you."

With Michael out of the room, the dean reached into his desk and pulled out the letter. Julian did not comment about the fact that the letter had been opened. He understood the dean's position. Mr. Parker hesitated to give the letter to Julian. "By rights, Mr. Wallace, I should be giving this to Raphael's mother, but under the circumstances, I am going to trust you with it. The police have read the letter as well. They took a copy for their files and left the original for Raphael's mother."

The letter was in an envelope addressed to "Mama." Julian gingerly opened the envelope and read the letter. It contained the answer to the question he had asked himself and discussed with his brother for over five years, and it had solved the mystery to Raphael's suicide.

"I understand," said Julian to himself. "I understand completely. Sir, I thank you. Now I need to see my nephew."

After going to the morgue to identify Raphael and make arrangements for his body to be released to him, Julian walked out into the evening air and breathed in deeply. He let the tears flow at will. "Lottie," he said, "why didn't you tell me?" Julian sat down on one of the benches lining the walkway. He ached with pain. He felt betrayed by Lottie and was surprised by her lack of trust in him. He could have helped both her and her son. Whatever her choice (to take the blame herself or to make sure Raphael was provided with what he needed legally), he would have been there right by her side. The whole family would have helped. Julian could not wrap his head around Lottie's decision. Perhaps it would have been better to tell the truth at the time. "Such a loss," he said, shaking his head. "You both lost, Lottie—you and Raphael."

His sister had lost years off her life, and her son had lost out on the counseling and retribution he needed to save his own life, his very soul. "Oh, my darling Lottie, what will you do when you read this letter? Will you feel guilt and blame yourself for Raphael's death?"

Julian realized that the only good thing about the situation was the fact that Lottie could be released from jail sooner; although, she was only a few months away from serving her entire five-year sentence. Nonetheless, she would no longer have to pay for something that she didn't do.

Julian decided to finish his business at Vanderbilt and the police department the following day. He would board a plane with his nephew's body and fly home. That evening, however, he decided to explore Nashville and his feelings.

CHAPTER 9

Lottie

L ottie kept a sardonic smile on her face as she was being fingerprinted and photographed. The process had nothing to do with her. It seemed to her to be happening to someone else. She was just an observer, not a participant. Her arraignment had been predictable. She had confessed to the murder and was sentenced to fifteen to twenty-five years in prison on involuntary manslaughter. Her attorney had been able to reach a plea agreement with the prosecutor, and her sentence had been reduced to five years.

The perfunctory shower felt soothing to Lottie. She held her long hair in her hands and made a momentary decision to cut it off. She asked the assigned officer to do the honor. The officer questioned Lottie thoroughly about what she thought was a rash decision. Lottie assured the officer that she wanted to be rid of the bothersome tresses.

The clang of the steel bars behind Lottie sent a chill up her spine. The cell was drab, and Lottie felt claustrophobic. She looked around at the small room and observed two bunk beds stacked. The top bed was made up with a blanket and a single pillow, which she assumed belonged to her cellmate. The bottom bed was stripped and obviously hers. The cell contained a small desk and a chair, and a toilet occupied the corner of the room, with a single shelf over it where toilet paper had been placed. Lottie wondered about her ability to survive. She lay across the bed and stared at the peeling paint on the ceiling. Silent, warm tears trailed down her face. She wrapped herself in her arms and uttered, "All of this is necessary, Lottie. You can deal with this. You just have to be strong. This is for Raphael. Remember that! Always remember Raphael."

Time hardened Lottie to the realities of prison life. She was assigned laundry duty, which she found to be good therapy. It kept her busy and exhausted, allowing her to sleep a few hours at night. She tried her best to stay to herself but found that impossible to do. Not only did she need the companionship of her fellow inmates but they also insisted upon hers. It was difficult at first. The women teased and taunted her about her relationship with her uncle and his murder. Lottie endured it all. It was her endurance that finally brought her peace and their acceptance.

Lottie met her cellmate Lillie Johnson when the woman came back to the cell from work duty. Lillie was of medium height. She had a full figure and brown skin, and she wore her midlength braided hair. She was a pleasant woman and welcomed Lottie into their "home," as she called the cell, with a chuckle.

"What you here for, girlfriend?" she asked Lillie.

"I killed my man and the father of my children," said Lottie frankly.

"Must have been an asshole," said Lillie, "'cause you look like a cool lady. I myself shot this motherfucker I was seeing 'cause he raped my twelve-year-old daughter. His ass lived, but they gave me three years for trying. Just finished one year. How much time they give you?"

"They started out with fifteen to twenty-five, but they reduced it to five," said Lottie.

⸺✐⸺

Lottie stood leaning against the prison fence in the courtyard, breathing in the fresh air, and soaking up the sun. It was wonderful!

She was thinking about her children when out of the corner of her eye, she saw a half-dozen women approaching her.

"So you that bitch who was fucking her uncle," said one of the convicts.

"You that hard up, pretty woman, or was that dick that good?" asked another, which caused everyone in the group to laugh at Lottie.

"What you kill him for, princess?" asked the same woman. "Caught him banging your daughter? Gotta keep that dick in the family, you know."

"Yea, that's what my fucking stepdaddy was doing to me. He started getting on me when I was twelve. I had to run away from home when I was fifteen just to escape his ass. You's a low bitch fucking your own uncle and having his babies and shit!" she spat.

Lottie never responded. She just smiled as if she were in on the jokes and taunts. Eventually, the teasing stopped when the women realized they couldn't get a rise out of her. She befriended as many as she could by complimenting them and listening attentively to their stories. Her sympathy and compassion eased them. They found a friend in a tarnished soul.

Lottie further surprised herself when she turned down Lillie when she offered to score cocaine for her. She wanted those days to be over. She did not want to self-medicate anymore. She craved the escapism of getting high, but she wanted and needed a clear mind. She had to stay on top for her children's sake.

Millie and Julian's visits kept Lottie sane. Information about her family was provided by her brother and dear friend. Julian sometimes brought her letters from the kids. As part of their counseling and therapy, they were encouraged to write their mother and express their feelings, thoughts, and activities to her. Buddy had come to visit her a few times while she was imprisoned, just enough to let her know that he loved his only sister. He carried a lot of guilt and regret because he had not been there for her and the kids. Lottie explained to him that he could not have helped, because she would have not let him. Buddy was relieved to hear Lottie say that to him.

Julian had offered to bring the kids to see her, but Lottie declined. There was no way she would allow her precious babies to come and see her in prison, in prison clothes. Julian told her that he had been unsuccessful in getting Mamie to come visit. Their mother was still angry and upset with Lottie for taking her brother's life. Lottie understood her mother's attitude. She was grateful that Mamie had risen above all that and had consented to raise the kids in her absence.

When Millie told Lottie about Vicky's rape, she was pained to the core. The rape was another example for Lottie of how she had never been able to protect Vicky. She was in jail because she could not protect Vicky, her only daughter. She had not even been the one who saved her from Spanky. Raphael had done that. Lottie imagined the violent attack on her daughter in her mind and grew sad and angry and sad and angry and finally disgusted. Vicky had needed her mother, and her mother was not there. How could she ever show Millie her gratitude? Her friend had been the one who rescued Vicky and helped her heal. Millie had always been like an aunt to the children. Lottie's benevolence toward Millie was intensified, knowing that her daughter had had Millie to turn to—someone she trusted with her life and her children's lives. She had gotten Vicky to the hospital and assisted her with making a police report. Vicky had stayed with Millie at her house for a month, and Vicky was the better for it. Vicky's letter to her mother about the horrible incident had been encouraged by Millie. The letter was limited in emotional revelations and the physical acts perpetrated by the young men. Vicky's desire was to spare her mother further grief. Soon after receiving the letter, when Lottie made her weekly call to her children, all she could say to Vicky was that she was sorry. Lottie choke on her own tears and remorse. Vicky tried to assure her mother that she was fine.

Lottie was proud of her kids. Each was making strides over time. They had finally accepted their mother's incarceration and were moving forward with their lives. She was not surprised at all about Teddy's propensity for show business. He was born for the stage. Raphael had been so much like Julian in his academic acumen. She was happy to see him follow in his uncle's footsteps. She also worried about Raphael a great deal. She didn't know how he would react if he were to remember that early morning.

Lottie tried to suppress memories of Spanky. She could not yet accept his death. At night, when she was vulnerable to thoughts of him, she sometimes couldn't fathom, couldn't grasp the thought that he was dead. She could still feel his hands touching her body and feel his breath close to her face, but it took deep concentration for her to fashion his face, his features, his eyes. When she had courage, she would glance at his picture hidden beneath her mattress. She could not bear to keep it out in the open like she did her kids' pictures. She did not want Spanky that available to her, even in death. After all, he had wounded her deeply. Lottie remembered that fatal night vividly.

Lottie had been high at the time, true enough, but reality had not totally escaped her. She knew what she saw and still could not believe her eyes. She saw Spanky move his hand up and down Vicky's legs and settled on her crouch. He held his hand there as his daughter struggled in her father's arms. Spanky kissed Vicky hard on the lips. Vicky pulled away and screamed, "Stop, Daddy! Stop!" Lottie grew horrified and ran into the living room and snatched her daughter from Spanky's arms. She lashed out at him, and he struck her. Lottie placed Vicky on the floor. She returned to Spanky and smacked him in the face with her fist.

"Bitch!" he said. "I'll . . ."

Lottie dashed to Vicky, who was sitting on the floor crying. Lottie had turned away from Spanky, leaving the rest of his rant trailing off into nothingness. Spanky left the room unnoticed. She soothed Vicky and took her to bed.

The shots rang out. Lottie sprinted from the bedroom and ran into the living room. She stopped there and listened for another sound. She wasn't convinced that what she heard was a gun. When she knew for sure that she had heard gunshots, she tried to remember how many she had heard and where the sound had come from. Lottie walked slowly into the kitchen. A shadow in the garage caught her eye. Fear compelled beads of sweat to accumulate on her forehead and drip into her eyelids. She quaked as she crept toward the garage. She made it to the garage door and peeped inside and saw a transfixed form before her, clutching a smoking revolver. Lottie shrieked. She walked toward Raphael, intentionally not looking sideways at the bundled body on the floor, for she knew who it was. She reached her son and eased the gun from his hand and held him in her arms. Raphael was dazed and nonresponsive. She led him inside and put him to bed. Raphael fell asleep immediately. Lottie slowed her steps as she walked back to the garage. For the first time in her life, she prayed to God that Spanky was still alive. She waded in his blood as she examined Spanky's body. He was gone! His eyes were open, and the expression on his face was shock. Lottie could no longer stand to look at him, so she went back into the living room and sat down. She had no tears; she couldn't cry. She was in shock. She didn't know what to do. She could not let anyone know that Raphael had shot Spanky. He was a little boy, just a little boy.

Lottie decided that the best thing to do was nothing at that moment. She looked down at the heavy metal that she had placed on the coffee table and picked it up. She made a momentary decision to hide the gun. But where? She went from room to room. Every place she picked seemed an obvious place for the police to look. Her bedroom next occurred to her. She walked about searching for the ideal place. Suddenly, she saw it—her panda bear. With desperation as her motivator, Lottie ripped the backside of the bear, removed some of the stuffing, and stuck the gun inside. She replaced as much of the stuffing as she could. Sitting on the side of her bed, Lottie was considerably calmer. She painstakingly sewed the bear's back together and placed it on the dresser, where it had been before. She balled up the remaining cotton and flushed it down the toilet. Now that there was no weapon, she could let the police think what they wanted. If they pointed the finger at her, she would have no choice but to confess, but she would not tell them what had happened to the gun.

Lottie picked up the phone to call the police then realized there was something else she had to do. She called Millie and asked her if the kids could come to her house, that Spanky had been killed, and the police would be coming soon. Millie told her she would be right over.

"Lottie! What has happened to Spanky?"

"I can't explain right now, Millie. The police will be here soon, and I don't want my children traumatized."

Lottie and Millie went from room to room and roused the children. They were fussy and out of sorts. They were sleepy and objected to being taken out of their bed. Lottie carried Vicky, and she and Millie ushered Teddy and Raphael out of the house. The two women placed the children in the same bed in Millie's spare bedroom.

Lottie rushed to the door but stopped long enough to give Millie a large hug. Both women were in tears, and even though Millie was thirsting for some answers, she held herself in reservation and watched her friend leave her house to enter into something unimaginable.

Once inside, Lottie picked up the phone to call the police; however, once again, she couldn't make the call. Instead, she called

Julian. She told her brother something tragic had happened, and she needed his help. Julian told her he was on his way.

Lottie looked at herself in the bedroom mirror. Her hair was frayed, her eyes were red and swollen, and her gown and robe were caked with Spanky's blood. Her first impulse was to take a bath and change clothes, but she couldn't. She didn't want the law enforcement to think that she was covering something up. She sat on the side of her bed and pulled out her vial of cocaine and the miniature spoon and inhaled a large dose of the drug.

Lottie heard Julian's car. She opened her door and ran toward the bright headlights into her brother's arms. "Oh, Julian," she cried. "Spanky is dead! He's lying on the garage floor, dead!"

"What happened, Lottie?" asked Julian. "How did he die?" Julian tried to mask the fear and terror that had risen in him as he gently led Lottie back inside. He had her sit while he went to the garage to see Spanky's body for himself. He kept his distance and observed the scene from the doorway. Julian held his breath and let out a deep sigh. He went back to Lottie and asked her again who had killed Spanky and by what means. There was so much blood.

"He's been shot, Julian."

"Did you shoot him, Lottie?"

"I don't know, Julian. I don't think so. I heard the shots, and I saw Spanky lying there obviously dead."

"What do you mean you don't know? Did somebody come to the house and did this?"

"Julian, I am confused. I don't know!"

"Did you call the police?"

"No, I tried, Julian, but I was too afraid."

"We have to call them, Lottie." With that said, Julian picked up the phone and dialed 911.

Julian stayed with Lottie during the interrogation. His mind raced as he watched the exchange between Lottie and the two investigators. His sister must have shot Spanky herself. Why wouldn't she admit it?

Lottie sat at her kitchen table with one officer while another stood nearby as he tried to keep track of what was going on in the garage and hear her account of the event at the same time. The house was swarming with police. A crime team had assembled in the garage, and a medical examiner was on the way. Lottie looked nervous and tired. She fidgeted with a drawstring on her robe. A cup of freshly made steaming coffee awaited her. The police had declined Julian's offer of refreshments.

"So, Ms. Wallace, let's take this from the beginning."

Lottie told the officer what had taken place.

"Did you kill Mr. Fielder?" asked the detective.

"No," said Lottie.

"Did you see who did, Ms. Wallace?"

"No, I didn't," said Lottie. "When I came into the garage, he was lying on the floor in a pool of blood."

"Was anyone else present in the house?"

"My children were, but they slept through everything."

"How old are your children, Mrs. Wallace?"

"My oldest is ten, my daughter is seven, and my baby is four."

"Are the children here now?"

"No, Officer. I took them to my neighbor's house. She's watching them for me."

Lottie was stingy with her responses, answering questions, but not elaborating on them. The second officer leaned over the lead investigator and whispered something into his ear.

"Ms. Wallace, we have not been able to find the weapon used to kill Mr. Fielder. Where is that weapon, confirmed by the coroner to be a gun?"

"I don't know," said Lottie, looking downward and still playing with the string on her robe.

"Once again, Ms. Wallace, did you kill Mr. Fielder? There has been no forced entry into the garage. In fact, the garage door had been down when we arrived. Your doors are secure in your house. Did you have visitors last night or this morning?"

"No!" said Lottie impracticably.

"What about your brother?"

"I can answer that, Officer. Lottie called me after she found Mr. Fielder's body and asked me to come over."

"When did you report the crime, Ms. Wallace, before you called your brother or afterward? Before you took your children out of the house or after?"

Almost inaudibly, Lottie said, "After I called my brother."

"We are missing important information, Ms. Wallace, and that makes me suspicious."

Lottie offered no additional information to the officer. It was obvious to the officer that this closed-mouth woman was not going to cooperate fully.

"We're going to finish this preliminary process soon. I'd like for you to come down to headquarters with me to make a formal report," stated the lieutenant.

"I need to change clothes first, sir," said Lottie.

"I can't allow you to do that, Ms. Wallace. Your clothing may contain evidence."

"Will my sister be arrested, Officer?"

"Not at the moment. We have to complete our investigation."

"Lottie, I'll meet you there. I'm going to wait until they finish here first. I'll check on the children and gather you a change of clothes."

Lottie thanked her brother then walked out of the door, escorted by the detectives.

The ensuing time was grueling for Lottie. She sat through six hours of grilling. She was so tired that her head and shoulders ached. She twisted and turned in her chair. She drank several cups of coffee. She grew angry but held it within. No matter how many times and how many ways they asked her the same questions, Lottie's answers never changed. They fingerprinted her, took a mug shot, tested her for gunpowder residue, and took all her outer clothing, including the house shoes off her feet. They replaced her garments with a baggy orange jumpsuit. She was given a pair of clogs to put on her feet. She was so happy when Julian arrived with her clothes; at which time, she was given permission to change.

"Well, Ms. Wallace," said the lieutenant, "you may go home now, but we are far from finished with this matter. You are a strong suspect in this murder. Please do not leave the state because we will be in touch with you soon."

The morning had turned into evening by the time Lottie and Julian got to her house. The police were gone, and Spanky was gone. She was overwhelmed by heartache. She stood and cried heavily. Julian took her in his arms and held her as she heaved and suffered. He carried her to her lonely bedroom and helped her undress. Lottie fell asleep when her head hit the pillow. Julian crept out the room and closed the door behind him. He was on his way to see their mother.

When Lottie awakened the following afternoon, she was exhausted. She crawled out of bed and went into the bathroom. Her children were on her mind. She wanted them with her; however, she was not ready to bring them home. She was especially paranoid about Raphael being in the house. Oh, the thought of that garage made her retch. She got on her knees in front of the toilet as her stomach turned. She started vomiting, but nothing came up but bile. She was so sick that she lay on the marble floor, where it was cool. She rolled back and forth while holding her upset stomach. Lottie lay there for a while. Her head was swimming, and sweat dotted her forehead. Eventually, she made it to her knees and went back into the bedroom and climbed back in bed. She didn't sleep; she just needed to feel better.

The phone rang. Lottie reached over and answered it with a hoarse voice. It was Julian.

"Hey, sis, how are you?"

"I'm not feeling well, Julian. I'm lying in bed hoping to feel better."

"You have been through a lot, Lottie. Are the kids with you?"

"No, no, Julian. They can't come home yet. I don't want them near that garage before I can clean it up. I am going to call Millie soon. I'll talk to them then."

"You don't have to worry about cleaning up, Lottie. I have arranged for someone to come over at three this afternoon to do the cleaning."

"What time is it now?"

"It's one o'clock. Listen, you take your time. I'll be over soon so that I can supervise the cleanup. Do you need anything?"

"No, Julian. I'm going to work on pulling myself together."

Lottie reached inside of her dresser drawer and took out her vial. She looked at it and realized that she would need more soon. She would call Spanky's partner and club manager, Dewy, to get more. She suddenly realized that she needed to get in contact with Dewy immediately to let him know about Spanky's death.

Overwhelmed, Lottie took a couple of the tiny spoonfuls of cocaine and sniffed it up her nose. She sat on the side of the bed and tried to empty her head, for a moment at least. Unable to erase the vision of Spanky lying dead on the garage floor, Lottie clutched her aching chest. Pain rumbled through her body and settled in her heart.

Unrestrained tears ran down her cheeks. Falling on her side, Lottie curled up in a fetal position and cried until her throat ached. Finally, she sat upright.

Lottie got up and showered and washed her hair. She put on a pair of jeans and a T-shirt. She had not let her hair dry completely. Her beautiful tresses reached down her back and dampened her shirt. When she went into the kitchen, Mrs. Whitfield, the housekeeper, was there making breakfast for her. Lottie felt ill and had no appetite at all. She sat at the kitchen table and silently sipped on her coffee. She felt a little more rejuvenated. She told Mrs. Whitfield that Spanky had been killed. Lottie told her as much as possible. The housekeeper was shocked, to say the least. She sat at the table in a state of disbelief. Shot in the garage.

Mrs. Whitfield pondered the situation. In all honesty, she wanted to grab her purse and run out of the house screaming. However, her love for Lottie and those precious children sealed her fate. She could not quit her job when they were going to need her more than ever. She never liked Mr. Fielder, and the hours he spent away from home meant that she rarely had contact with him. Ultimately, when she found out what he had done to Vicky, she abhorred the man.

The housekeeper was wondering where the children were. They had not been in their rooms when she got there, nor were they watching television as they normally were when she arrived at the house. She was returning from her day off. Mrs. Whitfield, who was a widow in her early forties, actually resided with the family and had been there from the time Spanky bought the house. Her deceased husband had been the first cousin of Spanky's club manager and partner, Dewy Whitfield. She had her own bedroom and private living accommodations on the lower level of the house.

"Where are the children, Ms. Lottie?"

"They are with Millie. I don't want them here until everything has been cleaned up." Lottie noticed Mrs. Whitfield's expression of horror when she mentioned cleaning up. "No, Mrs. Whitfield," said Lottie. "You and I are not cleaning up the garage. Julian is sending a cleanup crew to the house. They should arrive soon. In fact, my brother is on his way as well."

"Thank God, Ms. Lottie, because I don't think I could have done the job."

"To be honest, me either," said Lottie. "You should just go on with your usual routine. In fact, if you want to take the day off, you can."

"No, Ms. Lottie, I don't want to leave you alone."

Lottie thanked Mrs. Whitfield and hugged her with gratitude.

Lottie picked up the phone and called Millie. Just as Millie's phone was ringing, Julian came into the house. He came over and kissed his sister on the cheek.

"Hello, Millie," said Lottie.

"I am so glad to hear from you, Lottie. I have been one worried woman," said Millie.

"I am so sorry to have worried you, Millie. When I come and get the kids, I'll tell you what's been going on. How are they?"

"They're used to Aunt Millie, so they are fine. I told them that you had to take care of something, but you would be back. Lottie, they heard the police activities and wanted to know what was going on. I told them there had been an accident, but everything was fine."

"Thank you, Millie. However, I am far from fine. Can they stay a little longer with you?"

"As long as you need, sweetheart."

"I'm going to come by after a while to see them. I'll bring them a change of clothes and give them a bath." After Lottie hung up the phone, she turned her attention to Julian. "Hi, little brother," she said.

Julian looked at his sister and determined that she was too upbeat for someone who had lost the love of her life in such a horrendous manner. He knew that she was lit, but he decided not to acknowledge it by chastising Lottie. "Have you eaten today, Lottie?" Julian asked.

"No, Julian. I'm not hungry yet. What time are the cleaners coming?"

Julian looked at his watch. It was three o'clock exactly. "Any minute now. You should eat something, Lottie. You don't want to get sick," he admonished her.

"Julian, I'll grab something later. I haven't contacted Spanky's partner yet to let him know what has happened. I'm going upstairs to call him, then I am going to Millie's to see my children and help get them bathed and dressed," said Lottie.

"Are you bringing them home?" asked Julian.

"Not now. I'll bring them home when everything is clean and back to normal. Perhaps this evening," she said.

"Things are not normal, sis. They've lost their father," said Julian.

A transparent wave of pain rushed across Lottie's face. "I'll tell them eventually, Julian," whispered Lottie, because her voice had cracked and she could barely utter a word.

Julian held Lottie in his arms while she composed herself. "We'll tell them together," he said.

Lottie labored to climb the stairs. She gathered the kids' belongings then went into her room to call Dewy. She called Dewy's house and was told by his wife that he had already left for the club.

By the time Lottie had taken care of her children, it was early evening. She jumped in her car and drove quickly to the club. She wanted to get there before the crowd came in. She entered through the employees' entrance. Dewy was not at all shocked to see her there. He grabbed Lottie into his arms. He tried to keep his emotions in check but found it impossible to do. He cried softly on her shoulder.

Lottie pulled back and looked at Dewy incredulously. "You know?" she asked.

"The story is on the third page of the *Sun-Times* newspaper, Lottie. One of the employees saw it and called me. I waited to hear from you."

"The newspaper!" said a shocked Lottie.

"Not just that. His death has been announced on the radio stations and television news channels. They named you, his girlfriend, as a person of interest to the police," said Dewy. "Spanky was an important business man, Lottie, with a lot of investments. People knew him and respected him. You would be surprised."

Lottie was at a loss for words. She looked at the tall, dark-skinned, middle-aged man like he was an alien from another planet. "I need some stuff, Dewy," she said.

He went into a locked cabinet to retrieve the substance and handed her an ample supply. She opened the aluminum foil and used her fingernail tips to sniff some of the content up her nose.

"I hadn't even considered that all of this would be in the news. I hope my children haven't seen or heard anything. I haven't told them about their father yet. However, knowing Millie, she probably has shielded them from seeing anything on the television about the incident."

"What happened, Lottie?" asked Dewy.

"I'm not at liberty to say right now, Dewy. Suffice to say, it was an accident."

As curious as he was, out of respect for Lottie, he did not pursue the matter. "You know I got your back as far as Spanky and my business interests go, Lottie," said Dewy.

"Knowing that gives me peace. I trust you, Dewy," she said. "But I have to meet with you and the lawyers and the accountants to see what all is involved. I am also going to ask my brother Buddy to represent my interest as well. He owns his own business, you know."

"I thought you trusted me, Lottie" said Dewy. "Do you need to involve him?"

"Dewy, I don't know what's going to happen as a result of the police's investigation. In addition, I have my children to raise. I can't run a business right now. I hope you will try to understand my position," said Lottie. "Dewy, I have to go now. I really have not thought out any of this. I'm talking off the top of my head. We'll talk about everything when it is appropriate to do so."

When Lottie went downstairs the following day, she was surprised to see Julian, the kids, and Mrs. Whitfield sitting at the kitchen table eating.

"Hey, sis. Excuse the mess, but we were hungry. Here, take a sit and join us. Mrs. Whitfield and I went and got the kids from Millie and decided it would be a good idea to get in the car and drive by McDonald's. We bought enough for you too. Sit," said Julian, avoiding eye contact with his sister.

Lottie circled the table, pecking her little ones on the checks. She bent down to eye level with Raphael and gave him a kiss and a special smile. "How are my darlings?" she asked, never breaking her gaze with Raphael.

"Where is Daddy, Mama? Isn't he going to work today?" asked Vicky, who was accustomed to seeing her dad leave for work around their lunchtime.

Caught off guard, Lottie blindly grabbed for a chair. She had to sit. She looked at Julian with a questionable stare. She hadn't fully determined what she would tell the children about their father. She searched Julian's eyes for an answer.

"Your father has gone away," said Julian.

"Where?" asked Teddy.

"Do you remember the bird you guys found on the porch last summer?" asked Lottie.

"Yes," said Raphael. "He was stiff, and he couldn't fly. Mama, you told us he was dead, and he would never come back to life, so we buried him in the backyard. Is that what has happened to our father?"

"Yes, sweetheart," said Lottie as tears spilled from her eyes.

"Daddy is dead?" said Teddy. "How did he die, Mama?"

"There was an accident, and your father got hurt real bad. No one could save him," said Lottie.

"Then he is never coming back," said Raphael.

Teddy began to cry. He ran to his mother and climbed onto her lap. Vicky started to cry as well. Raphael was misty-eyed but stoic. He was in a state of shock. Julian grabbed Vicky in his arms and rocked her gently. Lottie looked at Raphael in amazement. He truly had not remembered shooting Spanky.

"Listen, guys," said Julian. "Remember what Mama and I told you about the bird? We said that we would be sad for it but also happy, because the bird's spirit had risen and he would be free to live in a new world where there would be no harm, and he could fly high and wide anywhere he wanted to." They stopped crying as they imagined the free bird soaring. "It's the same way with your father. He's free and happy too. He misses you guys and will always watch over you from the other world."

Lottie had never been more grateful for her brilliant brother. He had cast a spell of love and hope over all of them. Even Mrs. Whitfield gazed upon Julian admirably. She wiped the soft tears from her eyes and began to clear the table. She warmed up a cheeseburger and placed it in front of Lottie with a look that commanded her employer to eat it. She sat a cup of coffee on the table and took a seat in front of Lottie. Teddy was still in Lottie's lap, Vicky was still being held by her uncle, and Raphael rested his head on Mrs. Whitfield's shoulder.

Lottie ushered the children into the living room and encouraged them to play with their toys. She returned to the kitchen and asked Mrs. Whitfield to make them a pot of fresh coffee. After serving the two of them, she left the kitchen; she told Lottie that she would be in the living room with the children.

Two years passed before the district attorney presented Lottie's case to the grand jury. The investigators had put together all the evidence, but the case was not airtight. The gunpowder residue on Lottie's hand was insufficient to prove that she had shot the gun. The results only indicated that she had held the gun used to kill Mr. Fielder. In addition, no weapon had been found. The state prosecutors found themselves in a precarious position; nonetheless, they decided to move ahead with an indictment of Lottie. The grand jury agreed that the case should go to trial.

Lottie's lawyers wanted Lottie to go to trial. They felt that they had a strong defense and that the state's case was weak because of the lack of a weapon and their inability to prove that Lottie had fired a weapon. Lottie, on the other hand, did not want to send her family and children through what would likely be an arduous process. She directed them to go for a plea deal. Abiding Lottie's request, they were able to get her sentenced time reduced from ten to twenty-five years down to five years. Lottie was given thirty days to get her affairs together and turn herself in to the police.

As her time in prison passed, Lottie grew discontented with just doing laundry. She started spending her extra time in the library, where she read voraciously. Eventually, she compiled her résumé and made an appeal in writing to the warden to work in the library, even if it meant dual duties. Her request was granted, and instead of doing laundry, the warden asked her to create a literacy program for the inmates and to teach reading herself. Purpose. Lottie had found purpose.

Lottie had just begun. She enrolled in an online degree program at the University of Chicago, where she had once been a student. She had almost completed her master's degree in education when she dropped out at Spanky's behest. Lottie completed the coursework and obtained her degree. She immediately began her doctoral pursuit in prison education systems and how education can lead to total rehabilitation.

Although she had been given a challenging job, Lottie still found time to spend with the other inmates. She attended movie night and met with them in the activity room. Lottie was always available to talk to the women about their personal lives: their children, their desires, and their hopes for the future.

She engaged with them academically as well and helped them research job possibilities and requirements and the skills needed to do the jobs. She helped the inmates to develop strategies to prepare for the world outside, to meet the demands of a world that was not going to be their friend. The women took correspondence classes that focused on their area of interest.

Lottie's time in prison was going by fast. She was so busy and all-consumed that she was not paying attention to the clock and calendar. Lottie was happy and thriving.

Lottie had been on an extreme emotional high and was looking forward to seeing her brother Julian, whom she hoped was visiting her that day. She put on makeup and pulled her long hair into a ponytail. After almost five years in prison, her long tresses had grown back.

Lottie spotted her brother right away as he sat in the courtyard waiting for her. She ran to Julian and threw her arms around him. She kissed him on the cheek and sat down across from him. She noticed when he grew quiet and serious.

"Lottie, I have to give you some bad news. Mama is going through some changes right now that we don't fully understand," said Julian.

"How is Mamie?" asked Lottie.

"She's a mess," said Julian. "Buddy is with her right now. We both spent the night at the house last night. She won't talk. She won't eat. She just sits there crying."

It has just been too much for their mother to bear, thought Lottie. Julian's account of Mamie's condition came as no surprise to Lottie, and it bothered her. For the first time, she could weigh just how much Spanky's choice to be with her had wounded Mamie. For the first time, she felt guilt.

Mamie had been doing a great job with Lottie's children while she was confined. Lottie could relax about their well-being. Mamie was aware of the children's interests and activities. She had placed limitations and expectations on the kids just like Lottie would have done herself. All was well.

"It has all been too much for Mamie, hasn't it, Julian?" said Lottie. "You say she changed when she got the message that Granddad had passed? She rarely mentioned him and Grandmother, and she had not gone to visit them. That I am aware of," said a confused Lottie.

"Spanky has been dead a while now too, so I don't know, Lottie. Buddy and I assume it's guilt that is plaguing her. Maybe she thought she had more time to mend her relationship with her father. Remember when I went to visit him that summer before I started college?" asked Julian.

"I do," said Lottie. "She was very upset with you for going."

"She was upset because there were things about her and Spanky's lives that she didn't want anybody to know about. I told you some things, but not all of what had happened there. It was real bad, and I don't think there had been forgiveness among the family," stated Julian.

"I hate that Mama's past is afflicting her, but I'm worried about my children, Julian. I'm locked up here. Who is going to care for them? As far as that goes, who is going to take care of Mamie?" Lottie asked. "You can't. Buddy can't. And I can't ask Millie to take on that burden."

"So far, we're managing. Vicky helps her bathe, and her bedding and room are kept clean. She also cooks sometimes too, despite Teddy's dismay." Julian chuckled. "I'm over there every day, and I bring them food and spend time with Mama and the kids. Let's not worry right now. If things get too complicated, I'll call on Mrs. Whitfield."

"You know, she comes to visit me every month," said Lottie. "I love that sweet lady."

"Yea, she visits the kids too," said Julian. "She's a good friend."

Lottie relaxed a little. She was able to continue with her life without constantly worrying about her children. One night, she got into bed and reached for Spanky's picture beneath her mattress when she felt something rough and familiar. She pulled from beneath the mattress a folded foil containing cocaine. Lottie kicked the mattress over her head, awakening Lillie, her roommate.

"What is this shit?" she shouted at Lillie. "You know I don't indulge anymore, Lillie. Why would you try to tempt me with this?"

"Hold on, girlfriend," said Lillie. "Sometimes a girl needs to escape from it all. You do so much for us, Lottie, that I just wanted to do something special for you. I'm not trying to get you back on drugs, but I wanted you to have that in case you need it."

"Oh, Lillie, it's kind of you to think about me, but I can't accept this."

"Keep it, Lottie," said Lillie. "Life can get hard sometimes."

Lottie begrudgingly placed the foil back beneath her mattress. She was too sick to argue with Lillie.

Something was wrong. Lottie felt anxious, and her stomach was upset. As hard as she tried, she could not focus and concentrate. Her head was cloudy, and her thought process was compromised. She couldn't hold on to a single word.

After her last class for the day, she went into the library and sat on a couch and tried to read Toni Morrison's *Beloved*, but she couldn't arouse herself enough to continue reading. She put the book down and went back to her cell. She lay across the bed and drifted to sleep.

Lottie did not sleep peacefully, but she slept deeply. She dreamed that she was in the forest, walking slowly and brushing branches from the trees aside as she tried to make her way through to an opening. The moon was bright and hung low. She saw a panda bear dangling from a bamboo tree. He reached for Lottie, but she was too fast. She ran past him into an open clearing. She was suddenly surrounded by a hedge of red roses. She reached for one and was pricked by a thorn. Blood gushed out of her finger onto the ground. She was wearing a white nightgown. Pulling at the lace hem of her gown, Lottie tore the fabric off and used it to wrap around her finger. The blood soaked through. She needed help, so she ran through an opening in the hedges in search of someone who could stop the bleeding. She was running so hard and so fast that she almost didn't notice the boy standing at a crossroad at the end of the forest. He held his hands out to Lottie, and she ran to him. She fell to her knees. She was exhausted but happy to see the boy. An aura of light encompassed the boy, and the smell of cedarwood rose from him. He lifted Lottie's hand and unwrapped the bloodstained cloth off her wound. He turned her hand over and kissed her finger, and the bleeding ceased. Lottie kissed the boy on his cheek in gratitude before he left and disappeared into the woods.

When Lottie awakened, she realized that she was in the infirmary. A nurse stood next to her, taking her blood pressure.

"Well, look who's back in town! It's good to see those beautiful eyes open, Ms. Lottie," said the woman with kindness and joy.

"How long have I been here?" asked Lottie.

"Two days so far," said the nurse. "We're not through with you yet, my dear. You had a viral respiratory infection. The doctor worked hard to keep it from turning into pneumonia. How are you feeling?"

"I feel weak and exhausted," said Lottie.

"We are going to remove your tubes today and try to get some nourishment in you. No steak, but maybe a little broth or soup."

Lottie fell asleep again and had the same dream.

Lillie and the other inmates in Lottie's cell block clapped and cheered when she was returned to her cell five days later. She was happy to see her friends too. The kitchen staff had made a cake, the guards brought balloons, and everybody joined together to celebrate Lottie's return.

Lottie had been on a high for weeks. She had totally put her illness behind her and was striving at and accomplishing her goals. Lottie received a call from Julian and could barely wait to speak to him. She was hoping he was calling her to announce a visit.

"Hi, Julian. I'm so glad to hear from you. Are you coming for a visit today?"

"Hey, sis. I wish I could come to see you. I'd rather talk to you in person, but I don't have the time," said Julian.

"Are you all right? Is there something wrong, Julian? Is Mama okay?" Lottie asked.

"Mama is the same. I don't know how to tell you what has happened, Lottie, so I am just going to say it. Lottie, Raphael is dead. He committed suicide."

The earth shifted beneath Lottie's feet. She shook her head vehemently. The words she wished to speak would not leave her mouth. The desire to scream was agonizing, for nothing would escape her being. Everything had collapsed inside of her.

"Lottie, are you there?" said Julian. "I am so sorry. I am especially sorry that I am not there with you. Say something, sis."

Lottie sobbed and slid to the floor, her back pressed against the wall for support. Through snotty nose and a congested throat, she managed to say, "I'm here."

"After I make arrangements for Mama and the kids, I will be on my way to Memphis. I should be able to get more information there, and of course, I am going to bring Raphael back with me." Lottie wailed! "Just hold on, sis. I'll be back as soon as possible."

Lottie let the phone slide from her hand without disconnecting it. Lillie and her crew saw Lottie and immediately went to her. They lifted her body off the floor and escorted her back to her cell and put her to bed. The women sat on the floor and administered to their nonresponsive friend.

"Here, Lottie, take this," said Lillie as she raised Lottie's head and forced her to sniff some cocaine.

They propped Lottie up on a pillow and gave her water to drink. Another inmate wiped her face and helped her to blow her nose. The crew sat around and took some of the drug themselves. They sat in complete silence, observing Lottie for over thirty minutes before she was able to communicate with them.

"My son Raphael has committed suicide," said Lottie. "My brother Julian is on his way to Memphis to bring him home." Tears erupted from her soul, so she could not share with them any more information.

The women sobbed and cried out loud with her. They appeared as the women in an African village mourning the loss of a loved one. They passed the coke around and submerged themselves in their grief.

The time came that they had to report back to their cells. They each hugged their friend, exiting with heavy hearts. Lillie climbed in her bed and listened intently to Lottie's every move, every shift, every breath.

Julian called his sister when he returned and told her he would come to the jail as soon as possible, but first, he needed to speak with her lawyer. In light of Raphael's suicide note and confession, the district attorney petitioned the judge for Lottie's immediate release, effective the following day.

Lottie was surprised the following morning when the guard came to her cell. She had barely slept and was feeling groggy and crossed. She staggered from her bed and mumbled incoherently at the guard.

"You act like you don't want to leave this place," said the guard.

Lottie turned on her heels and looked inquisitively at the woman. "What did you say?" asked Lottie, who wasn't sure if she had heard the guard correctly.

Lillie shrieked and jumped out of her bed and jumped up and down for joy. She hugged the shocked Lottie. "You go, girl! You have earned this privilege. Now you can be home for your other children. This is marvelous, Lottie!"

"You have been sprung, Lottie, and you are going home today!" said the guard.

"That's not possible, Paula," said Lottie very suspiciously, addressing the guard by name. "Is this one of your stupid jokes?" said Lottie, still raunchy.

"I am not joking, Lottie. Your brother is waiting for you in the warden's office. Your release papers have already been signed by a judge."

"But I don't understand, Paula," said Lottie.

"I can't tell you more, Lottie. I was sent here to get you. Here, take your clothes and get dressed and gather your belongings. I'll come back for you in fifteen minutes," said the guard as she passed Lottie the same clothes that she had worn when she was imprisoned.

Lottie was suspicious of her release. She could not believe it. Part of her wanted to shout for joy, yet her other self felt the release was not possible. She turned to face a teary-eyed Lillie.

"I am so happy for you, Lottie, but dang, I hate to see you go."

A misty-eyed Lottie reached out to her friend and held her in a fierce hug. "Lillie, this is not the end for us. I'm definitely coming back to see you guys and help you anyway I can."

"You know you better," said Lillie.

Lottie moved fast. She got dressed and began pulling photos of her children off the walls and grabbing things from beneath her mattress and bed. She reached for the foil of cocaine and started to give it back to Lillie, but she put it in her jacket pocket instead. She reached underneath her mattress and took out Spanky's picture. She looked at him, wondering at the same time if she was being paroled or if Raphael had regained his memory and confessed.

Lottie was stricken by the thought that her freedom could have been gained by Raphael's confession. The dooming possibility that he had remembered that horrible night and as a result took his own life was seismic to Lottie.

Lottie was drawn out of her thoughts when the guard returned. She gave Lottie a bag for her personal items. Lottie gave Lillie a hug and left promptly with the guard.

As Lottie walked past the adjoining cells, friendly hands reached out to her.

"That's the way to go, girl!"

"You must have really laid it on that ole warden pretty hard, Lottie, for him to let you go free." One giggled.

"Best wishes to you, Lottie. Tell the world I'm still here," said another.

Lottie kissed some and hugged others. Her joyful and sad tears intermingled with those of the women who had become her friends.

"Write to us, Lottie. You know how lonely it gets in here," said Brenda, to whom Lottie slipped her foil of cocaine.

Julian was all Lottie saw when they entered the warden's office. She leaped in her brother's arms and wet his face with kisses. She turned to the warden and asked, "How is this possible?"

"Although we are sorry to see you go, Lottie, we all are so happy for you," said the warden. "Your brother is the reason you are being released today. Therefore, I am going to let him explain everything to you. Take a seat, you two."

"Raphael left a note for you, Lottie, and I'd like you to read it."

Lottie looked at the cryptic note and almost refused it. Her intuition told her that its content was painful. Her hand shook lightly as she took the naked note from Julian. "Caused you to suffer . . . hereby confess . . . Goodbye, Mama. I love you. So he remembered, and he could not bear his guilt," said Lottie. "In all my efforts to protect him, I couldn't protect him from the truth." Lottie's eyes stung from the birthing of new tears.

"Sweetheart, his truth allowed you to go free. After I came home from Tennessee, I went to see your lawyer and presented him with the letter. He took the letter to the district attorney, who took it to a judge, who granted your immediate release."

"I see," said a less-than-grateful Lottie.

"We are going to leave now, Warden, and wish to thank you for all you've done for Lottie," said Julian."

"It's been my pleasure, Mr. Wallace," said the warden to Julian. He walked across the room to Lottie and grabbed her hands. Holding them tight, he looked into Lottie's eyes and said, "After you have gotten through your loss and grief and are ready to work, I want you to consider rededicating your time to the women here at the prison.

You have done so much for them, in fact, for all of us, that I want to hire you permanently to continue the programs that you have started here."

"I think I'd like that," said Lottie. "I will be in touch, Warden."

Lottie's freedom brought her little joy. She didn't see the autumn leaves dipped in red, brown, and gold colors. She didn't notice how lonely the birds' nests looked as they hung shanty like upon the branches. She couldn't smell the sweetness in the fall air. She didn't feel the fall's crisp breath upon her cheeks. Invisible to her were the people who walked back and forth, going about the daily tasks of living. She only saw images of Raphael, her ten-year-old son, her firstborn, her love.

Julian had arranged for Raphael's body to be sent to Leaks Funeral Home. Five days after Lottie's release, they held a family-only funeral. The chaplain eulogized a young man he never knew. He spoke of the family being united again in heaven. He talked directly to Lottie about the challenge of losing one's own child and how one must leave him in the arms of the Lord. There was not a dry eye in the chapel. Even the austere Buddy gave in to his grief.

Raphael's body was cremated and delivered to Lottie in a beautiful leaf-covered urn trimmed in gold. Lottie placed her son's remains on the shelf over the fireplace in her mother's house.

The day that Lottie was released, Julian drove them to their mother's house. Lottie, who was lost in thought, had not noticed where they were going until they had arrived. "Why are we stopping here?" asked an irritated Lottie.

"Lottie, your house is boarded up. No one has lived there in years. You can't possibly go there."

"Oh yes, I can, Julian! That's my house. I won't stay anywhere else."

"Sis, be realistic. Your house is not suitable to live in right now. We didn't know you were going to be released, so no one prepared it for you. Not counting the fact that you would be alone, and I just don't think it's a good thing for you to be alone right now."

"Who's going to be alone?" spat Lottie. "I still have two living children. They are going to be with me. We have to put our lives back together, Julian."

"Not in one day, Lottie. Not today. The kids just can't be uprooted at the drop of a hat. They have been through much too much already. And what about Mama? Don't you think she needs some time to get used to losing her family all over again?" asked Julian.

Lottie sat pensively. "All right, Julian," she finally said. "The kids can stay for a while, but I surely won't. I'm going home as soon as I check in on my children."

"Lottie, I am worried sick about Mamie. I'm especially concerned now that you are talking about taking her grandchildren away from her. It'll kill her, Lottie."

"Don't you know that I died a little every day for five years? No way I'm going to live without them now, Julian," she said.

"What if they want to stay with their grandmother, Lottie? Will you force them to go with you anyway? They love Mamie and are stressed by her decline as well."

Lottie was visibly hurt. The idea that her children might not want to live with her never crossed her mind. Little had. She had not even had a chance to get used to being out of prison, furthermore where she would stay. She assumed that she would take one step into what life had been like before. She had envisioned her children being overjoyed to see her and wanting to be with her again.

"Julian, do the children know that I have been released?"

"Of course, Lottie. I told them first. They are thrilled to have you coming home."

Lottie was suddenly anxious to see Vicky and Teddy. She got out of the car and outpaced her brother to Mamie's house. When Lottie entered the house, Teddy leaped from the window seat where he had been observing his mother and uncle as they sat in the car talking and went and stood by his sister. Lottie hesitated at the door. She had become less than confident about how she would be received. Going inside as bravely as possible, she noticed that Vicky and Teddy were nervous too.

"Mama?" asked Teddy, who was still very young when Lottie went away. He was holding on to Vicky's arms. As he got older, he let go of his fantasy that his mother had left to pursue acting. He realized that she had been in prison all along. He had spoken to her numerous times and had written to her. Raphael's adventitious suicide was still a complex to him. He hadn't understood some of the circumstances leading to the disaster that had struck his home like lightning. Nonetheless, the whole incident had brought his mother home, and he was happy about that.

"Yes, Teddy, I am your mother," said Lottie as she extended her arms to him.

Teddy bolted from his sister's side and ran into the embrace of his mother's arms. Lottie's body rattled from the sea of emotions that had seized her. She looked hopefully at Vicky, who stood quietly with tears streaming from her eyes. Vicky drifted over to her mother and touched her head lightly to authenticate her presence. Lottie released Teddy and grabbed her daughter to her. This was what was left of her children.

Julian had waited to enter the house. He wanted Lottie and her children to have time alone with one another. When he entered the living room, he found the three of them nestled together on the floor.

"Where is Mamie, Julian?" asked Lottie.

"She's in her room. I told her that you were being released and coming home today. I can only hope that she understood. It's hard to tell," stated Julian.

"She understands." said Vicky. "I can tell, and she's happy about it too."

"I don't know how, but Mama seems to communicate her feelings to Vicky and Teddy. She never speaks, but Vicky and Teddy seem to understand what she needs and wants," said Julian.

Lottie looked at her children incredulously. She got up off the floor and went to her mother's room. She had to see for herself this mysterious Mamie everyone spoke of. She wavered formality and walked directly into the room. Upon the bed lay this shell of a woman who resembled her mother.

"Mama," called Lottie. "Mama, it's your daughter. I'm home."

Mamie did not move or speak. Her eyes followed the sound of Lottie's voice. Lottie moved closer to her mother and sat on the side of the bed.

"What is this all about, Mama?" she asked. "Are you trying to kill yourself? Why are you playing this cruel joke on everybody? For attention? Well, Mamie, you definitely have gotten everybody's attention. Still got to be the pampered one. I've never given in to you, Mama, and I'm not going to start now. I want you to snap out of this!" said Lottie as she grabbed her mother and shook her.

Lottie grew angry rather than sympathetic. "Listen, old lady. I just had five years of my life taken away from me. My oldest son is dead, and my remaining two kids barely know me. I don't have time for this shit of yours. Wake your ass up, Mamie!" shouted Lottie.

Lottie sat back on her mother's bed and let her head rest on the headboard. She was exhausted. She looked sideways at her mother and groaned out her frustration. Mamie did not respond. Lottie took her mother's hand in hers and fell asleep.

CHAPTER

10

Mamie

amie awakened to Lottie's misery. Her daughter shook spasmodically in her fitful sleep and sweated profusely. Mamie placed a loving arm around Lottie. None of them understood. Yes, she could speak if she wanted to. She had nothing to say. Words were useless. They lacked the capacity for the truth. They encouraged deceit and demanded shallowness. Mamie was beyond pretense. All her life, she had lived on pretense. She pretended that it didn't hurt when her mother gave her to Calvin Wallace. She pretended that it didn't hurt to not see her brother for years and years. She pretended that it didn't hurt when Spanky left her for Lottie. She pretended that it didn't hurt when the love of her life was killed and she was left all alone—alone in a friendless and unkind world. She pretended that it didn't hurt to see her daughter hauled off to prison for killing the one and only person she had loved above herself and all others. Did she think Lottie really killed Spanky? She didn't know what she thought. She only knew that she didn't know. She hated Lottie at times, true enough, but not because of Spanky's death but rather because of all the unhappiness her daughter caused her. It was not within Mamie's reasoning strength to accuse or blame anyone for Spanky's death, for whoever killed him surely destroyed her. How does one continue to love the person who annihilates them? When Mamie had been told about Raphael's suicide and the reason for it, she felt oddly relieved, because she didn't have to go through a test of her love for her grandson. She didn't have to wave through any mixed emotions.

She didn't have to abhor him. Raphael's death ended it all for Mamie. The pretenses were then completely behind her.

Mamie brushed back the lock of hair that had fallen in her daughter's mouth. Not even that bit of nuisance was enough to awaken Lottie. Her obvious pain didn't awaken her either. For the first time, Mamie considered the many pains Lottie had had to suppress in order to survive her ordeal. So apt her daughter had become. For a moment, Mamie felt bad about not being more of a comfort to Lottie but quickly returned to her former attitude. Ruefulness had no place among the many ashes of Mamie's life. Her time must be spent now on bringing about a quick end to her life, and not speaking was the first step in that process. Mamie's approach to suicide was to hold her breath and desire it. If one does not breathe, one dies. How can one hold his or her breath? Breathing was involuntary. Although the body forces life on the breath holder by making one breathe, one still had options, such as placing plastic over the head or breathing in exhaust in an enclosed garage by running the engine of a car. Inevitably, Mamie's option was to always be mindful of the destruction her love for her brother had caused. Memories alone would kill her.

Once she's gone, her family can begin to live normal lives (whatever that may be). Her mother told her that hell awaited. Mamie, a nonbeliever in such things, was unaware of the many facets of hell. She had been enlightened by time. Mamie never had many expectations of life. In fact, she had none at all. She lived for Spanky and him alone. Even when he left her for Lottie, she felt she still needed to exist for him, that one day he would realize his error and return to her. Why she chose to live beyond his death was a mystery to her. She learned to live and would have continued trying to learn if her father hadn't died. Mamie couldn't understand why his passing had affected her so severely. She began to feel like she was the only thing keeping an otherwise closed book open. She wanted to put the

Fielders to rest. She wanted Lottie Wallace and her family to have a fresh start, to not have to contend with the past, to not have to stare any longer at Mamie and Spanky's love for each other and the consequences of their relationship. The least she could do was die. Why wouldn't death come to her? How many more mornings must she awaken? The daughter that lay in her arms was not enough, Buddy was not enough, Julian was not enough, and her grandchildren were not enough. Mamie envied Raphael, Spanky, her mother, and her father's peace. Turmoil, trouble, pain—these things were over for them. How could they have left her behind?

"Ooh! Ooh!" moaned Lottie. Cuddled beneath the covers, she rocked like a baby. Mamie intensified her grip around her daughter. "I need my stuff!" said Lottie, not yet awake. "I can't! Raphael, wait! Don't! No, Raphael, no! See the panda in the tree?"

Mamie rocked Lottie and buried a kiss in her hair and let her tears flow freely.

Linked

ottie had awakened that first morning after being released from prison in her mother's bed. Mamie was huddled next to her, stroking her hair while smiling sadly. Lottie couldn't control the shaking or arrest the horrible gnawing in her stomach. She extracted herself from her mother's arms and ran to the bathroom. She reached it just in time. Bile erupted from her stomach. She felt dizzy and clammy. Lottie was dismayed. She thought she had conquered her addiction in prison. It had been months since she had experienced withdrawal. She surmised that the reemergence of her problem had been caused by the death of her son. She was too weak to fight this obstruction again. She would go see Dewy.

Lottie got into the shower and let the tempered water flow over her body. She found it difficult to hold on to the bar of soap she was using to lather herself. She had to pick it up from the bottom of the shower several times. She managed to complete her grooming and got dressed.

It was midafternoon, and she didn't know whether or not she could reach Dewy at the club. Nevertheless, she would surely try. She was about to reach for the phone when Teddy seized her from behind.

"Good! You're awake," said Teddy enthusiastically. He was so happy to have his mother home.

Lottie quickly composed herself and turned around to face him. She gave her youngest child a kiss. She held him away from her so that she could take him all in. "You have grown so much, Teddy," she said to him then pulled him back into her embrace.

"Vicky and I have already fixed some food for you. We made sandwiches, and we have potato chips and coffee too."

Lottie didn't want to eat. She had one thing on her mind, and it wasn't food. The idea of food made her nauseous; however, she did not complain to Teddy. She let him lead her into the kitchen, where she was shown a place mat with a huge sandwich on a plate and chips in a bowl. Teddy went to the coffee maker and poured her a steaming cup of coffee. In an attempt to delay the chore of eating, Lottie reached for the hot coffee and began to drink it black. She realized she needed the stimulant.

"Where is Vicky?" she asked. "She helped you, didn't she?"

"Oh, she took Nana a plate of food. She won't come out, you know, so we take her food to her," said Teddy nonchalantly.

Lottie tried to pick up her sandwich, but her hand was shaking so severely that she grew ashamed. She placed her hands on her lap to gain some control. Teddy, who was very perceptive, did not ask his mother what was wrong. He assumed she was stressed out. Instead, he went to the refrigerator and poured himself some juice and excused himself by saying he had to rehearse for an upcoming engagement.

Lottie breathed a sigh of relief when Teddy left the room. She rose from the table and went to the window and stared out of it. In her mind, she saw Raphael outside playing baseball with Julian. He was really good; therefore, she had not been surprised to learn that he was playing on his high school team. She cried in earnest, and the aching in her heart enhanced her need to get ahold of some cocaine. She told herself that she needed drugs to get through Raphael's impending funeral. She would go view her son's body on her way back from the club. She felt so guilty about looking for drugs at that time. Her children had been a surprise to her. They were indeed self-sufficient, but they were, after all, children. With the loss of their brother, they needed her more than ever. She didn't know what to do. Temptation and obligation battled for her soul.

Engrossed in her thoughts, Lottie did not hear Julian when he came into the kitchen. She was startled by his touch. She turned into his arms. After giving his sister a hearty embrace, he looked intently at her. "You don't look so good, old girl," said Julian.

"This old girl don't feel so good either, Julian. I need a fix real bad, little brother. I need help! Please help me, Julian," implored Lottie.

"You have got to make a decision, Lottie," said Julian. "You have got to choose between drugs and your children. They deserve the better of you, Lottie. They have been through enough. I won't sit back and let you destroy them."

"You don't have to tell me that!" responded an irritated Lottie. "I know what my responsibilities are, Julian, but I also know that I am sinking fast. I can't do this alone. I can't ignore the gnawing in my gut. All I want to do is get high. I know you don't understand brother, nor can you empathize with me. Just look at me, Julian. I am a wreck. Look at my hands. Look at my face."

"Would you consider a drug rehab program, Lottie? I happen to know about one place in particular that I would like to recommend. Rehab may be the only place where you can get help with letting this habit go for good," said Julian.

"How do you know about this place?" asked Lottie.

"Christine told me about it. When you were incarcerated, I told her how well you were doing as you were avoiding drugs and conquering your habit. She admonished me to not get too excited about your progress, because you had managed to involve yourself with getting your degrees and teaching. Things were well there and at home. She felt that the challenges you may face on the outside would set you back, Lottie, so she gave me the name and number of the director of the program whom she housed with in college," explained Julian. "Why don't we go see what they have to offer."

Lottie was pensive. Fear and uncertainty about making a commitment to go through a rehab program stopped her from even wanting to go to the center at that moment. "Julian," she said, "let's go tomorrow. Today I want to see my Raphael. Should we take the kids with us and Mamie?"

Julian sighed. "We'll all go, Lottie."

Lottie did not sleep that evening. Viewing her son's lifeless body and the reality of his death further destroyed her, as well as the rest of the family. Mamie came home and went straight to her room. Vicky followed to help her grandmother to undress and get in bed. The rest of the family gathered in the living room, exhausted by the grief and emotions that had seized them. Vicky came to join them just as the front door opened. It was Buddy. He could not go with the family to the funeral home because of his work. He had gone by later. His solemnness expressed his utter devastation. He sat with his family as they mourned.

After Julian and Buddy left and Vicky and Teddy had gone to bed, Lottie went into the kitchen and made coffee. She spilled her first cup while pouring because her hands were unsteady. She was sweating profusely, and the heat from the coffee caused perspiration to roll down from her forehead into her eyes and mouth. Lottie choked on her salty tears that ran down her throat. Pulling herself together eventually, she drank more coffee.

Lottie thought about tomorrow, when she had agreed to go to rehab. She knew in her heart that she would go. Lottie sat until the morning sun peeped into her kitchen window. She had spent the evening reliving Raphael's short and valuable life. She was on a merry-go-round from his birth to his death.

The Chatham Rehabilitation Center was nothing like Lottie had suspected. They drove into the parking lot on the side of a huge brick house. When they entered the house, they walked into an open lounge where a small group of people had gathered to casually watch television, play cards, read, and play games with a handful of children. Everyone spoke to them. A tall, dark-skinned, impressive woman rose to greet them personally.

"Hi, I'm Dr. Regina Baldwin, founder and manager of this center. How can I help you?" she asked as she extended her hand to Julian and Lottie respectively.

"Hello, my name is Julian Wallace, and this is my sister, Lottie Wallace," said Julian.

"We're not very formal here," said Dr. Baldwin. "May we use our first names?" she asked while talking to Julian but looking at Lottie. "Who referred you?"

"My girlfriend, Christine Williams. You two shared a dorm in college."

"Yes, I know Christine. Our paths have crossed since college. In fact, she serves on the board of my foundation, which is the flagship of this center. Come with me," she said. Regina led them into a large dining room and asked them to take a seat at the table with her. "Christine is a magnificent woman!" she said. "Very intelligent and energetic, she gets things done. You're a lucky man, Julian."

"I am indeed," replied Julian, obviously proud.

"She hasn't referred anyone to me in quite a while. Plus, she usually calls first," insisted Regina.

"Normally, she would have," said Julian, "but she left last evening on a business trip. She gave me your information and sent her apology for being unconventional with this referral. She knew you would understand. Also, this involves her family."

"I do understand, Julian, and it's all right."

"Regina, it's Lottie here who needs your help," said Julian, redirecting the conversation to the subject of their visit.

Regina was very aware of Lottie, and she had already identified her as the one who needed her help. Her goal in diverting everyone's attention from the purpose of the visit was to give Lottie the opportunity to relax and adjust to her surroundings. She could tell that Lottie was beyond frightened and intrepid.

"Lottie, how are you?" Regina asked.

Lottie took in a deep breath then released it before she spoke. "Nervous," she simply stated.

"Are you a user, Lottie?" the doctor asked.

Lottie could not bring her eyes up to meet Regina's inquisitive stare. She spoke to her hands, which still shook. "This relapse was a surprise to me, Regina," she said. "I haven't used but one time in the past five years. I was in prison. Yet I was home for one night when systems of withdrawal seized me, and my need for a fix intensified. To stop me from going out and satisfying my cravings, my brother brought me to you on this, my second day of being freed."

"Lottie, I am a clinical psychiatrist. Therefore, I don't just out-and-out diagnose a person without medical and mental evaluations, both of which I am going to do with you. Five years of sobriety is a wonderful thing. It's not surprising that you feel the need to use again, because addiction is a lifetime disease. Believe me, you have come in here today better off than most of the women I see. I'm going to go so far as to say to you, you may be experiencing panic attacks," said Regina.

"Panic attacks?" asked Lottie.

"Listen to me carefully, Lottie. I'm not saying definitely that that is your problem, but I am saying it could be one of the components of your overall condition."

"I am probably a bundle of mental issues," said Lottie.

"We will see," said Regina. "We start tomorrow morning at 9:00 a.m."

"Tomorrow is good for me, Regina," said Lottie.

"Let me tell you more about this center," said Regina. "Look around you, Lottie. This is no prison. It is a home. You are among friends. We are a family at Chatham Rehabilitation Center. There are no more than twenty-five participants at any time. Five live here because they have special needs. Eventually, through our various initiatives, they will transition into society fully equipped to navigate their lives. Everyone else are here on an outpatient basis. They go and come as they please. We offer individual and group counseling. Our medical needs are met through our association with Trinity Hospital—I issue no drugs from this facility.

"As you know, Lottie, a large part of conquering addiction is individually inspired. Each struggle is different. You or any other patient will be judged. I consider those who come here as participants rather than patients. My main goal is to inspire, assist, and provide the means for those entering this house to leave here healthier, happier, stronger, and ready to live fulfilling and meaningful lives. Do you have any questions, Lottie?" Regina asked.

"There are children here, Regina," noted Lottie. "Are they being counseled too?"

"No, they are not," said Regina. "Women are encouraged to bring their children with them if they want to or need to do so. The women help each other out by babysitting while the mothers are engaged. They prepare the children food, read to them, and play with them during the time they are here."

"That's wonderful!" said Lottie, impressed by what she had heard and seen.

"Let's take a tour, Lottie," said Regina.

They picked up Julian, who was sitting in the living room, and began the tour in a spacious chef kitchen. The kitchen was modern and enhanced by stainless steel appliances, granite tabletops, and marble floors. They observed three bathrooms, six bedrooms, an attic apartment, an outside deck, a large backyard, a three-car garage, and an office that was positioned in a bright sun porch.

Both Lottie and Julian had been truly impressed and pleased with their experience with Regina. Lottie was all in and felt that she needed what Regina had to offer, as well as her approach.

As the months rolled by, Lottie was benefiting greatly from the counseling that she was receiving. Learning to take control of her own life was an integral part of her therapy. As her first initiative, she decided to become more than a silent partner in her businesses. She would run the nightclub herself and establish herself as the head of the liquor stores, properties, and other businesses that she then owned, thanks to Spanky.

Lottie decided that she needed preparation for such an undertaking. She enrolled in business classes and attended seminars designed to help those who wanted to start a business. She saturated herself with finance classes and investment strategies. For over a year, Lottie focused all her time on becoming authentic as a competitor in the business arena.

When Lottie walked into the club, she was pleased to find the place in good condition. Dewy had truly run the place as if it were his own. He had been Spanky's partner but not on a fifty-fifty basis. He was as dedicated as if he were an equal investor. The club was empty when Lottie arrived. She sat arbitrarily at a table and gazed about her. She could not immediately muster up the courage to go into Spanky's office. A deep sense of nostalgia seized her, and sadness prevailed upon her. Emotions swelled like pools inside of Lottie. She fought back the tears that sprang up in her. This was not the day for sorrow but rather one of sweet victory—the first day of her new life. The many nights that she had sat at the bar under the watchful eyes of Spanky and his leering customers rushed upon Lottie like a gale of wind. She suddenly felt naked and cold. It prevailed upon her at that moment to close the club down and have it completely renovated, to paint over the walls and tear down the bar and start over, creating new memories. She wanted the club to reflect her personality, to have her personal signature. Lottie made a mental note to meet with her accountant first thing.

Spanky's was a dark place. With its decor of burgundy and green, the club was much too solemn. Lottie would change that. She would use rose and mauve and mirrors and gold. Resolved, she went into the back of the club and entered Spanky's office. The office was clean but cluttered. Evidently, Dewy did not have a filing system, she thought. She brushed the papers aside and sat down behind the desk. Pink and green and beige were the colors that Lottie saw as she sat there taking in the scenery. Lottie hesitated for a moment. Are her colors too feminine? She would give her ideas more thought.

The bell to the back door rang. It startled Lottie, who was lost in her visions. She could not imagine who might be at the door. It was still too early for Dewy; however, he had keys to the club. Lottie opened the door.

"Hello. I didn't mean to disturb you, miss. I just happened to be passing by when I noticed the car parked outside. I thought maybe Dewy was here," said the man, surprise registering on his face.

"Who are you?" inquired Lottie.

"Forgive me for my lack of manners, miss. My name is MacArthur Benson. I'm the liquor distributor for this club."

"Well, hello, Mr. Benson. My name is Lottie Wallace, and I am the owner of this club," said Lottie, smiling. "May I be of assistance?"

MacArthur Benson was obviously stunned. He had known that Spanky's lady had inherited the club after his death, but he never really expected to see her there. Lottie's beauty had not escaped him. In fact, he found her irresistible. How was he ever going to do serious business with this woman while hiding his attraction to her?

Clearing his throat, he said, "It is a pleasure to meet you, Mrs. Wallace."

"That's Ms. Wallace," said Lottie, establishing her independence. "Likewise. What can I do for you today?"

Trying to not appear too surprised by Lottie's correction of her handle, Mr. Benson said, "Nothing really, Ms. Wallace. I drop in on my customers occasionally to see if everything is satisfactory."

"Well, I truly cannot answer that. This is my first day on the job and haven't taken stock of things yet. However, I think you should know that I will be closing the club down in a few weeks for renovation. I'll have Dewy contact you before we reopen, if not before, depending on what the club's needs are."

"I see. So you will be managing Spanky's yourself?"

"With Dewy's help, yes. Will that pose a problem for you, Mr. Benson?" asked Lottie.

Far from it, thought Mr. Benson, but he elected to say instead, "It'll be my pleasure to work with you, Ms. Wallace, as well as continue my association with Dewy."

Lottie was pleased and extended her hand as a show of faith.

"Will you be closing the liquor store as well, Ms. Wallace?" asked Mr. Benson.

"I don't think that will be necessary at this point, Mr. Benson," said Lottie.

"Once again, Ms. Wallace, it was a pleasure to make your acquaintance," said Mr. Benson. "I will go now so that you can get back to work."

"I appreciate that, Mr. Benson," said Lottie warmly.

"And it has been indeed my pleasure to meet you."

"Indeed, it was," said Lottie as she returned to her desk.

Lottie had never once looked at a man other than Spanky. She was surprised to learn that she could actually be attracted to someone else. She felt different somehow. The tall, handsome, lean, well-dressed Mr. Benson had definitely stirred something up inside of her. She went into her private bathroom and looked at herself in the mirror. *A little war-torn,* she thought, *but still attractive.* Anyway, she wouldn't even know how to act socially with a man. Suddenly, she felt depressed.

"Oh, Spanky!" she said. "I can't do this life without you. I don't want to do this without you."

On her way home, Lottie decided to drive to her old house. She wanted to see Millie, but she especially wanted to take a look at the place that she and her children once lived with their father. She had to make a decision as to whether or not she wanted to live there again. She parked her Cadillac on the street. She couldn't even make herself pull into the driveway. She sat motionless in her car, eyeing the boarded-up structure. It only took a few minutes for Lottie to decide that she could never live there again.

Lottie started the car and drove the short distance to Millie's house. She pulled into her old friend's driveway and got out of the car. Millie was surprised and happy to see her closest friend. Although she had visited Lottie numerous times, she had not been able to persuade Lottie to visit at her house, which was so close to Lottie's old life in proximity and spirit. Millie understood Lottie's desire to not see the place where Spanky had died; therefore, she never pushed the issue. This day was a pleasant surprise. They gazed intently at each other then hugged. For moments, it was as if time had not changed, as if the two were about to embark upon one of their daily routines. They cried in each other's arms like babies. Millie led the overwhelmed Lottie inside and offered her something to eat or drink; however, Lottie declined, opting instead for just coffee.

After drinking some of Millie's familiar brew, Lottie pushed back from the table and breathed a satisfactory sigh. "How have you been, Millie?" asked Lottie. "I'm sorry that it has been a while since we spoke last, but life has been a whirlwind."

"No need to apologize, Lottie," said Millie." I can only imagine how your life must be right now. I am well. I just miss you and the kids. You look wonderful!"

"I feel wonderful too," said Lottie, really meaning it. "Millie, I went by the club this afternoon. I'm going to take over the club. I have to talk to Dewy about my plans. I left before he got to work. I plan to remodel Spanky's and introduce live music and stand-up comedy."

"That sounds wonderful, Lottie!" enthused Millie. "Maybe Teddy can do his act there too."

"Yeah, when he is age-appropriate," said an amused Lottie.

The dear friends roared with laughter. Millie saw a Lottie she never knew existed. She was so happy for her friend. Lottie rarely smiled, much less got idiotically excited about anything.

M amie understood everything they were saying to her, "repressed aggression, hatred for her mother, suicidal tendencies," and on and on. Don't they understand? She simply did not want to talk; didn't they understand that she had nothing to say and no need to say anything? Everybody kept pressuring her to seek professional help. Lottie wanted her to try the Chatham Rehabilitation Center, where she was going. Mamie refused. She would, however, make a compromise; she would come from behind her citadel and live in cohabitation with her family, since she hadn't achieved annihilation through physical death. Maybe that would lessen her family's concerns. She would live her life outside of her bedroom.

Mamie begrudgingly admitted to herself that she was glad that Lottie had decided to live with her and not take the children away. She did not relish the thought of her daughter and grandchildren living in that house where Spanky's life had ended. Initially, Lottie had planned to stay with Mamie for a short time. It had then been almost two years that they all had been together, and in Mamie's estimation, they had been good years for all of them. Julian was constantly visiting, and Buddy had come by more than he had in years.

Mamie was still conflicted about her feelings for her daughter. She knew for sure that she loved her, and she was convinced that Lottie loved her too. She just had not been able to resolve the issues that Lottie had caused her to have with Spanky. She was aware of Spanky's philandering with other women, but when he built a life with Lottie instead of her, she grew bitter toward her daughter. Lottie should have never let that happen. Mamie blamed her for all the loveless nights she spent because Spanky was with her. Something in the abyss of her soul told her that her daughter's relationship with Spanky was only symbolic of her brother's true character. She knew for sure Spanky would have left her cold and needed eventually. Some women would have taken his attention away from her. In this particular case, it was her daughter, Lottie.

When Spanky died, Mamie was at a loss. She no longer had hope that he would come back to her. It was her love for and devotion to her three grandchildren that gave her life purpose. She loved those kids more than she had ever loved her own. Her grandchildren did not compete for her love and attention; however, with her own children, she resented that they took time and energy away from her, when all she had wanted to do was to serve Spanky. She never felt resentment or guilt when it came to her grandchildren. Mamie would never admit it to anyone, but Teddy was her absolute favorite. His free spirit was abounding, and his love for his family was beyond limits and expectation. Vicky was willful but devoted to her grandmother. She always felt the need to watch over Mamie and help her. Mamie lacked the energy to combat Vicky, so she was freehanded with her when Vicky insisted on having her own way. She worried constantly about Vicky's welfare. Losing Raphael was more than Mamie could bear to think about. He was the quiet one, the timid one, the one who never gave anyone trouble. He was so brilliant, so much like his uncle Julian.

A lump grew in Mamie's throat every time she thought about poor Raphael taking his own precious life. He had always been withdrawn and frightened to death of girls. Mamie inwardly chuckled at her reveries.

Her family had survived a great deal. She thought intensely about Lottie and the changes she had seen in her. Lottie had practically turned her whole life around. Her daughter just didn't understand. Unlike Lottie, Mamie was not capable of riding the world by herself, so she chose to fade into the background of life. It was the only way her family could achieve a new start, a chance to put the past behind them and move on. She was the last link to that old life, and she refused to be the one thing that tied them to it. Love had always resulted in loss for Mamie Fielder Wallace.

igh school was a blast for Teddy. He sailed through the hallways with more than a modicum of confidence. He was, after all, a local celebrity. Not only had he been a frequent talent around the city but he also had landed a future appearance on *Star Search*. The girls were ridiculous; there were so many seeking his attention until Teddy elected to stay away from all of them. He really didn't have time for that type of socializing, nor did he want the distraction. He could always date later. Between his studies, rehearsals, and performances, Teddy barely found time to sleep. He relied heavily on his family, and they relied on him, especially his nana. He felt safe with his mother and uncles and sister. He could be himself without judgment; he could come off stage and just be Theodore Fielder.

Teddy considered himself to be the man of the house now; therefore, it was his responsibility to keep an eye on the women in the family. He did this covertly however. The Wallace women were a stubborn and independent group of individuals. He was proudest of his mother. Over time, Teddy had garnered more particular and intimate information about his family's history. Instead of being embarrassed, he was smug about it. They were actively building a new life from one of tragedy and pain.

Teddy had never thought much about drugs. He knew people who indulged, but he never wanted to try them himself. He was much too high on life as it was. He and his siblings had been in counseling for years, and they did not stop when their mother came home. She wanted her children to have mental health. He knew now it was because of the extremities of life, which with they were confronted.

Therefore, he understood his mother's addiction, to a degree. Counseling had helped him comprehend her issue. He had come to appreciate his mother's efforts be sober and stay sober. He remembered when he was younger and his mother was arrested, his uncle Julian and grandmother put Vicky, Raphael, and him in counseling almost immediately. As kids, they hated it and were reluctant to attend. They wanted to obey their mother's wishes, so they cooperated as much as possible. None of them liked the idea of revealing themselves to a stranger. They were uncomfortable about that. He wished when Raphael left for college that he had continued the process. It was obvious to him that his brother needed help.

Teddy was the first of the three of them to open up to the counselor. He had been so young when his family had fallen apart that he had few scars. He was practically a baby when his father died. He had problems holding on to his mother's presence when she went away. The photos he had of her helped to keep her image fresh in his mind. He had grown so close to his sad, pained nana that she became his mother figure. He had received much love from his grandmother, as well as Vicky, Raphael, and his uncle Julian. His uncle Buddy was not around very much at that time, but he was happy that he was a part of his small family. At first, when it came to discussing his brother's death with the counselor, he was not able to talk about it. He didn't want to allow himself to think too much about Raphael. The pain and sadness he felt was drowning him in a bottomless sea.

Vicky and Julian had done their best to explain to him why Raphael had taken his own life; nonetheless, the reason did not abate the loneliness. Teddy still felt like someone or something had come and plucked his brother off the face of the earth without warning him. He felt the extraction as if it were he himself being taken away. It was surreal.

When Raphael died and Teddy was given the reason why his brother had chosen to take his own life, he hated Spanky. He could not remember his father very well, but he hated him for being the cause of his brother's demise. Teddy loved Raphael tremendously. He never tried to emulate Raphael, because he could not imagine being as introverted as his brother was. One had to dig to find Raphael. Teddy wore his whole being on his sleeve, so to speak. He could not remember even one occasion when he had asked his brother for help and had been refused or sought his attention and had been turned away. When Teddy performed, Raphael was there, encouraging him. He had been so afraid that Teddy might falter that he never relaxed and laughed with the audience. Teddy could never judge whether or not his jokes were funny by Raphael's reaction, because there was no reaction. "That was great, Teddy!" he would say when they got home, as he placed a proud arm and warm hug on his brother.

Teddy had sent Raphael off to college confident that he would be home as soon as Thanksgiving. He still found it difficult to believe that his brother had come home dead. Teddy was in pain for his nana too. No one knew better than him how much Raphael's death had affected Mamie. Teddy and Vicky stuck close to her during that time. They kept a visual on Mamie at all times. He was glad his mother had come home. The time she spent with Mamie, trying to coax her into sharing her grief with the family, gave Teddy and Vicky time to deal with their loss. His mother's return was the only good thing he could find amid the tragedy.

Teddy watched grief at its most treacherous self during those first days, weeks, and months of Lottie's return. His uncle Julian literally took care of all of them. He practically anticipated their needs and provided for them. Teddy had never felt so helpless in his life. There were plans to be made for Raphael's funeral. The family's visit to the funeral home had established the fact that his brother was truly dead.

He watched his mother become a basket case. She didn't sleep, and what she ate would starve the average person. His nana had become even more withdrawn, refusing the food that they brought to her. He and Vicky did the best they could, but they, too, were burdened by their sorrow.

After Raphael's funeral, things began to improve slightly. The family was beginning the process of letting go, and life slowly picked up a new routine—life minus one. He still worried about his mother. She was restless, pacing the floor day and night. She would embrace herself and just sit and rock. She would perspire regardless of the temperature. She would go into the boys' room and sit on the side of Raphael's bed hour upon hour. When he or Vicky would approach her, she would hold them tenderly to her chest and cry dry tears. They tried to give her space yet let her know that they loved her. Teddy felt that she would get better. He was well aware of the personal investment his mother had made into Raphael's life when she chose to go to jail in his stead. In actuality, his mother had gambled on what seemed to be a sure bet and lost. She had lost a great deal, not only her son but also five years of her life and five years of her children's lives.

Uncle Julian immediately sought help for his mother. He had taken her to a rehab center and to see a doctor. She had been placed on sedatives; however, they did not seem to be working. What was the most difficult for Teddy to deal with was her isolation. His sister Vicky was affected even more than him when their mother started to pull away from them.

It was hard for Teddy to resume his old life at first. Some of his fire had been extinguished. He found very little about which to joke. He refused several engagements offered to him by his agent. When he talked to his nana about his feelings and not going back to work, she shook her head no and pushed him off her bed, her way of saying, "Get back to work!" Teddy complied. Fortunately, his grades had not suffered. He absolutely found refuge in his studies. School occupied a part of him that would otherwise have been consumed in depression and chronic sorrow.

Teddy was glad to be graduating from junior high school that June. He was looking forward to being in high school that fall. There were a host of activities to keep him busy. The event was only a few weeks away, and he wanted very much for his family to be there. He was timid about bringing the subject up with them. He watched daily to see if there were any improvements or changes in his mother's spirit. There were few notable changes other than the fact that she was no longer perspiring, rocking, and pacing the floor. She was just overwhelmingly sad. It had been almost six months since they buried Raphael, but the atmosphere around him did not attest to that fact. It could have been just yesterday. Teddy decided that he had no choice other than remind his mother that the day was quickly approaching for his graduation. Prior to the graduation ceremony, there would be a luncheon, and he needed suits for both occasions. Teddy felt that he had given his mother enough time and space. After all, she owed him a part of herself, as well as the rest of her family. It was time for him to see whether or not this woman, whom he had loved and believed in always, really loved and believed in him too.

"Mama," broached Teddy, not raising his eyes to meet his mother's eyes, "I graduate in June, so I wanted to know if my family was going to be there."

The lengthy silence caused Teddy to have heart palpitations. He raised his eyes, and there sat his mother, disheveled and vague. He lowered himself to his knees, touched his mother's shoulder, and looked deep into her very soul. He found there shattered love. "Mama, did you hear me?" he asked.

Lottie reached for Teddy's face. She placed a hand on his cheek and smiled. Tears chased each other down her face and landed on Teddy's arm. She grabbed him and rocked him back and forth. Tears stung Teddy's eyes, but he held them back. He fought the pity, anger, and hatred that swelled up inside of him. He pulled back from his mother's embrace and sat back on the floor, away from her.

Lottie got up and grabbed him by the neck of his shirt, pulled him off the floor, and dragged him with her to his nana's room. He was almost afraid of her. "Mama, Teddy is graduating from junior high in a few weeks. I'll get to see my baby boy graduate!" she said proudly. His mother went to her mother and hugged and kissed her. Lottie let out a fantastic scream as she danced around Teddy. Her behavior even solicited a smile from Mamie.

When Lottie first came home, Vicky didn't know how to act or what to feel. She didn't even know what to do, so she withdrew a little. Her heart went out to her mother, yet she was ambivalent about her behavior. The initial relief that Vicky had felt at first slowly turned into stress, her hope into resentment. Everyone was concerned about her mother; however, it seemed to Vicky that her mother catered to no one. Her uncle Julian had taken her to a doctor, planned her son's funeral, and had gotten her in a rehab program, and she and Teddy waited on her hand and foot.

Vicky had to admit that things had gotten somewhat better with the advent of Teddy's graduation from middle school. Her mother's spirit had lifted. Nonetheless, Vicky had not found herself an intricate part of her mother's life. Her mother spent a great deal of her time with Teddy, perhaps rightly so considering that her brother needed her to plan and execute a proper graduation experience for him. She held on to her uncle Julian for dear life and spent time with their grandmother, trying to bring her around, but Vicky received hugs and sad smiles. It was as if her mother didn't know what to say to her.

Evidently, her mother did realize what was happening to her relationship with her daughter. One evening, she knocked on Vicky's bedroom door. "May I come in, Vicky?" she asked.

Vicky opened the door and said, "Come in, Mama."

"Vicky," said Lottie, taking her daughters hand in her own, "these are complicated times for me and the whole family. I love you, sweetheart, and I know I haven't been there for you. It has not been intentional. I feel a great deal of guilt when it comes to the type of mother I have been to you, Vicky. I was away, and you got hurt really bad. You experienced abuse at the hands of your father, and I was not there to protect you. My best friend had to become mother to you because I was not there. Whether my reasons for not being available to you are valid or not, I had put someone else ahead of you, and I'm doing it again with Teddy. Please forgive me. I am going to get better as your mother. I won't neglect you again."

Vicky looked into the depths of her mother's eyes and met the love, the pain of disappointment, and her heart almost broke. "Thank you, Mama, for explaining your feelings to me. I love you so much, and I don't blame you for the bad experiences that I have had in my life. In fact, I have been feeling guilt as well."

"Vicky, what could you possibly feel guilty about?" said an astonished Lottie.

"Mama, I am the reason my brother killed our father, I am the reason you had to go to jail, and I am the reason my brother took his own life," said a distraught Vicky.

"My goodness, Vicky!" said Lottie. "None of that is true! It is not your fault that your father was corrupt and of low character. The only one to blame for you being in that type of situation was me."

Vicky had not immediately known the circumstances of Spanky's death until she overheard her uncle Julian and mother discussing it on the day that her mother got home. In fact, none of them had even known who killed her father. She had assumed that it was indeed her mother. It hurt Vicky to the core to find out the truth. What could her father have done to her to cause Raphael to kill him? Had Spanky been the cause of her nightmares? Was the dreams about the big hands about her father? There was so much to sort out. She desperately needed her mother to help her understand.

Vicky remembered how easily Teddy had gotten their mother to come out of her stupor. Her mother had gone through the house announcing Teddy's graduation, a fact that everyone else seemed to know but her. She came to Vicky's room and said, "My baby is graduating from middle school, Vicky! We're all going, and we have a lot to do. This will be our first time out as a family, except for Raphael's funeral. Let me call Julian and Buddy. They must come too."

At that time, Vicky grew hopeful. Perhaps life would go back to normal again.

"You're Teddy Fielder's sister, aren't you?" the students asked her constantly. Vicky was beginning her junior year at Hirsch, where she had been for three years, yet she had now become Teddy Fielder's sister. Vicky had prided herself on her immense popularity. She was active in several extracurricular activities and knew most of her peers. She could practically date whomever she chose and was the envy of every girl in her classes. Suddenly, she was just Teddy Fielder's sister. Vicky was beginning to feel that there was no place where she could shine.

Vicky lay across her bed and looked at the ceiling. She tried to remember when was the last time she felt loved and wanted. It didn't take much time for her to figure it out. It was with Terrence. They had spoken often since Raphael died, but she didn't get to see him through the Thanksgiving holidays because of the circumstances. Things had been so chaotic for her family that the summer had gone by without the opportunity for them to be together. She no longer feared telling her family about their relationship, because she believed the only person who would have been offended by their being together was Raphael. Now she had to wait for another holiday to see Terrence. His phone calls were the only things that made her truly happy. She had been so numbed by her brother's death that she didn't feel that she had conveyed to Terrence how much she loved and needed him. During the ensuing time, Vicky was ready to put the last year behind her and to feel better about her life. She wrapped herself in velvet thoughts and let her memories of being in Terrence's arms embrace her. She rolled over on her stomach and reached for the phone on the nightstand. She brushed the hair from her face with one single stroke and dialed Terrence's number. He was not in his room, so she left him a message to call her.

Vicky rolled out of bed and left her room. She noticed that her mother's bedroom door was opened. She peeked inside and noticed that her mother was not there. Her mother had been spending much of her time with Millie at the club. They were redecorating it for some kind of grand reopening. She went into the living room and was taken aback to see her grandmother sitting there in the lounge chair.

"Grandma, you're out your room!" she said.

Mamie smiled and beckoned for Vicky to come and sit with her. She folded herself in her grandmother's arms and breathed in her musky order. She brushed back the silver-gray patch of hair that had fallen in Mamie's face.

"Grandma," she said, "Do you think Mama loves me?"

Mamie frowned and cocked her head to the side, indicating to Vicky that she was confused by her question.

"She doesn't really talk to me, Grandma, nor does spend time with me. She barely knows that I am around. There are a lots of things I'd like to talk to her about and a lot of things I want to ask her."

Mamie etched a question mark in the air.

"I want to know what our father did to make Raphael shoot him," said Vicky. "I know it had something to do with me when I was younger, but I don't know exactly what. Mama said that my daddy hurt me. I just want to know how."

Her grandmother looked intently into Vicky's eyes. She didn't quite know what to do. Mamie was surprised that after all this time, Lottie had not told Vicky the entire truth. She mouthed the words,

"Ask Julian." Mamie understood how difficult the conversation would be for Lottie; however, Vicky deserved the whole truth. Vicky kissed her grandmother and left the room.

Julian customarily worked until about six o'clock. Vicky wanted to be at the bank when he got off work. She stood outside and watched the people as they paraded by her. She saw an elderly lady who reminded her of her grandmother. This lady was outside in the fresh air and the sunlight, going about her day. She hobbled slightly because one of her legs was shorter than the other; nonetheless, she was a happy woman who smiled at Vicky as she passed by. Vicky smiled back at her and suddenly felt bad for the matriarch of their family. Mamie would never venture downtown and walk its fair streets. A young man and woman went by her, whom she observed were not much older than her. They were laughing and pointing out sites to each other. Vicky's thoughts raced to Terrence, and her needs to see him and be with him were stifling. A man came from somewhere behind her and startled her. He walked undauntedly by her, brushing her shoulder as he passed by her. Vicky recognized the man and ran to catch up with him.

"Uncle Julian," Vicky called.

Julian turned around to see his niece waving at him. He stopped and waited for Vicky to catch up with him. "Hi, love," he said. He hugged his niece and pecked her on the cheek. "What are you doing down here?"

"I came to see you," said Vicky, happy to see her awesome-looking uncle. He was so tall. You could tell he frequented the gym, because his lean frame bulged with muscles. He had on a brown suit and shoes, a golden dress shirt, and an art-rendering tie that combined the colors of his suit and shirt, and he carried a brown leather Coach shoulder bag. His curly hair was neatly trimmed, and his copper-brown skin glowed in the sunshine.

"Is everything all right?" he asked Vicky. He was concerned. It was highly unusual for Vicky to venture downtown by herself.

"Well, yea. I guess so," said Vicky vaguely. "I need to talk to you about something, Uncle Julian, and I want to talk in private."

Julian was more than a little curious. "Why don't we stop somewhere and have a cup of coffee. I could use some coffee after a hard day of work."

Julian led her into the closet restaurant and chose a table near a window. As they waited for their waitress, he and Vicky observed the pedestrians as they strolled by on their daily quest. They found people gazing fascinating.

After their order had arrived, Julian gave Vicky his full attention. "Okay, sweetheart, tell me your story."

"Uncle Julian, something has been bothering me ever since Raphael died. I heard you and Mama talking about Raphael's suicide. I heard Mama say he killed our father because of me. What did my father ever do to me that would make my brother shoot him?"

Julian shifted in his seat, obviously nervous and disturbed by his niece's query. He had never deceived his niece and nephews, and he was not about to start then. Vicky was a young woman, and he knew that she could handle the truth. As always, he was very exact with his niece. "Yes, Vicky, Raphael shot Spanky because of you, but not you alone. Spanky was physically attacking your mother. Your mother and father were fighting because your father tried to molest you. Raphael heard their conversation and witnessed the assault. Your brother had not been aware of what he was doing nor could he remember afterward what he had done. So you see, Raphael's reacted to years of abuse of your mother by his father, so he snapped. So you see, Vicky, Raphael did not react the way he did directly because of you."

Vicky sat back in her seat and was quiet for a moment as she tried to digest what her uncle had just told her. She could not have even imagined the truth. She was relieved to hear that it was not her alone who had caused the tragedy, but she was still not convinced that she had been told the entire story.

"Uncle Julian, do I know everything now?" Vicki asked.

"Yes, you do. You know that I would never lie to you," said her uncle.

"Well, why does Mama blame me? Why is she taking this whole thing out on me?"

"In what way is she blaming you?"

"She's ashamed around me. She is either ashamed of me or herself. She won't talk to me, Uncle Julian. She doesn't even ask me about what type of day I had or what I did for the day. She wants absolutely nothing to do with me," said Vicky, wiping a stubborn tear from her eye.

Julian sat reflectively for a moment. He had always known Vicky to be a rational and sensitive child. Her feelings must have some merit. He was a constant presence in that household and had witnessed a bonding between his sister and her children, or so he thought. As he took a retroactive look at Lottie and her family, he had to admit that he had not seen Lottie and Vicky engaged in any mother-daughter activities. Lottie had struggled with mental issues when she first came home. She had reached a point where she was not participating in life; she was in a trance most of the time. She did not respond to those around her. Perhaps the sedatives she was taking contributed to her state of mind, but Julian felt that his sister suffered most because of her all-consuming grief.

"I was not aware of the problems between you and your mother. Whatever the problem is, sweetheart, it is not you. It has to do with something inside your mother. I will talk to Lottie," said Julian assuredly.

Inwardly, Julian felt depressed and inadequate. He could understand Lottie's behavior to a degree. Vicky had been her competition when Spanky was alive. In Lottie's subconscious mind, Vicky had been the cause of his death. The mother and daughter needed a trip to see Regina.

"Vicky, let's schedule an appointment for you and your mother with Regina, her counselor. During which time, you guys can sort through your issues with a professional," Julian suggested. Vicky agreed. "Come on. Let's get you home," said Julian.

Vicky went straight to her bedroom when they arrived home. Her grandmother had retired to her room, Teddy was in his room doing his homework, and she could overhear her mother and Millie talking and laughing in the kitchen. She picked up the phone and called Terrence. At last, he answered.

"Hello, Terrence," she said when he answered.

"Hi, sweetheart. It's nice to hear from you. I've been thinking about you. Man, I miss you," said Terrence.

"I've been thinking about you too," said Vicky. Both were silent for a few minutes. Those nests of love and joy still hung over them. Terrence was overwhelmed by the love he felt for this young woman, and Vicky was hopelessly in love with him and desired his presence. Being apart from each other only served to make their commitment to each other stronger.

"Vicky, I'll be home for Thanksgiving. Will I be able to see you then?"

"Oh, Terrence, that would be awesome! Thanksgiving is only a few months away. Yes, you can see me. Every day, all day long. I love you, Terrence," said Vicky.

"I love you more," said Terrence.

Vicky tried to find a place within herself to store her longings. She still had a long time to wait for Terrence. She took out her homework and submerged herself in her studies.

CHAPTER

15

J ulian was happy to have his sister home and safe. He would do everything possible to help her. He had never been as worried for Lottie as he was when she became nonrespondent for all those months after Raphael's funeral. Nothing seemed to lure her from the threshold of oblivion. It was an agonizing time for the entire family. Buddy had even been concerned enough to make more visits to see her and Mamie. Julian was glad that he and Christine had located a suitable rehab program for Lottie. He did not like the idea that Lottie's doctor had put her on sedatives. In his opinion, that prescription had caused his sister's malaise. However, the drug had stopped Lottie's panic attacks. Regina had been correct when she said that Lottie was suffering from a panic attack rather than withdrawals from her drug addiction. Lottie did eventually respond to therapy and went as far as to design a new life goal for herself.

Julian's heart strengthened as he thought of Christine. He loved her dearly. They had lived together for fifteen years, yet she never pressured him to marry. She traveled a great deal, and his time was consumed with his responsibilities at work and with his family. Julian knew that most women would not be as tolerant as Christine; therefore, he was absolutely committed to her. He remembered that fateful day when she walked into the bank, seeking to open a personal checking account. New at his job, Julian was working in new accounts and had the good fortune of helping her.

He had seen her almost immediately when she came into the bank and could barely take his eyes off her. She was striking in her tailored red suit, which framed her body perfectly. Single-breasted, the suit had a broad collar trimmed in black. She wore black pumps, which made her look taller. Her hips were narrow, her waistline thin, and she had the most magnificent swanlike neck. Her complexion was dark and her face oval. She had full, sensual lips. Her eyes were dark and knowing. She was sophisticated, almost too womanly for her age. Her hair fell in short, layered curls that framed her face. Julian was hopelessly in love.

When Julian heard the receptionist assign her to him, his heart skipped a beat and his head thundered. He offered Christine a seat and proceeded in a professional manner. Masking his emotions as much as possible, he found he was incapable of looking at her. He stole glances of her while she filled out forms. Whenever he leaned toward her, the perfume she was wearing made an indelible impression on his senses; he never forgot it. Her hands were slender. The ink pen she held glided across the page with little pressure or force on her part. Julian smiled when she lifted her eyes from the form. Christine was very aware of the handsome man sitting in front of her and returned him an encouraging smile. Once they had concluded their business, it dawned on Julian that this woman could walk out of the door, and he might never see her again.

"Excuse me, Ms. Williams," said Julian.

"Call me Christine," she said.

"Thank you. I will. I don't mean to be out of line, Christine, but would you have dinner with me some evening?" asked Julian.

"I would love to, Julian Wallace," she said, looking at his name tag.

Julian and Christine's relationship progressed rapidly. Each fell absolutely in love with the other. Christine trusted Julian, even though he was a true mystery to her for many, many years. Sometimes it bothered her that she had not been introduced to his family. The fact that he would not even discuss them with her irritated her more. Nonetheless, she was committed to Julian and assumed he would eventually open up to her.

L ottie was embarrassed and angry with herself. How selfish could she be, how neglectful? She listened intently to Julian as he relayed his encounter with Vicky and the content of their discussion. Lottie remembered how she felt when her mother was heavily involved with Spanky and how she and her brothers were pushed aside while their mother put her relationship before them. Had she turned into her mother? She never wanted her children to feel left out of her life. Everything she had done and was doing was for her children's legacy. She wanted to rewrite history, not reinvent it. She agreed with Vicky; she had lost her focus and indeed abandoned Vicky and Teddy. The mother and daughter, in her opinion, needed help to mend their relationship. She made an appointment for them with Regina.

The morning that Lottie and Vicky were meeting with Regina, Lottie was nervous. When she and Vicky got into the car, she turned to her daughter and said, "I love you so much, Vicky."

Vicky responded, "I love you too, Mama."

Vicky didn't know what to expect from this session with Regina. Would her mother be truthful? Would they walk out as best friends or forever enemies? Vicky, at all risks, planned to speak from her heart.

"Who would like to go first?" asked Regina.

"I think I should," said Lottie, "if it is okay with Vicky."

"I don't mind, Mama," said Vicky.

"Remember, Vicky, when we talked and I apologized for being neglectful of you and I promised things would be different between us?"

"Yes," said Vicky, "and I was very hopeful that things would change between us, but it didn't."

"I was hopeful too, but I never followed through. In fact, I allowed circumstances to degenerate more. I threw myself into my personal goals. I became too busy to concentrate on us, and I stopped being a mom and became business-oriented instead. That was my character flaw.

"I got out of prison not knowing who I was, Vicky, and I didn't get the chance to answer that question for myself. All I knew about myself was that I was a grieving mother, surrounded by a hurting family. I felt like bricks had tumbled over on me, and I crashed under the weight. I was mentally distraught and mentally ill. I didn't understand how grief can consume someone. So I sought out the person whom I felt needed me the most, and that person was my mother, when in essence, she was the person I needed the most. My heart grew cold to stop the pain. Even counseling could not help immediately. I lived as a ghost for far too long."

"So you became a disappearing act."

"In many ways, yes, until I found another purpose for my life."

"But that purpose was not inspired by your children," said an angry Vicky. "You are indeed the most selfish person that I have met in my short life."

The truth of Vicky's accusation stung Lottie like a cluster of bees.

"Did you know that I have a boyfriend, Mama? Something you never asked me about. Did you know that my menstrual cramps are so bad that when they started, the doctor had to prescribe medication for me that I still take to endure the pain? Did you know that I am an advent tennis player, that I have a chance to go to college on an athletic scholarship? Did you notice that I have never had my hair cut, therefore, it is too long, and that's why I wear it up all the time? Shall I continue, Mama?"

"No, Vicky, you have proven your point more than adequately, and I understand."

Regina asked, "What is the solution? Where do you two go from here?"

"Don't ask Vicky," said Lottie, "because I have a feeling that she would send me straight to hell." Lottie laughed, perhaps inappropriately, but it broke the tension, and they all had a good laugh. "Regina, since I took Vicky out of school for the day, she and I are beginning right now to be so close to each other that people will think we're glued together. She's going to use that brilliant brain of hers to help me redecorate my club, then she and I are going to take her brother out for dinner."

"That sounds like a plan to me, Vicky. What do you think?" asked Regina.

"Definitely a plan," said Vicky, grinning from ear to ear.

As they left Regina, Lottie said, "Now tell me about this mysterious boyfriend that no one knows about, especially Teddy, who tells everything."

Lottie and Millie pored hours into choosing the right materials for Lottie's club. They became familiar faces in the designing studios and supply stores throughout the city and outlining suburbs. They fanned through paint samples and samples of wallpaper. They went back and forth to carpet outlets, looking for the perfect colors. They sat on furniture and surveyed dishware. They slept little and ate even less.

Lottie's club was a spectrum, elegant and magnificent. One walked in on lush purple carpet. Glass tables, adorned by swiveling pink leather chairs, were placed strategically throughout the club. Small chandelier lights hung high over each table, and clear round bowls containing liquid fires were set in the middle of the tables. A large asymmetric glass bar with silver trims extended the length of the club, and high-back pink leather chairs with silver frames and legs were placed around the bar. A grand silver chandelier hung over the bar, and the glass mirrors behind the bar were etched with silver swans gliding across a lake. The gray walls were set abloom with small bouquets of violet, pink, red, yellow, and white flowers that had green stems highlighted with strokes of silver.

The entertainment area was in the back of the club. A raised platform served as the dance and performance area. Pink satin curtains framed the bottom of the stage, and the backdrop were mirrors that were etched with the same swan that hung behind the bar. To the right of the stage was a brand-new kitchen, equipped with modern stainless steel appliances. To the left of the stage and down the hallway were sizable male and female washrooms. Lottie's office was adjacent to the entertainment area.

Lottie's office was no longer a room with a desk and file cabinet. It had been recreated to reflect Lottie's style and taste. The carpet was the same purple color that was in the main section of the club. Pink- and purple-flowered wallpaper covered the wall behind Lottie's desk, and a wall of mirrors with her swan theme covered the wall across from her desk. The remaining walls were painted gray like the rest of the club. A pink leather chair officiated behind a large glass desk. The desk featured fresh long-stemmed pink roses in the center, and framed pictures of Lottie and her children faced her from every direction. A pink couch sat in front of the glass mirrors, and a glass table was placed in front of the couch, which displayed various magazines. Lottie's wooden file cabinet was close to her desk.

Dewy and Millie had been at the club during the entire process. Dewy had left the intricate details to the two ladies, but he supervised most of the labor and restoration process. Neither he nor Millie had seen the finished product. Lottie wanted them to wait to see the club in its completion. She was a little nervous about Dewy's response to the office because it was feminine, and he would have to work there as well.

Lottie asked Dewy and Millie to meet her at the club the following night. She brought with her Vicky and Teddy. Lottie was so pleased with their reactions. Vicky and Teddy best expressed their feelings with "awesome and fantastic." They touched everything and investigated the entire club. Millie, on the other hand, was frozen in place. She cried so hard that Lottie led her to a seat at a table so that she could compose herself. Dewy stood grinning with his chest poked out. He had always been a big man, but he stood as a giant that evening.

"Teddy, Vicky," said Lottie, "can you two stay out of trouble while I meet with Dewy and Millie for a while?"

"Yeah, Mama, we won't tear it down," said a playful Teddy.

Lottie kissed each of them then invited Dewy and Millie into the office.

"I gather that you two like what you see," said Lottie. She got no immediate response because Dewy was sitting on the most comfortable couch imaginable, so he was swelled with contentment and pride. Millie was walking around the office, saying "Beautiful" and crying unabashedly.

"Dewy," said Lottie, "I need you to contact MacArthur about stocking the bar."

"That's no problem," said Dewy.

"Millie," said Lottie, "let's run some newspaper ads, announcing interviews for a lead cook and cooking staff. We also need to place ads for performers."

"You got it, Lottie," said Millie.

"Dewy, I leave the hiring of bartenders and waitresses to you. You know best. We have several decisions to make. I only want to serve dinner on Fridays and Saturdays. We'll have two performances on those evenings as well. We can consider the details later. I'm going to have the lead cook offer up a few menus for us to consider."

"When will we open, Lottie?" asked Dewy.

"I don't know, Dewy," she said. "After we finish taking care of these tasks, we can choose an opening date. There is one last thing I wish to discuss with you tonight."

Lottie turned to Dewy and said, "I love you, Dewy. You were there for Spanky, and you have supported me with a warm heart and respect. You have not denied me anything. I am not totally sure of the arrangement you had with Spanky, but I wish to offer you twenty-five percent ownership in this club and the liquor businesses, as well as a salary, that is, if you find the offer agreeable."

"Lottie, yes! You have no idea how much this means to me. I was Spanky's partner in the operation of his businesses, but never was I offered a legal partnership by him. He paid me a salary, but other monies was given to me under the table. He paid me well. Nonetheless, you are paying me financially, and you are giving me status." Dewy rose from his seat, and so did Lottie. He grabbed her into a bear hug and let the tears flow.

"Millie," said Lottie, "my dear and true friend, my sister in soul and spirit. You have never required anything from me, yet you continue to let me and my children and my family be a part of your family. I wish to offer you five percent of my enterprise as well as a salary because I want you to be my assistant manager. Will you accept?"

"Everything you own, Lottie?"

"Everything I own, Millie."

Millie could only nod her consent because she could barely breathe from choking on her own tears. The two women embraced each other and soaked their clothing with teardrops of love.

The one aspect of the club that was not complete was the name on the marquee. Lottie still didn't know what to call her club. A sense of depression nibbled at Lottie's being. She had finished the largest part of her project. She sat at her desk, thumbing through her index file. As if by design, the rotary files stopped on the name and number of Spanky's drug supplier. Lottie had been sober for almost ten years, yet the urge to indulge in her old habit was overwhelming at times, and that surprised her every time. She finally understood what Regina had meant by "day by day." She realized that her battle to stay sober would never truly end. She gave the rotary a forceful spin, turning it away from the dealer's information. Someday, she would throw the card away, but not today.

Lottie forced her mind on the last few details of her club. She needed an opening date and a name for the club. It was no good; she wasn't really concentrating. Her mind was all over the place. She gave the rotary another spin, and it landed on MacArthur's card. The thought of him brought a smile to her face. Maybe she would see him when he met with Dewy. He had called her and left messages over the past months, but Lottie had not called him back. She had been busy and did not want the distraction of a man whom she found too irresistible. She was in fear of MacArthur.

Lottie decided to call Julian and Buddy to arrange for them to see the club. She reached for the phone but abandoned her decision to call her brothers when the doorbell rang from the back of the club. Lottie went and answered the door. Before her eyes stood the most magnificent man she had ever seen. It was MacArthur. Lottie smiled warmly at him then stood aside for him to come inside.

MacArthur followed Lottie into her office. "Wow!" he said. "This is amazing! Now this is what I call an office."

"Come with me," said Lottie. "I'll show around."

MacArthur followed her throughout the club. "You definitely can't wear blue jeans in here. This is most elegant, Lottie, and absolutely marvelous," he said.

They walked back to Lottie's office where she offered MacArthur a seat. "Thanks," he said as he walked around the office instead. He sat on the edge of her desk and spoke softly to her. "Ms. Lottie," he said, "I have called you several times, to no avail. I am glad I came by today, because after seeing all of the work you have done, I can blame your nonresponse on your being busy rather than an outright rejection."

Lottie giggled nervously. She beamed. She felt herself to be very silly thinking that she needed a drug to make her feel good. She had never felt so good as she did being in the presence of MacArthur. "I am happy that you came today, MacArthur," said Lottie. "In fact, I was just thinking about you. Forgive me for not returning your calls. I have been extremely busy, with not only the club and other business but with my family as well. I have two teenage children," she said.

"Call me Mac, Lottie. I know you must be a wonderful mother," said Mac.

"Thanks for the compliment," responded Lottie. "However, I'm learning every day how to parent my children, to be a better mother, and to provide them with their needs, especially my time and love."

"I hope to meet them someday."

"Dewy is supposed to call you about restocking our bar. Have you heard from him?"

"Yes, he has. We are meeting tomorrow morning here."

"Thank you, Mac."

"For what, selling you my products?" said Mac sarcastically.

Lottie paused. She feared getting too intimate with Mac.

"When will you open?" he asked.

"I haven't chosen a date or a name for the club, but I will be inviting you to the opening," said Lottie.

"So you don't know how long it will be before I see you again," said Mac as he locked eyes with Lottie.

"I suppose not," said Lottie, taken aback by Mac's intonation.

"Well, I am off, Lottie," said Mac. "I have an appointment to make."

Lottie sat silently and watched Mac walk briskly out of her office. Mac felt stupid. He had let his emotions get away from him. He had hoped to ask Lottie out on a date. When she did not return his calls, he jumped the gun and went to see her. After meeting with Lottie, it became apparent to him that she was not interested.

Mac had wanted Lottie very badly. He dreamed of her. Meeting her had placed his love life in peril. He didn't consider himself a player; however, there were a couple of ladies with whom he spent time. He had dated very little since he met Lottie. She was the only woman he wanted to date seriously. He had held on to his bachelorhood tightly, but when it came to Lottie, he was ready to commit himself to her. He knew at first sight that she was the woman for him. Mac was ready to make that uphill climb to be with her.

Lottie was hard on herself as well. She wondered why she had brushed Mac off like that. She wondered what was she saving herself for or for whom. These were the questions she was asking herself when the doorbell rang at the back door. Was it Mac returning? She opened the door to her brother Julian.

CHAPTER 17

The past two weeks had been gruesome for Lottie. She was tired. When she walked into her mother's house, she stopped at the archway and listened for a while. It was early, only 8:30 p.m., but the house was quiet, and she was glad. She put down her briefcase and looked around. Lottie went into the kitchen to make coffee. She sat at the round table and remembered childhood experiences there in the kitchen with her mother and brothers. Life was strange to her because she realized that her own children were sitting at the same table, developing childhood memories of their own.

Lottie saw visions of Spanky and her mother arguing with each other, usually about Spanky's long absences away from home. He never tried to hide his philandering from Mamie. He had just expected her to accept his behavior because he had no plans to change, and he had insisted that Lottie do the same when they were together. Roger "Spanky" Fielder was not to be questioned.

It had been in this very house that Lottie had become her uncle's lover, it had been in this house that she had inflicted the greatest pain on her mother and brothers, and it had been in this house that she had single-handedly split her family apart.

Lottie felt ill. She wanted to run out of the door and never return. Instead, she went to her daughter's room and knocked on the door. "Are you awake, honey?" she asked.

"Yes, Mama," said Vicky. "Come on in."

Lottie entered and plopped herself on Vicky's bed. She kissed her daughter on the lips. "Do you want to know what you, Millie, and I are doing tomorrow? I think I'll ask Mrs. Whitfield too since this is going to involve her in what I hope will be in a significant way."

"What?" asked Vicky.

"We are going to start our search for a new house."

Vicky fell back on her bed and started kicking her legs in the air and giggling simultaneously. Lottie fell next to her and laughed until she cried.

They drove around the suburb of Homewood, looking from the car at the few available homes that were there. Lottie saw about three that she liked, so they drove back around to those that they liked and wrote down the contact information. In the meantime, Lottie told Millie she would put Spanky's house on the market.

When Lottie and Vicky arrived home, they were greeted by a dozen yellow roses in a crystal vase. Stuck between the stems was an envelope that contained a beautiful card with a silver swan on the cover. Suspecting who it was from, Lottie let Vicky read the card.

"Who's Mac, Mama?" asked Vicki. "Whoever he is, he wants your attention. Listen to this, Mama. 'Take the time to smell the roses, preferably with me.' This guy knows how to romance a woman." Vicky threw her mother a wicked smile and left the room.

Lottie was impressed by Mac's gesture. The card lay in her lap. She knew that she should call him and thank him. With this display, she had no choice, and she was aware that Mac knew as much. Suddenly, she was irritated. She would not be manipulated into a situation for which she was not ready. She did not have the time for a man to be in her life. She had a home to buy, children to take care of, and a club, liquor stores, and properties to manage, and that didn't even include preparing for the grand opening of her club.

"Maybe later, Mac," she uttered aloud.

Lottie sat in the living room and looked out of the window at the ever-changing fall scenery. She needed to clear her mind and gauge her emotions. She got up and went outside. She inhaled the crisp air and stood, arms crossed. She walked to the driveway and leaned against her car. She closed her eyes and emptied her mind. A thrush of cold wind ripped around her and caused her to shiver. Lottie took a speedy retreat back into the house.

Lottie called the club in hopes that Dewy was there. When he answered the phone, Lottie greeted him and asked him for Mac's number.

"I'll give you the number, Lottie," said Dewy, "but if you want to speak to Mac, he is right here, going through inventory with me."

"Yes, I would, Dewy. Thank you," said Lottie.

"Hello, Lottie," said Mac.

"Mac, I want to thank you for the beautiful roses," said Lottie.

"I'm glad you like them, Lottie. When I saw them, they reminded me of you. So what's your answer?" asked Mac.

"Answer to what, Mac?"

"Will you take some time to smell the flowers with me? I know you are a busy woman, Lottie, but I was hoping—"

"Wait, Mac! Let's not get carried away. I only called to thank you for the flowers," said Lottie emphatically. With that said, Lottie hung up the phone. She felt badly about being abrupt with Mac, but she was not about to lead him on.

Lottie turned her attention to the club. She needed a name and an opening date. She picked up Mac's card and looked at the cover again, then she knew. She would name her club Silver Swan. She was so happy! Lottie looked at the elegant swan on the card again, and it caused her to think, this time about the most elegant time of the year. In Lottie's estimation, that time was New Year's Eve.

Lottie, Millie, and Mrs. Whitfield had narrowed their search for a house to two choices. Millie had arranged a tour of each. The second house they toured spoke to Lottie's heart. The house was in a gated community. One entered the main gate, which was guarded by a young man who asked for Lottie's identification. He checked Lottie's name on the list he had on his clipboard then allowed them to pass. The area was spacious, allowing for grand homes with spacious yards surrounding each house. Lottie pulled into a gated driveway at the fourth house, a colonial with an attached three-car garage. The house was a tan brick structure with large white columns. The porch was a veranda with space enough for an outdoor table, a couple of rocking chairs, a swing seat, and an abundance of flowers—a picture that Lottie created in her mind when she first saw the potential home.

When they entered the double doors, they walked into a massive hallway that led into the living room. The floors were a dark cherry oak. To the right of the living room was a formal dining room. A separate entrance led into a huge kitchen with a bar for stools and a recessed area surround by windows, which would accommodate a large kitchen table. All the appliances were new, and marble floors accentuated the modern feel of the house. On the first floor down the hall was a massive master bedroom with its own spa bathroom and shower. The room had a walk-in closet, which delighted Lottie the most. Adjacent to the master bedroom was a second master bedroom similar to the first, which Lottie wanted for her mother. Up the curved staircase, which separated the living room from the dining room, were three bedrooms. Two of the bedrooms had Jack and Jill bathrooms. One of these two bedrooms would belong to Teddy, and the other would become a guest bedroom. Lottie was reserving the third bedroom for Vicky; it had its own bathroom. Each of the three bedrooms had private balconies large enough for outdoor furniture and plants.

Back downstairs was a staircase that led to a finished basement. The family room was massive and could contain all their recreational needs. The laundry room was also downstairs. Beyond the common space was a delightful apartment, equipped with a living room, bedroom, kitchen, and private bath. This apartment was essential to Lottie because she planned to give it to Mrs. Whitfield. She would have a private entrance leading to the large patio outside and to the back gate of the property.

The landscape was awesome. Lottie really did not have to do anything to the property. The perennials were still in bloom, and mums in various colors replaced the dead annuals.

After the ladies had finished the tour, they stood on the veranda, amazed by what they had seen. Lottie turned to Mrs. Whitfield, who was wiping away tears, and said, "Mrs. Whitfield, I want you to come live with us not as a housekeeper but as part of our family. You have always been there for us, and we need you and want you around us always. I want you to take the apartment so that you can have your own private place."

"Lottie, I love you guys so much. I have always felt like family. That is how you all have always treated me. Yes, I'll stay with you, then I won't have to be alone anymore," she said.

"And you, Millie," said Lottie, "I want you and James to use that guest bedroom as often as you please."

"We will," said Millie. "You can count on that!"

Lottie put in her bid for the house that very day.

CHAPTER 18

Very early on a Saturday morning that November, Lottie set the house astir. She wanted the entire family to go with her to see the new house. Even though she had closed on the deal to buy the house, she still wanted everyone's opinion. She hoped everyone would love it like she did. Although she had already discussed the house with Mamie, her mother was reluctant to separate from the home she had had for many years. Therefore, Lottie drew protests from Mamie.

Mamie was still in bed even though she had heard Lottie calling everyone from their rooms and knew that she was next. She pulled a pillow over her head. Lottie entered her mother's bedroom and had to suppress her laugh. She went to her mother's bed and gently lifted the pillow off her head. Mamie pretended to be asleep. Lottie shook her mother until she sat up in obvious frustration and anger.

"Listen, Mamie Wallace!" said Lottie. "You and this entire family are moving out of this building. The move will be the best thing for all of us. I know you don't like the idea of moving from your home, but when you see our new home, I think you will be pleased."

Mamie got out of bed and folded her arms in protest. She shook her head stubbornly. Lottie grabbed her mother by the arms and set her down on the bed. She leaned into Mamie's face and said, "Mama, there are too many memories here in this house that are best left in the past. With the new house, we can pave the way for a brighter future and greater happiness. We need to let our broken hearts mend. Now, Mama, I won't take no for an answer. I hate to force you to move, but I will get Buddy and Julian to help me move your belongings out of here.

"I'm sorry, Mama. I don't really mean what I say. If you truly do not like the house and don't want to live with me and the children, you don't have to. I'll leave you here, but I need you to come with us today."

Lottie could see the dread and fear vanishing from Mamie's eyes and felt so proud and happy when her mother gave her a cursory nod.

Lottie watched her children take guarded steps toward the house as she ushered Mamie out of the car. She and Mamie walked arm in arm to the front entrance. Lottie opened the door with her keys to their new home. As she did so, Teddy and Vicky took off to explore the house. Lottie gave Mamie a perfunctory tour while Teddy and Vicky went in search of their room. Not surprisingly, each of them chose Lottie's intended bedrooms.

Lottie showed her mother the second master bedroom. Mamie smiled as she explored the space. She clapped her hands when she noticed that she had a private exit onto the large patio. Mamie nodded to express how much she liked the bedroom.

Next, Lottie took her mother to see her own bedroom. She pointed to Lottie's private patio with delight as well. The women went upstairs to see what Vicky and Teddy thought of their rooms. Each had chosen the very bedrooms that Lottie had chosen for them.

"This is what I'm talking about, Mama! And I really like the fact that I am away from everyone," said Teddy. "That way, when I do my thing, I won't be bothering anyone." Teddy gave his mother a big hug and a kiss.

Vicky's room was bright because of the abundance of sunshine coming in through her double windows. She opened the doors to her balcony and went outside and breathed in the rich air. "Mama, this is marvelous! I couldn't be any happier."

Vicky encircled her mother in her arms and kissed her cheeks. Lottie wiped the tears of joy from her daughter's eyes. Everyone was blown away by the expanse of the backyard. Even Mamie brightened at the open-spaced, well-groomed lawn. She pointed to a section of the lawn and, in the fashion of charades, indicated that she wanted a swinging bench there. Lottie could see that her mother liked the house and was very happy.

They went downstairs to the family room, where the children flipped out. Then Lottie led them to the apartment that was dedicated to Mrs. Whitfield. She informed the family that the former housekeeper would be living with them.

"Oh, Mama! It will be great to have her live here with us. She helped Grandma to take care of us when you were away," said Vicky.

"Mrs. Whitfield is family to me," said Teddy. "Bring it on, Mama."

Lottie's love for her family was so deep at that moment that her heart almost burst.

Because Lottie was opening the Silver Swan on New Year's Eve, she wanted the family to move in before Christmas. She told them that Thanksgiving would be their last family event in Mamie's house.

Moving day proved to be just as difficult as Lottie thought it would be. Her mother was a mess. She didn't want to leave. She didn't want to move in the cold weather. She had not liked any of the families who wanted to rent the apartment. She didn't want to use a real estate agent. Lottie arbitrarily spoke to her brother Buddy, who still lived on the third floor of the building, about taking on the additional responsibility of renting out Mamie's apartment. Buddy had managed the building for his mother for years. He knew everything he needed to do to get the job done. Therefore, Mamie did not have to worry about the apartment, and furthermore, she could eliminate that issue of her "This is why I can't move" list. With only a couple of hours before the movers were to arrive, Mamie was still laboriously packing her things. She had not trusted the moving staff to pack her personal items. Lottie decided to leave Mamie to her task. She would, instead of stressing over Mamie, go to the club and do some work.

Lottie was very agitated when she arrived at the club. She could hear Dewy talking to someone; however, she had no interest in finding out who. She decided to go over the talent and agenda for opening night. She had used Teddy's agent to obtain her performers. He had been kind enough to introduce Lottie and Millie to an affairs specialist who worked diligently with them to schedule the performers and the publicity for opening night and the club in general. Lottie had left the back-and-forth communications with the publicist to Millie. All Lottie had to do was sign the contracts and agree to the intricate details.

As Lottie sat at her desk going over her books, she was amazed as usual about the business and financial structure that Spanky had established. He had been rich for a long time and had left Lottie a very wealthy woman. She was pleased that she had prepared herself on every level of running a business. Yes, she had an accounting firm to handle her money, but she was proud that she could check and follow up on her own finances. She toyed for a moment about buying a new car but decided to wait until after the new year. She was buying Vicky her first car so that she could drive Teddy and herself back to the city for school. Vicky would graduate from high school at the end of the school year, and Lottie didn't want them to have to change schools.

Lottie chuckled aloud as she looked at the opening night's lineup. Teddy would warm up the audience for the special appearance of Gladys Knight. When that bit of information had hit the public, the Swan Lady had more requests for reservations than it could accommodate. Many of Spanky's previous patrons had already secured their place to be present when the new club opened. Lottie had to hire additional staff to help Millie just to handle the calls. The club was booked all the way into the spring of the following year.

"I thought I heard someone laughing in here," said Mac as he peeped into Lottie's office.

At first, Lottie became rigid, but something in Mac's eyes, something warm and inviting, engulfed her. She actually beamed at him. "Good morning, Mac. You're here early today."

"Just wanted to finalize everything with Dewy," said Mac. "I don't want you to have any last-minute issues. Your shipment will arrive in two days."

"Mac, I really appreciate your efforts." Lottie rose from her desk and came around to face Mac. "You are coming to the opening, I hope."

"I wouldn't miss it for the world," said Mac. "Will you be my date, Lottie?"

Lottie almost melted under Mac's expectant gaze. "No, Mac, that won't be possible. I will be too busy working to entertain a date."

Mac moved closer to Lottie. "Why are you so afraid of me, Lottie?" he asked. "Why won't you give me the slightest chance to get to know you and you to know me?"

Lottie moved to turn aside and found herself a prisoner in Mac's arms. The scent of his spicy cologne rose to her nose, and she swooned. She sensed his intentions too late. He kissed her lovingly, softly. She leaned closer to him and accepted his kiss. His lips were sweet and warm as they pressed against hers. Lottie raised her arms and let them circle Mac's neck. He lifted her off the floor and pressed her body to him. Lottie shivered as feelings arose in her that had lain dormant inside of her for years. Mac released her gently. Their eyes stayed on each other. Lottie's heart pounded. She stepped away from Mac so that she could breathe.

"When will you be ready for me, Lottie? Spanky has been dead for many years now. He won't be back. It's time for you to move on."

"Maybe I am reluctant because of Spanky, but I don't think so. I don't know, Mac. All I know is that my love for him was an endless well. Mac, I have never known a man other than Spanky. Frankly, I don't know what to do, especially about you and me," said Lottie.

Mac lifted Lottie's face and pecked her on the lips then left and went back inside the club.

Seeing Mac made Lottie more stressed. She arrived home before noon to find her mother still packing and the movers hanging out at their truck, waiting for her. Lottie stood at Mamie's door unnoticed for the longest of time. She stood fuming as she watched Mamie methodically wrap each item and label it before neatly placing it in the box. When she could bear no more, Lottie went into the room and snatched the picture frame that her mother held from her hand and threw it into the box. Mamie looked horrified at her daughter.

"You are doing this shit on purpose, Mamie!" shouted Lottie. "You are deliberately doing everything you can to delay this move. Now you either get a move on or stay here forever!"

With that, Lottie left the room. Mamie was shocked to see her daughter in such a rage. She quickly wrapped her remaining belongings and placed them in the box.

Lottie went to check on the other rooms and found them empty of the things that they were taking with them, as her mother's room should have been. Most of the furniture was being donated to Goodwill. She walked outside and encountered Teddy and Vicky sitting on the steps, laughing. Lottie sat down with them and took several deep breaths to help calm herself down. The gnawing in her stomach was too familiar. She stood up and paced about. She wanted to get high, or so she thought. She sat back down and gave her children a playful push. They laughed heartily as they struggled to sit upright again. Lottie leaned forward with her face in the cups of her hands and her eyes closed. Suddenly, she was back in Mac's arms. It was at that point that she realized that what she felt was not withdrawal but her desire for a man, for Mac. She wanted desperately to make love with Mac.

The Christmas holiday came fast. It was a busy time for the Wallace/Fielder family. They were still unpacking and trying to decorate for the holidays after the arrival of the new furniture. Regardless of the bevy of activities, things seemed well for the first time in a long time.

The family was happy, and joy abounded. Teddy had received word from his agent that he would appear on *Star Search* that January. Vicky was spending a great deal of her time with Terrence. (Lottie had met him for the first time in Thanksgiving and found him to be a worthy young man.) Mamie, on the other hand, worried Lottie. She was once again confining herself to her bedroom, sulking, in Lottie's estimation.

Lottie was spending much of her time at the club. If not for Mrs. Whitfield pitching in wherever she was needed, she would have been exhausted and dismayed by the process of moving and opening up the club. She was demanded everywhere. Every time someone entered the club, her heart would leap. She had anticipated a visit from Mac, but he never came.

Lottie was tired. She was getting very little sleep. She only had to wait a few more days for the opening. She was looking forward to the family's trip to California for Teddy's performance on *Star Search*. The trip, coupled with some vacation time, would do a world of good for each of them.

"Vicky, sweetheart, what are you doing up at this hour?" asked Lottie.

"Waiting on you, Mama. This is the only way I can get to see you and talk to you privately. You are gone when I wake up in the morning, and I am asleep when you come home at night," said Vicky.

"I'm sorry, Vicky. Your mama has a lot on her plate right now, that's all. The club opens in three days, you know. I got a lot to do. Let's go into the kitchen and have some coffee. Mrs. Whitfield usually has some waiting for me when I get home," said Lottie. Lottie poured a cup for each of them. "I figure this will keep us alert while we talk. Tell me, honey, what is this personal problem you are having?"

"Mama, I am in love with Terrence," Vicky ventured.

Her declaration drew a broad smile from Lottie. "From what I have seen between you and Terrence, I think you might be too," said Lottie with suppressed laughter in her voice. "I don't mean to lessen the importance of what you told me, but I have a tendency to get giddy when I am tired."

"Well, I'm serious," said Vicky, slightly annoyed with her mother. "Mama, Terrence wants to go all the way, but I am afraid that he will hurt me like those men did. However, I am more afraid of losing him."

Lottie could hardly bear the conversation. The image of her daughter being brutally attacked by those three men made her stomach turn. She pushed the coffee aside and reached for Vicky's hands. "You must forgive me for everything, sweetheart. I'll never forgive myself for not being here for you."

"Mama, I don't blame you for what happened to me. It would have happened whether you had been home or not. It was a routine day. I was on my way to school. I am better now. It's just sometimes when Terrence wants to be close, I can't stand for him to touch me. It hurts me to see the rejection and disappointment and confusion in his eyes. He doesn't know about the rape."

"You know, Vicky, you and I are more alike than you know. We both have been scarred very deeply. It is going to take time for us to heal," sympathized Lottie. "Tell Terrence about the rape, Vicky. Take the pressure off. He will have to wait until you are ready. At least he will know why you behave as you do, and if he truly loves you, he will wait for you. Vicky, there is a man whom I want to be with desperately, but I, too, am not ready to be touched. I want to be ready, but I'm not," said Lottie. "I won't give you the spiel about being too young, Vicky. The deepest love and the only love I have ever had happened for me when I was your age. That love also proved to be a tragedy. I am saying take your time, Vicky. Take all of the time you need."

"Are you talking about our father, Mama?" asked Vicky.

"Yes, my daughter. Spanky was and is the only man I have ever known. It's hard for me to get past your father, to get on with my life. Do you think you should talk this over with Regina? I know the day is coming when I will have to lay on her couch, so to speak," said Lottie.

The two laughed at the impossibility of that happening. Laying on Regina's couch was not the counselor's style.

"You are right, my love," said Lottie. "Heaven forbid just needing to lie down and be psychoanalyzed."

The mother and daughter laughed until their bellies ached, indeed relieving a lot of pent-up tension.

19

CHAPTER

amie was accustomed to change. It was the one sure thing she could count on. However, the whirlwind that Lottie had created unnerved her. Her home had become the base for a myriad of activities. Teddy demanded more of her attention; he needed an audience to practice his routine. Vicky, earlier on, nestled under her like a fragile bird falling from its nest. Millie and Lottie raced around and huddled together, discussing the renovation of the club. Julian made his daily visits, brief as they were. Buddy had even become more attentive than ever before. Mamie rued the day she got out of her bed and stepped out of her room.

Then came the talk of moving into a new house. Whose life was it anyway? Didn't she deserve a say in what she would do with her life? Every inch of Mamie's house held a special memory for her. It was her haven. As painful as it was at times to remember the past, she did not want to live anywhere else.

Every item in Mamie's home carried Spanky's spirit. On the living room beneath her feet was the very spot that Julian was conceived. She used to sit in that same living room and comb Lottie's hair. She would sit and read in her favorite chair, which still sat in front of the living room window. From that spot, she could see Spanky as he advanced toward the house. She knew that she would move when the time came because of the children. They needed her, or so she thought. For a while, when Vicky didn't think that her mother loved her, she had found solace in Mamie's arms. When Teddy was not locked away in his room, he sat at Mamie's feet, watching television or reading.

Mamie had to admit that she loved Lottie's new house. It was huge, and the backyard was extraordinary. The garden area definitely was the place for an outdoor swing. Mamie envisioned herself sitting in the breeze under the protection of the large tree nearby. She could read there or daydream there and be alone there. She wanted to extend that space to create a vegetable garden, one which she would grow herself. She imagined herself digging in the dirt, producing marvelous tomatoes and greens and carrots. The idea took her back to the past when she and Spanky would tend to their mother's garden. Mamie sighed. She would have to wait until the spring before she could see her dream come true. What, however, would she do with herself until then?

Unfortunately, Mamie's clear purpose and role in the family shifted. After the move into the new house, everyone became consumed with placing furniture, decorating, and Christmas dinner and the opening of the club. Suddenly, no one was aware that she even existed. In addition to moving, Vicky's time was also taken up by her boyfriend, Terrence. She developed a closer relationship with her mother, who had also become Vicky's confidant. She no longer relied on her grandmother. Teddy had been his usual self until he got his *Star Search* confirmation. Then he placed all his time and energy into preparing for the event, as well as working on his opening act for the club. Lottie was never home. She left before Mamie got up in the mornings and did not return home until after she was asleep.

Aside from unpacking, there was little for Mamie to do. Mrs. Whitfield did most of the cooking. The few times that Mamie volunteered to help with dinner, she ended up drinking coffee while Mrs. Whitfield did all the work. She felt useless in the kitchen too. Lottie had a cleaning service that she used to keep the house clean. Mamie hoped to eventually fit in somewhere. In the meantime, she would once again retreat to her room. This time, Mamie was not seeking isolation. She enjoyed being around her family very much.

She was trying her best to adjust to her new life. Her bedroom was so outstanding that she relished spending time there. She would put on a heavy sweater and sit outside on the patio. She had a television in her room, and she had her library of books that she would sit on her lounge chair and read. Mamie shared meals with her family and was otherwise available to them. Her family was afraid that she was falling back into her old self—the dark, dying-in-spirit self. However, if her family was waiting for her to speak, Mamie Wallace still had nothing to say.

～ℋ～

Teddy was lit up like a neon sign. He was amused by the household in which he lived. He had one definite thing to say about his mother: when Lottie Wallace decided to do something, she did it with gusto. Teddy was proud to see some of himself in the woman he called mama. He realized that the sad, dependent, and confused person he once knew had been replaced by this lively, happy, and ambitious female hurricane.

For the first time in a long time, Teddy was free of his concerns for his family. His mother was renovating her club and buying a new house. Vicky was in pursuit of a romance, a relationship with Terrence Coleman, which he thought he would never approve of, because he was the boy who beat up his brother years ago. Nonetheless, after seeing his mother take to this man version of the once boy, Teddy acquiesced. He, on the other hand, continued to spread his energies between school and his performances. He was thrilled that his mother was going to let him perform at her opening night. His nana was nervous about moving out of her home; nonetheless, she had agreed to come with the family when they move, which pleased Teddy a great deal. His family would continue to be together in their new dwelling.

Greater than any joy for Teddy was when they moved into the new house, and he received his own private wing. The first thing that he did once he was ensconced in his room was to go out on his balcony. He stood erect, secure, and proud as he gazed across the vast property that was now his home. He inhaled the crisp December air. Teddy closed his eyes and let his soul be transformed by the loveliness of his new surroundings. Happy thoughts prevailed in his mind, but there was one drop of rain on his parade: he felt sorry for his nana. She seemed a little lost. He felt that deep down his nana had looked forward to the move, but so much of her life had been lived at their old address.

Teddy remembered the day that they moved. His mother had been in an absolute tizzy. His nana had not helped the situation with her procrastination. He and Vicky had not known whether they should help his nana or not. They chose to move themselves from the fray and just wait outside. Teddy wished he had more time to spend with his nana, but the pressure of preparing for two major events and the demands of the holidays made it impossible for him to be there for her. Before he knew it, his nana had reverted back to her old ways. He hoped with all his heart that she would come out of her bedroom and stay out among her family. Surely, she must have known that they loved her dearly and enjoyed her company. He was definitely going to try to persuade his nana to go out to California with them. It was because of the encouragement that he got from his nana that had given him the confidence to pursue his dreams.

⌒✌⌒

Vicky was so inspired by the changes her mother had made as it related to their relationship and the challenges that she was confronting as she strove to make a new life for herself and her family. There was so much to be excited about: Terrence was coming home for Thanksgiving, her grandmother was up and about, Teddy was busy with his career, her mother was redecorating and reopening her club, and to top it all off, they were buying a new house. Vicky was as elated as a child on Christmas morning.

Vicky and Terrence spent their Thanksgiving holiday having dinner with her family and going to a movie that evening. Terrence detoured into the night after they had left the movie. Instead of taking Vicky straight home, he drove to the lakefront and parked the car. They stared out into the open night. It was cold outside. A blanket of stars lay against the distant sky. A strong wind disturbed the sturdy car, causing Vicky to become cold inside her skimpy jacket. She snuggled up to Terrence, and he circled his arms around her. She smiled up at him and accepted his kisses unabashedly. She felt his hand as it moved about her body. She was relaxed as Terrence explored her body, secure in her belief that what she offered, her love, would be all that he required of her. She cooed as his tongue brushed against her lips. She shivered when he thrust it inside her waiting mouth. She liked the taste of him. She swooned from sheer ecstasy.

Long moments passed before Vicky felt the cool night's air against her skin. She pulled from Terrence's embrace to find her blouse unbuttoned and her breast exposed. Terrence had adroitly unhooked her bra. When she realized the state she was in, Vicky hurriedly fixed her bra and, with shaking hands, managed to rebutton her blouse. She was distressed.

"This is getting out of hand, Terrence," she said with an edge.

"I thought you wanted me too, Vicky," said a confounded Terrence. "I didn't mean to insult you. I thought you were in to me as well. Are you afraid, babe? You know that I will care for you."

"It's not that, Terrence," said Vicky too quickly. "Maybe I am afraid. I don't know. Just don't ask me to explain myself right now, Terrence, please. I can't explain."

Vicky shut down on Terrence. She felt badly later, because she had not spoken to him on their way home. She had bewildered this man

273

she loved. She was not ready to have sex with him, and she was sad that he felt rejected. She hoped that she had not lost him entirely. Her heart ached, and she sobbed silently. She loved Terrence so much.

Vicky had not anticipated Terrence's call the next afternoon. She had spent the morning in her bed. She had no appetite and didn't want to talk to anyone. She was glad that her family was busy so that she would not have to fake pleasantries. Mamie had been her only visitor. She could deal with her grandmother, because once she ascertained that Vicky was all right, she left her granddaughter alone.

Vicky picked up the phone on the second ring. She still did not want to talk to anyone, but she knew that her grandmother would not answer the phone, and the call could be from her mother checking on her or one of her uncles. When Terrence greeted her, Vicky perked up immediately. The long pause after she had wished Terrence a good morning alerted Vicky to what was next. Dread seized her heart. She felt, without a doubt, that Terrence was calling to end their relationship. She was losing the love of her life because she could not yet tell him that she was scared to death of being intimate with a man.

"Last night, I thought about some things, Vicky," said Terrence, tempering himself as he spoke. "I think our problem may be our age difference."

"Terrence, that's absurd," said Vicky. "You talk like you are twenty years my senior. You are only three years older than me," said Vicky in defense of her maturity. "I'm a lot older than you think, if you know what I mean."

"Then you must have rejected me out of fear. We are both virgins, Vicky, at least I am, and I am assuming that you are too. I want our first time to be really special. So if you are not ready, neither am I."

Vicky was exasperated by the entire issue. "Terrence, I trust you to take care of me, but I am just not ready to have sex. I need some time to get where you are."

"How long will it be before you are ready for us to be together, Vicky? Will it be when you are twenty-one or when we are married? What are we waiting for?" asked Terrence, compounding Vicky with questions—questions that were difficult for her to answer.

"Terrence, I—"

"Stop, Vicky. I am wrong for pressuring you," said Terrence. "You let me know when you want to make love with me." With that said and done, Terrence hung up the phone.

Vicky held the dead receiver to her ear. Something about the disconnection buzz captured her. It held her and kept her from putting down the phone. The ending of her conversation with Terrence was warranted in Vicky's estimation. She deserved such an abrupt ending because she was making Terrence suffer. His misery clung to her.

Vicky watched a movie with Teddy and her grandmother in Mamie's room. After it was over, she went to her room to read. She was restless, and sleep evaded her. She needed to talk to her mother badly. She took her book and went downstairs into the kitchen. She glanced at the clock. It was almost midnight. Her mother probably would not be home for hours. She poured herself a glass of milk. She read the calendar, which dictated their lives. Lottie had written down everything that was on the family's agenda for the month. Then she turned her attention to counting the 405 ceramic towels that lined the kitchen walls. Reluctantly, she went and sat at the kitchen table to read some more. Little of what she read registered with her because she could not concentrate. Her thoughts kept wandering back to Terrence. She was not sure at all whether or not she would hear from him again.

When Vicky heard her mother's keys in the door, she immediately looked at the clock. It was after three o'clock in the morning, but she did not feel the least bit tired or sleepy. She inhaled deep breaths to still her beating heart. She had to find the courage to talk to her mother about the most intimate aspect of her life.

Vicky felt much better after talking to her mother. They were still laughing about Regina as they escorted each other through the hallway, where Vicky departed from her mother and went up the stairs. Neither of them cared about waking up Mamie and Teddy. The joke about Regina's couch, or lack thereof, had shattered the anxiety that had sprung up from their deep conversation. When Vicky reached her room, she smiled at herself in the mirror. She was happy and proud of the image before her. Not only did she look like her mother but she also felt and thought like her too.

Vicky arrived at the rehab center; she arrived alone. She sat down in the living room area. She immediately took Mrs. Flores's baby from her lap and started bouncing her up and down. Little Angela giggled with delight. She stole away with Angela into the nursery, giving the baby's mother a much-needed break. She relieved Mrs. Flores for half an hour as she lost herself in the joy of watching Angela and the three other children who were there with one of the mothers. Regina stood at the door and observed Vicky. On the rare occasions that Vicky and Teddy had come to the center, they played with the little ones. The two of them were very loving toward the children who were there. When Angela's mother returned, Vicky left with Regina.

"Those babies adore you, Vicky," said Regina, "and Teddy too."

"I adore them as well, Regina," said Vicky. "In fact, I was just thinking about volunteering some of my time here after school to help some of the mothers out."

"We would love to have you," said Regina. "So what brings you here today? It's a sure bet that it wasn't little Angela."

"I need to talk to you, Regina, about something personal," said Vicky.

When they walked into Regina's office, Vicky, for what seemed to Regina as no apparent reason, started laughing. She laughed so hard that her eyes moistened. Regina was amused but confused.

"I'm sorry, Regina," said Vicky, "but your office has become the subject of a private joke between me and Mama. It's the couch thing. You don't have one in here." With sudden awareness, Regina smiled and offered Vicky a chair. "I'm sorry, Regina," said Vicky, still on the edge of hysteria. "I just need a moment to compose myself. I feel awfully goofy."

"Tension," said Regina.

"Yes, I suppose so," said Vicky.

"What's happening with you, Vicky? You seem happy," observed Regina.

"I am happy, Regina, for the most part, but I am frightened," said Vicky. "I have been in love with this young man for some time now. However, something always seems to get in our way. First, he went away to college, then my brother died, and now . . ."

"Now what?" asked Regina.

"Now there is the matter of sex or rather my inability to have sex. Do you think I am too young to be intimate with a man, Regina?"

"It is not my place to answer that question, Vicky," responded Regina. "Do you think you are too young for intimacy with a man?"

"I want to be with Terrence—that's my boyfriend's name. I want to be with him more than anything, but I can't go through with it. I get lost in him, then without warning, I draw back. I'm back, and I am afraid. I know that I can trust Terrence, Regina, but it's the feelings that I have when we get too close physically that I cannot bear. Instead of seeing him, the person, I see abstract faces and foreign hands clawing at me. I have to stop myself from screaming, Regina," said Vicky. "I don't want to scream. However, I am afraid that I just may someday. I don't want to scream. I don't want anyone lying on top of me. I don't even want to be naked before a man. Yet, Regina, I want to feel the way Terrence makes me feel. I want the love he offers me.

"When I first entered high school, after the . . . after I was attacked, I felt like I had no value. I had been used and discarded. Whenever boys noticed me, I thought they could tell that I had been used, and perhaps they thought it would be easy for them to use me too. I loved teasing them and then turning my back on them. It was, 'Yeah, you were wrong, weren't you? Don't you know that I hate you, fool?' Eventually, I got bored with the charade and just started ignoring them altogether. Surprisingly, there came Terrence, my brother's classmate and sometimes nemesis, an unlikely candidate for love. Somehow, we worked through all of that, yet we hadn't even scratched the surface.

"He is going to grow tired of me, Regina. Terrence is so handsome. He could have any girl he wants, but he wants me . . . for now anyway," said Vicky, saddened by the possibility of not just losing Terrence but tearing his heart apart as well.

"Do you live with the assault daily, Vicky? Is it not just a blur?" asked Regina.

"It is a distant nightmare, Regina. It is the kind of nightmare that you don't remember when you are awake, but there are sweeping images that dance about in a haze before your eyes that block the face of a loved one at the moment of a kiss. You brush the nightmare away before it can take the joy of that kiss away from you," said Vicky.

"Vicky, do you think these nightmares may be at play in your relationship with Terrence?" asked Regina.

"I suppose they have to be," said Vicky. "Terrence has a way of consuming me, until I bring myself back to reality."

"You give me the impression that you trust Terrence, Vicky, but you really don't. Because of your experience, it is going to be hard for you to trust any man, whether you love him or not," said Regina. "Terrence is going to have to earn your trust by waiting until you are ready, and believe me, Vicky, someday you will be ready. I think if you told Terrence about the attack, it would help him understand better why you are reluctant to being entirely intimate with him."

"That's what Mama said too, that I should tell Terrence everything. I guess you great women think alike," said Vicky.

"indeed so," said Regina.

"I rue having to have that conversation with Terrence. I am so embarrassed about that incident," said Vicky, sending a guttural groan into the air.

"Now that I don't want to ever hear again, Vicky Fielder!" said Regina. "You have survived a vicious attack by three thugs. That was not your fault!"

Vicky went around Regina's desk to where she sat and hugged her and kissed her cheeks. "I'll come in for two hours three days a week when school starts back," whispered Vicky, still clinging to Regina's neck.

"Thank you, Vicky. I'll look forward to seeing you soon. Remember, sweetheart, we can talk anytime you need, by phone or in person," said Regina.

"Thank you, Regina," said Vicky.

Vicky did not go home when she left the center. Instead, she paid Terrence a visit.

"Hi. I've been calling you all morning," said Terrence when he opened the door for Vicky.

"I went by the center for a while. I am going to volunteer there three days out of the week after school to help the mothers with their children," said Vicky.

"That is nice of you, sweetheart," said Terrence. "I love that great, big heart of yours. Have a seat. I'll get us something to drink."

Vicky watched Terrence as he played host to her. He was tall and muscular. He had always been athletic, and it showed. His smooth brown skin was augmented by light-brown eyes. His heart-shaped lips begged to be kissed. His smile was ingratiating, and he swaggered slightly when he walked. Vicky yearned to be with him.

Terrence took his usual position on the floor at her feet, with his arm resting on her lap. Vicky moved her hand through his hair and met his smile with a conservative kiss on his smooth lips.

Vicky spoke softly, "Once upon a time, a thirteen-year-old girl decided to venture out into the big bad world alone. She usually walked to school with her brothers, but on this occasion, she was running late and decided to walk to school by herself.

"On her way to school that day, she was abducted by three men who saw her by herself. They pulled her into an alley, raped her more than once, and beat her severely."

"Wait a minute, Vicky! I don't think I like your story. Is this a true story or a movie you watched?" asked an alarmed Terrence. "Who is this girl you're speaking of? Vicky, tell me you are not speaking of yourself," said a horrified Terrence as he stood on his feet.

"Yes, Terrence, I am talking about myself. It's my story, and it is my personal experience," said Vicky as quiet tears streamed from her eyes.

Terrence drew Vicky to him and held her to his chest for the longest of time. Vicky could feel the elevated beat of his heart and his heavy breathing. Terrence was incensed. Holding Vicky away from him, he took a deep dive into her eyes. His reaction was worse than Vicky had imagined. Once he was calm enough to speak, he had one question.

"Did they catch these punks? Are they in jail as we speak?" Terrence asked.

"No, the police never did catch them. There were no witnesses, and the description I gave them matched most of the men on the south side of Chicago," said Vicky.

"Those son of a bitches need to die. Now I understand that you are very afraid to be with a man, and you have a legitimate reason for feeling the way that you do, Vicky. It takes time to recover from something like that."

"I have had a lot of help over the years. I went to counseling, and Millie and Uncle Julian and my grandmother were there for me all of the time. My mother talked to me about it. I felt so sorry for Mama. Because of the fact that she couldn't be with me, she suffered much guilt and pain."

"Baby, I thank you for sharing your experience with me. I am sorry if I was forceful with you about us having sex. I'll never pressure you again, Vicky," said Terrence, "and I'll never leave you. We will be together forever, my love."

Vicky sat with Terrence on the couch and let his warm embrace and sweet kisses console her. Hours passed before they were ready to part from each other. Terrence drove Vicky home in time enough for her to have dinner with her family. Vicky asked Terrence to join them, which he did because he was not ready to let her out of his sight.

The Christmas holidays were very special for Vicky. She and Terrence had spent every day together. She could not remember the last time she was so happy. She took time out every day to sit at her desk in her bedroom, writing in her journal. Regina had suggested that Vicky keep one, and the exercise had helped her to have a broader perspective of herself and her world.

⌒✐⌒

"Good evening, old folks," said Teddy, grinning. "Welcome to the Silver Swan. I am Teddy Fielder, the son of the fabulous owner, Ms. Lottie Wallace. There she is over there. Not her," he said, pointing at another woman sitting in proximity to his mother, "the pretty one." He pointed directly at Lottie, and everybody stood and clapped for her.

"Okay, okay, that's enough. You don't want that head of hers to get bigger, do you? It's big enough in my opinion. I've never been in a room full of old folks before. Damn, I can smell the Bengay all the way up here. How many of you have your original teeth? Raise your hand if you do. Um, two out of three hundred is pretty bad. Sir"—he pointed to a gentlemen in the audience—"I'll hold that cane for you when you dance. We don't want you to accidentally trip your dance partner.

"Don't y'all get me wrong. I love old folks. My nana is my best friend, mainly because she won't talk, so I get to do all of the talking. You know how you all like to talk, especially about the good old days. What good old days? 'You kids just don't know how good you got it.' What's good about running to and from school every day because somebody is after you? What's good about being held upside down while somebody is emptying your pocket of all your money? And what's good about wearing uniforms to not show gang affiliations? Don't you know that the gangs know who they are?

"There is my nana over there, with her fine self." He pointed to his grandmother. "Don't get any ideas, you old buzzards. I know some of you still try to have sex after taking those little blue pills, and I'm not going to have you humping my nana. Dirty old son of a bitches. Sorry, Nana. She doesn't like me to curse. How did folks come up with that children-shouldn't-curse shit when everything that proceeds from an adult's mouth is a cuss word?

"'Mama, do you have my bus money?'

"'Motherfucker, I done told you a thousand times that your black ass is walking those little ole five blocks to school.'

"Even when we are babies, you curse at us. 'Come on, little Junior, take your bottle 'cause my motherfucking ass is tired, you little son of a bitch.'

"I have to give it to you old men. Y'all know you be running the women. You guys hit on these ladies, flash a little money, show them your Cadillac and Lexus, and they become yours right away, as long as that money don't run out. But don't mind me, I am just jealous. Girls just don't like peanut and jelly sandwiches.

"You have been a splendid audience, and I thank you for indulging me. Now I am going to turn this thing over to my mother, your host, Ms. Lottie Wallace."

As Lottie proved herself more capable, Julian started to focus on his own life. He drew pleasure from the small conversations he had with Christine—small, for the greater issue of his background was still a closed subject between him and the woman he loved. What astounded him most about Christine was her brave tenacity and her appreciation of his privacy. Julian sensed that she was aware of his faithfulness and love for her; therefore, she trusted him. Nonetheless, he was still concerned about the fact that she never probed him about his past and his family. He planned to come clean to her about everything.

Julian sat across from Christine at their dining room table, pondering how he should approach the matter and how much he should reveal to her at that time. "Christine," he broached, "Lottie's opening for her club is New Year's Eve. I'd like for us to attend. It's about time you meet my family. They all will be attending."

Christine wanted to burst out of her skin. She had long awaited Julian's invitation to meet his family. She contained herself as best as she could. She smothered the burning currents inside her. Her success with Julian was due, in part, to her unobtrusive behavior, this she knew, for she had always wanted to know the secrets about Julian's family that he was keeping from her.

"I would love to go, Julian," she said. "In fact, it would be an honor. Julian, remember the last time we went out with my parents?"

Julian loved Christine's parents and enjoyed every time they all were together. Mr. Williams was a lawyer, and Christine's mother was a high school counselor. He respected and admired the both of them. Her brother Paul was serving in the military in Iran; therefore, Julian did not get to see him often.

"Yes, sweetheart, I remember," said Julian.

"The subject came up again about your family afterward. My parents wondered, for the hundredth time, why they had not met your parents over the years. They didn't question your love or loyalty to me. Nonetheless, they accused you of hiding some type of secret from me," said Christine. "I know you adore your family, Julian, especially Lottie."

"Lottie needed me, Christine, and her children needed me even more," said Julian.

"I am not jealous of Lottie or your family," stressed Christine. "I learned from watching you care for your family that you are an honorable and charitable person. What else did I need to know to love you?"

"My family has a dark past, Christine," said Julian, "a past that is so engraved in my soul and memory that it is difficult for me to talk about. Someday, I may be able to talk about it and not be mortified, but that day is not today. Instead, I want to set a course for my own life, my future."

Julian dropped to his knees and pulled a small black velvet box from his pocket. He took Christine by the hand and said, "Christine, will you marry me?"

Christine was so shocked that she could not speak right away. She saw the seriousness in Julian's eyes and was surprised by his nervousness. She stood up from her chair and went to Julian. She held his face in her hands and said, "Yes. Yes, Julian, I surely will. You have made me so happy!"

The future husband and wife held each other close and kissed. Christine opened the box and found inside a five-karat marquise diamond ring. Julian put the ring on her finger. She was so busy admiring her engagement ring that she almost overlooked the other content of the box. Inside the box was a multijeweled friendship ring.

"Oh, Julian!" she said. "How beautiful!"

"You are the only best friend I have ever had," said Julian tearfully.

"I have always dreamed of a Valentine's Day wedding, Julian. Would that be too soon?" asked Christine.

"I think that would be a perfect day," said Julian. Julian was buoyant. He felt free. He felt like a man who had finally took control of his life. He felt like the happiest man in the world.

Lottie's sequined red dress hung on her closet door. She roamed through her jewelry drawer for her diamond drop necklace. The diamond earrings she held in her left hand. Clad in her red lace underwear, she moved from drawer to drawer, fighting among their contents, and ultimately going back to the first place she had looked. She reached into the back of the drawer and pulled out a long black velvet box. Inside was the cherished necklace that Spanky had given to her years before. Lottie gazed upon its delicacy and the brilliant reflections of the diamonds. It had been many years since she had worn the jewel. The necklace had been given to her by Spanky as a piece offering upon returning home after weeks at Mamie's house. She felt it very appropriate to wear the necklace on such an occasion. After all, Spanky was the sponsor of the evening's event.

Lottie sat at her vanity and put on her jewelry. As usual, she wore very little makeup: some lipstick, rouge, mascara, and eyebrow pencil. She dabbed Chanel No. 5 cologne behind her ears and behind her knees. With a single twist, she pulled her hair into a chignon and garnished it with a rhinestone comb. She put on her stockings, dress, and silver slingback heels. She grabbed her silver clutch bag and put her lipstick and perfume inside and then walked out of her room.

"Ooh la la!" exclaimed Teddy.

"Oh, Mama, you look exquisite!" raved Vicky.

Lottie grabbed her children on each side of her and hugged them. "You guys are nothing to shun tonight," said Lottie. She admired Teddy's silver-and-black tuxedo jacket and black pants. True to form, he had on silver-and-black shoes. Vicky had chosen a golden spaghetti-strapped, wide-skirt dress to show off her splendor. She wore black pumps and carried a black clutch bag. Lottie was so pleased with her mother. Not only had Mamie agreed to attend the affair but she also graced the occasion by wearing the new dress that Lottie had bought her. The dress was a sequined black dress, sleek and long. Mamie wore gold shoes and carried a small gold shoulder bag. Her luscious hair was swept to one side and was swung over her right shoulder. Wearing only lipstick, Mamie was still a stunning woman, and Lottie and the children did not hesitate to tell her so. Lottie draped a black mink shawl over her shoulders, and Mamie donned a long black mink coat. Vicky and Teddy wore black wool coats with identical silver swan stick pins attached to their lapels.

The family's limousine was waiting for them outside. They stopped and picked up a dashing Terrence, clad in a black tuxedo and coat, and headed for the club. They arrived at the club ahead of the guests. The door was to open 7:00 p.m. Lottie situated her family at the first two tables. She left room for Buddy, Julian, Millie, and their guests. She also reserved a smaller table for the star of the evening, Gladys Knight, for her to sit.

After Teddy's performance and introduction of his mother, Lottie welcomed her guests then introduced the band. The band played, and the guests danced freely on the dance floor. Lottie floated across the room, meeting and talking to the many people who sought her attention. She had been so busy that she had forgotten about MacArthur. Glancing around the room with only a half hour left before dinner would be served, she wondered if he had come at all, for she did not see him right away. She noticed that Julian had arrived, with whom she assumed was Christine. Buddy sat next to his date, observing everyone and everything. Lottie started toward them and suddenly stopped. She had seen MacArthur. Her heart pounded thunderously as she watched Mac glide across the dance floor with a very extraordinary-looking woman. Little missiles attacked Lottie's heart, leaving the throbbing sensation of pain. She struggled along her path to Julian and Buddy. She sat for a miserable moment with them, a waxy smile on her face. They had been there for Teddy's performance and were discussing how much they had enjoyed his act and what they thought was inappropriate. Lottie cut short Julian's conversation and excused herself. She left the table abruptly and fled to her office.

Julian followed Lottie out of concern. "What's wrong, sis? You look disturbed."

"I have lost him, Julian, before we could ever get started. I lost him."

"Lost who, Lottie?" asked Julian.

"That's a lie, if I am true to myself. I was given a chance, to be honest, but I couldn't get myself together enough to take him up on his offer. He asked to come with me tonight, and I said no, because I would be too busy to spend time with him. What did he do? He brought someone else instead," said Lottie tearfully.

"Who are you talking about, Lottie?" asked Julian.

"Who he is is no longer important, Julian," said Lottie. "I'm going to pull myself together, then I want you to take me back inside, please."

Millie and James had also arrived, later than Lottie had expected, but they had been there for Teddy's routine. Lottie had hoped that Millie would come early in case there were some late complications. However, at the moment, their tardiness was not Lottie's concern. She whispered to Millie that they must talk. The two feigned a trip to the ladies' room. They almost made it to the office when the affairs specialist grabbed them and led them to the dressing room, where Gladys was in the process of putting on her wardrobe.

Lottie spontaneously helped the star with her gown. The two chatted like old friends. Lottie and Millie sat with Gladys and drank champagne. After getting the star's permission, Lottie asked an assistant to bring her family and Millie's husband to the dressing room to meet the singer. Gladys signed autographs and flirted with Lottie's two brothers, which drew smiles from their dates rather than ire. She hugged Mamie and placed a kiss of honor on her cheek. She told Teddy that he was the best opening performer that she had ever had. She would be watching him closely in the future. Teddy beamed his enthusiasm. Lottie broke up the friendly gathering, citing Gladys's need for some quiet time before going on stage. She shrugged her shoulder at Millie, an indication that they would have to delay their talk. Millie's concern for her friend was not lessened by the show of goodwill that Lottie had exhibited to all.

At exactly eleven, Lottie introduced Gladys Knight to the audience. When Gladys began to sing, Lottie was enraptured, as was everybody else. The setting was very intimate. One felt like the performance was an individual privilege. Even Mamie sat in awe of the singer. Vicky promised to buy every record that Gladys had ever made. When Gladys finished singing "Midnight Train to Georgia," the crowd was in an uproar. They stood on their feet and clapped and whistled and jumped for joy.

Lottie looked around behind her for the source of the heat on her neck. She discovered it in the passionate rays of McArthur's eyes. She snapped her head back around in utter disgust and anger. Needless to say, she was at a loss for words later when he came to her and held out his hand for a dance.

After performing, instead of disappearing into the dressing room, Gladys sat down with Lottie at the table that had been reserved for them. She greeted those who approached her graciously and warmly. She signed autographs for them and shared champagne with Lottie and her family before heading back to the dressing room to change and depart. Lottie, Millie, and the affairs specialist helped Gladys and were given hugs and kisses before the assistant and guards led her to her limousine.

Lottie had just returned from seeing Gladys off when Mac approached her. She looked up at him with distrustful eyes. Mac put his arm around her waist and guided her to the dance floor. He increased his hold on her as they danced with their eyes locked on each other. Lottie searched Mac's eyes deeply. She thought she had glimpsed pain in them. Yet in another moment, she thought that she had seen love in them. She did not doubt the anger she saw when it appeared in all its fiery intent, blazing from his gaze. She knew too what her eyes told him.

Lottie looked over Mac's shoulder at his date. The woman glared openly at her. Lottie returned her an equally vicious look. Mac buried his face in her neck. He inhaled her essence and shuddered. Lottie grew dizzy from the closeness. Mac kissed her neck and her face. He glued his lips to hers and sucked her breath away. Lottie's knees buckled beneath her. Mac secured her in his grip and released her burning lips. Lottie lay her head against his chest and fought tears of agony. Without provocation, she pushed away from him and escaped into her office.

Lottie sat for a long time at her desk, shielding her eyes with her hands. Millie, who had followed her to the office, sat patiently for her friend to compose herself. "You got it bad, don't you, girlfriend?" said Millie. "Lottie, I know you are hurting, but didn't you tell Mac you were not ready for a relationship?"

Lottie nodded.

"If that is true, doesn't Mac have the right to date other women?"

"Not at my club, Millie! Not on my opening night! I'm going to have security throw him out!" shouted Lottie petulantly.

"Don't do that, Lottie," implored Millie. "I will just go out there and tell him it would be best if he and his date left discretely."

Lottie sat in her chair and swirled it around and around, as if to promote or compound dizziness.

"Do you want Mac, Lottie?" asked Millie.

"I don't know yet, Millie," said Lottie.

"I suggest you give it some thought. Personally speaking, I think you are already in love with Mac."

"Whatever I am, Millie, I will not be manipulated into having a relationship with anyone. All I have asked for is time. I did not ask to be included in Mac's relationships with other women. I had enough of that with Spanky. Another woman will never, ever again be the issue between me and a man," said Lottie.

Millie came back to the office and told Lottie that Mac and his date had left quietly. Lottie went into her private bathroom and refreshed her makeup then rejoined her family and guests. She had the limousine, which had brought them to the club, to take Mamie and the children home. Julian and Christine, Buddy and his date Karen, James and Millie stayed with Lottie after the club had closed for the night. They drank coffee and ate croissants and laughed and talked. As the sun rose on them, they decided it was time to go home. Lottie declined a ride home and stood watching the couples leave to begin the new year together. She felt so sorry for herself and alone. The idea that Julian would soon be a married man added to her sense of sorrow and loss. For she knew in committing himself to Christine completely, Julian had reduced his role in her life. She would no longer be his primary concern—a realization that brought tears to Lottie's eyes.

Lottie stretched out on her office couch. She kicked off her shoes and released her hair. The club was empty of all employees, except for Dewy. So exhausted was she that she fell asleep immediately. The late afternoon sun was setting and pulling darkness in its wake. Lottie's psyche recognized the change in time, but consciousness eluded her. In her sleep, she brushed away what she thought was a fly on her face, even shifted her position to stop the pesky fly from pestering her to no avail. Finally, she willed herself to awaken and was startled to find

Mac leaning over her, blowing gentle breezes on her face. She did not move as he tenderly kissed her. Mac stood back and waited for Lottie's reaction. Events from the previous night became alive in her mind, and she grew angry. Still groggy, Lottie sat up slowly on the couch. She looked up at Mac with all the ambivalence a soul could bear.

"Get away from me, MacArthur! How dare you show your face here! Who let you in my club?" she stormed.

"Dewy did. I came to apologize, Lottie," said a wounded Mac contritely. "If it's any consolation, last night was the most miserable of my life. I had wanted to show you that I didn't need you, that I didn't want you."

"You damn well showed me that much. You humiliated me and embarrassed me!"

"We can't . . . I can't go on this way, Lottie. My god, I want you more than I have ever wanted anyone. I need you, and I don't want to go through life without you."

"What about my needs, Mac? My need to be respected and considered? I tremble in your arms. You know you affect me, but instead of waiting until I can freely be with you, instead of nurturing and appreciating the effect you have on me, you chose to use my weakness against me just to prove a point. You are a selfish asshole. Get out!"

With all said, Lottie opened the door, an invitation for Mac to leave, which he did in a most remorseful manner.

Time moved swiftly for Lottie. The club was a massive hit. She was so busy that she had little time to deal with the aggravation she felt for Mac. She had ignored his calls, donated his flowers to the rehab center, and engrossed herself in her family and business. She prepared herself for the family's trip to California, where Teddy would appear on *Star Search*.

The trip to Los Angeles was marvelous. Lottie was so proud of Teddy. Her only regret was that Julian and Buddy could not be there with the rest of the family. She had expected to go and come right back home, but when Teddy made it to the next round, they decided to stay until his next performance. If he won on that occasion, they could return home until the finals.

When the knock came at her hotel door, Lottie thought it was Teddy. She was getting dressed for dinner and was only wearing her underwear. She threw on a rob and answered the door. She was utterly shocked to see MacArthur standing outside of her room.

"May I come in, Lottie?" he asked.

Without a word, Lottie stepped aside to let him enter. She went to the bed, retrieved her dress, and went into the bathroom to put it on. When she emerged, she was fully clothed in a long, sleeveless black dress. She sat on the side of the bed and slipped on silver pumps, never once allowing herself to meet Mac's eyes. She rose and ran a comb through her hair, put on some lipstick, grabbed her purse and coat, and left the room.

Lottie met Teddy and his agent in the hotel lobby, and the three of them left for dinner. When they returned back to the hotel, Teddy made an escape to his room. Lottie, on the other hand, lingered downstairs, talking to Teddy's manager. After a few drinks at the hotel bar, she returned to her room. When she opened her door, she was totally outdone by the sight of MacArthur asleep on the couch. He awakened when Lottie turned on the lights. Lottie stared at him with absolute unbelief.

"You have been here all of this time, Mac," said Lottie. "Are you jet-lagged?" Mac did not answer. "I want you to leave, Mac," she said. "What do I have to do, call security?"

Mac rose and stood so close to Lottie that his breath blew strands of her hair into her face. "I can't leave, Lottie. I can't bear this torture any longer."

Lottie felt weak and tired, tired of running from this man. He sensed this and pulled her into his arms. He groaned as his passion for her intensified. With little effort, he led Lottie to the bed and stretched himself over her. His eyes locked upon hers. He held her face in his hands and kissed her warmly then brutally. Lottie let his hands roam her body at will. She held him tightly. She kissed his neck and nibbled at his ears as he unclad her. She did not let go as he freed himself of his clothing. He possessed her hungrily. With her own desires equaling his, Lottie surrendered herself to Mac.

21

CHAPTER

LINKED

O n the Fourth of July, Lottie hosted an outdoor barbecue. The weather was splendid. It was hot outside and cloudless. On her spacious patio, flowers, which Mamie had nurtured and grown, adorned the outside space. Chairs and tables spread out from the patio to the luscious lawn. Her children had decorated with balloons and flags. Mamie's swing was the focal point of her abundant vegetable garden, which had provided them with the vegetables for the salad and grilling.

The entire family was engaged in the preparations for the feast. Mamie and Mrs. Whitfield were the grill masters. Lottie brought out to her the marinated meats, hot dogs, hamburgers, steaks, fish— there was no end to the array of foods that were being offered to the guests. Teddy, Vicky, and Terrence were in charge of the music, and Regina had been asked to sing, for she had a most marvelous voice. Her husband would accompany her on the piano.

Lottie had invited several of her friends and their guests, over one hundred people. Dewy and his wife arrived early because he was in charge of the libations and would serve as bartender. Millie and James arrived on the heels of Dewy and his wife. Next came Buddy and his fiancée, Karen, with Julian and his new wife, Christine. They had married the previous month, on June 1. They had married at their new church, Trinity, before a small group of one hundred guests. The wedding was so elegant, and Christine had been the prettiest bride that

Lottie had ever seen. Mac was the next person to come. He and Lottie had become an item. The buzz was that an impending engagement was soon coming, but they were taking their time.

Lottie finally found time to sit and enjoy her friends and family. She watched Mamie and Mrs. Whitfield as they grilled without ceasing. Mamie still did not speak, but it was obvious to all who knew her that she had finally achieved some level of happiness. She smiled more often and would laugh out loud at Teddy's inappropriate jokes. She could also be caught humming and swaying to the beat of music.

The following Monday, Lottie rose early. She had a two-hour drive to Stateville prison, where she would meet with the warden. When she arrived, she happened to see some of the guards who had worked there when she herself was in prison. She had gotten there on time for her nine o'clock meeting with the warden.

"Lottie, my goodness, I am so happy that you could come this morning," said the warden as he embraced her.

"Warden, I would have been here before now, but things have been complicated for me, and I just couldn't find the time," said Lottie.

"I understand," said the warden. "I have read in the papers about some of your endeavors, and needless to say, I could not be more proud of you."

"I owe you a great deal, Warden. You gave me the opportunity to advance myself while I was her, and I am forever grateful."

"And look what you did with those opportunities. You used them to become a blessing to the women here, and I will always be grateful to you for that."

"I want to thank you for keeping me abreast of the rehabilitation and literacy program."

"You mean the Lottie Wallace Rehabilitation and Literacy Program," said the warden, "the one which would never have existed without you?"

Lottie smiled with pride.

"You know, we had stopped offering the program for a while because of the lack of funding and coordination."

"I know, but we couldn't have that, could we? It had been my plan to come back and volunteer a few days a week. I was disheartened when you called me about ending the program."

"Once again, you came to the aid of the women here, Lottie. Because of your generous donation and consequent funding, our program has grown exponentially," said the warden. "It was an act of genius when you introduced me to Mrs. Regina. Her team came in here and set our program in a forward motion."

"Regina is the best," said Lottie.

"Thanks to your proposal and extension plans, we have partnered with potential employers from numerous businesses and charitable organizations that have provided our graduates with clothing and housing as they try to rebuild their lives."

"I am very impressed with the number of women who have completed the program. Who would have ever guessed?" said Lottie.

"Over a hundred women have graduated from the program, Lottie, with either their GED or AA degrees. We have five women who have gone on to receive their bachelor degrees in social services and are now working in the program, two of which are friends of yours."

"Believe me, I know about. We have kept in touch with each other since our prison days. I love that some of the inmates have obtained early release because of their tenacity and assistance to their fellow women."

"So, Lottie, are you ready for the barrage of request that have been made by the governor, Prison Review Board, notwithstanding the national interest by prison reform advocates, for you to meet with them and speak publicly about your dreams, hopes, and plans that stemmed from your own personal experiences?" asked the warden.

"Let's not forget the media, Warden. No, sir, I am not ready. You get ready too, because I will be dragging you and Regina along with me. Time is still an issue for me. We all will have to be on call for these occasions. We all will discuss our successes with the public. The first thing you and I have to do is schedule our appointment with the governor," said Lottie.

As Lottie drove home that afternoon, she let the flashbacks of her life stream like a movie in her mind. She was amazed at how events had unfolded into a life that she could never have imagined. She thanked a god that she never knew. In her heart, she felt that God could be the only reason for her abundant and blessed life.

ABOUT THE AUTHOR

E laine Chandler-Harris is a freelance writer of several genres. Although this is her first novel, she has written personal articles that were published by the Chicago Sun- Times Newspaper, Black Enterprise Magazine, and others. Her poetry has been published in anthologies that include Chicago State, Illinois State, and Jackson State Universities. Ms. Chandler-Harris has always had a creative mind and will, indeed, delve into mysteries of life that others may find intimidating. As a professional, she holds a Bachelor's Degree from Chicago State University, Post-education credits in Media Communications, and a Masters Degree in Education Administration from National-Louis University.

Printed in the United States
by Baker & Taylor Publisher Services

Printed in the United States
by Baker & Taylor Publisher Services